Praise for Susan Meissne...
readers and reviewe...

W...

Tracy Farnswort... ...t the Kleenex, you are certain to need them. Susan Meissner's debut novel is... impressive and leaves me hungry for more."

A book group leader in Tennessee reports: "It was one of [our] favorites out of all the ones we have read...We discussed in depth the characters, and how you made them so real...Only a few books have been as well received by this bunch as was Why the Sky Is Blue."

A Minnesotan says: "Wow! What a brutally honest, beautifully expressed, compelling book! I simply could not put it down. I will definitely recommend it to many, since I work in my local public library. This book is so personal that I thought I was reading a diary or personal letter."

Bo... ...005"

THE REMEDY FOR REGRET

Kelli Standish, focusonfiction.net, says: "Meissner's incredible gift with words has never shone truer...a must for any discerning reader's library."

Publisher's Weekly says: "The novel is readable if not deeply involving, and it refrains from the high melodrama present in many contemporary Christian novels for women."

IN ALL DEEP PLACES

Author Mary DeMuth (Ordinary Mom, Extraordinary God) says: "Loved the book. Couldn't put it down...lyrically written, sensitively wrought...Captivated me from page one."

Jamie writes: "Once again, you created a cast of characters that made me feel..!"

ArmchairInterviews.com writes: "Susan Meissner has once again skillfully examined the basic truth of what it is to be alive in the world, with all the good and all the bad that is there. But she doesn't leave it at that. She gently reminds us that it is God's grace and love that will see us through the night...Meissner's books are must-reads."

NovelReviews.BlogSpot.com writes: "In my opinion, Ms. Meissner writes christian fiction the way it should be written, with threads and hints and God webs interwoven into not very rosy pictures of broken lives."

WIDOWS & ORPHANS

SUSAN MEISSNER

HARVEST HOUSE PUBLISHERS

EUGENE, OREGON

Scripture quotations are taken from the HOLY BIBLE, NEW INTERNATIONAL VERSION®. NIV®. Copyright © 1973, 1978, 1984 by the International Bible Society. Used by permission of Zondervan. All rights reserved; and from the New American Standard Bible®, © 1960, 1962, 1963, 1968, 1971, 1972, 1973, 1975, 1977, 1995 by The Lockman Foundation. Used by permission. (www.Lockman,org).

Cover by Left Coast Design, Portland, Oregon

Susan Meissner: Published in association with the literary agency of Alive Communications, Inc., 7680 Goddard Street, Suite #200, Colorado Springs, CO 80920, www.alivecommunications.com.

This is a work of fiction. Names, characters, places, and incidents are products of the author's imagination or are used fictitiously. Any resemblance to actual persons, living or dead, or to events or locales, is entirely coincidental.

WIDOWS AND ORPHANS
Copyright © 2006 by Susan Meissner
Published by Harvest House Publishers
Eugene, Oregon 97402
www.harvesthousepublishers.com

Library of Congress Cataloging-in-Publication Data

Meissner, Susan, 1961-
   Widows and orphans / Susan Meissner.
      p. cm. -- (Rachael Flynn mystery series)
   "Published in association with the literary agency of Alive Communications"--T.p. verso.
   ISBN-13: 978-0-7369-1914-2 (pbk.)
   ISBN-10: 0-7369-1914-7 (pbk.)
   1. Trials (Murder)--Fiction. 2. Women lawyers--Fiction. I. Title. II. Series.
   PS3613.E435W54 2006
   813'.6--dc22

                                    2006007606

Printed in the United States of America

06 07 08 09 10 11 12 13 14 / LB-MS / 10 9 8 7 6 5 4 3 2 1

ACKNOWLEDGMENTS

I am thankful to work with an amazingly supportive editorial team at Harvest House Publishers. Nick Harrison is the best kind of editor: honest, direct, and insightful—and he never lets me settle for mediocrity.

My agent, Don Pape of Alive Communications, is truly an encourager extraordinaire. Every writer should have such a friend and cohort to cheer her on.

Judy Horning, my proficient proofreader, is also a terrific mom, friend, and booklover. I am fortunate to have such a willing reader to catalog all the errata and still enjoy the story.

Pam Louwagie and Dan Browning, staff writers at the *Star Tribune,* co-wrote a series of news stories in October 2005 on the very real problem of the victimization of Hmong girls in the St. Paul area. Their stories made me cry. My words are fiction; theirs are real. These commendably written, troubling articles provided me with the insights I needed to craft a tale that would ring true.

Attorney and fellow writer James Scott Bell answered many of my initial questions about legal procedure and never laughed once. Attorney Dione Talkington-Fletcher also lent me her insights as a public defender practicing in the state of Minnesota. I am grateful beyond words to Clayton Robinson Jr., a prosecutor with the Ramsey County Attorney's Office in St. Paul, for his patient assistance with every question I posed, every scenario I envisioned, every detail I dreamed up. I could not have written this book without his help. Any liberties I have taken with regard to Minnesota criminal law or process are my responsibility alone.

"Religion that God our Father accepts as pure and faultless is this:
to look after orphans and widows in their distress
and to keep oneself from being polluted by the world."

JAMES 1:27

"The Christian ideal has not been tried and found wanting—
it has been found difficult and left untried."

G.K. CHESTERTON

What's Wrong with the World

ONE

Rachael Flynn had just laid her two-month-old daughter down for a nap and had walked back into her living room when the ringing of the telephone split the early afternoon quiet.

She pushed aside the stack of legal briefs she had been perusing earlier that morning, which were strewn about the coffee table and hiding the cell phone that beckoned her. Rachael mentally reminded herself as she unearthed the phone that maternity leave meant she wasn't obligated to wade through any of the files. But the polite plea that she stay current with the firm's caseload while she enjoyed McKenna's first six months at home had needled her that morning. She had grudgingly succumbed to the call of duty, even though it was a Sunday. She grabbed the phone and sat down on the couch. Her mother's number blinked back at her on the phone's tiny screen.

"Hey, Mom."

"Rachael…" Her mother's voice on the other end was thick with panic.

"What is it, Mom? What's wrong?" A sliver of fear pierced the calm. Rachael's first thought was that something terrible had happened to her father.

"Joshua has..." Her mother's voice broke away in a sob.

Joshua.

Rachael's younger brother by five years. The missionary to the downtrodden. The hope of the homeless and fatherless. The zealot for social justice. The religious fanatic. The troublemaker.

Joshua was in trouble. Again.

"What has he done, Mom?" Rachael inquired. She didn't even raise the end of her sentence in the curlicue way a question is spoken. She was tired of hearing the answers.

Her brother, Joshua, was a study in contrasts. A good man, a man of compassion, a man whose credo was easily "first do no harm." He lived to ease the suffering of the most vulnerable. But he was a man who brazenly took the law into his own hands whenever he perceived it might right an injustice. For all the good he did, he seemed forever in trouble. Joshua had a criminal record in four Minnesota counties for being empathetic to a fault.

My brother is the only decent man I know who knows what it's like to be in handcuffs, Rachael had said to Trace, her husband, on their first date, when he had asked about her family. She had learned it was best to be up front with people from the get-go when it came to explaining Joshua.

"Rachael, it's...he's..." Again her mother's voice faltered.

As her mother's words fell away half-spoken, Rachael exhaled heavily. She was continually torn between a lifelong desire to shelter Joshua from the cruelties of the world—like she did when he was young and she had influence—and wanting to clobber him for being so stubbornly independent. She wasn't sure she wanted to know what new offense Joshua had committed in the name of God and all things holy. She had lost count of how many times he had been arrested for being where he shouldn't, doing what he ought not, and saying what he technically wasn't free to say. Her mother was no doubt calling to ask for her legal advice yet again. What more could she say than what she had already said a hundred times over? As long as Joshua persisted in exercising his own brand of social justice, he would continue to land himself in jail. There wasn't any way around it. She could only protect him from so much.

Rachael waited for her mother to finish. She eased back into the couch, tossing her infant daughter's burp cloth onto the coffee table in front of her. She mentally flipped through the catalog of Joshua's past offenses: blocking entry to abortion clinics, resisting arrest, obstructing legal process, interfering with police procedure, trespassing, breaking and entering, loitering, making false statements to the police. Mere misdemeanors and strongly worded citations. He had spent more time in court than in actual jail. What could he have possibly done this time?

When her mother remained silent, Rachael began again. "Mom, what did he *do?*"

"He's...oh, Rachael, I can hardly say it!"

"Mom, please tell me!" Rachael exclaimed. Above her she could sense Trace looking down upon her from his art studio in the alcove above the living room.

Her mother's voice wasn't much more than a whisper. "He's confessed to murder, Rachael! He told the police he killed someone!"

The air in the apartment stiffened around her. Echoes of the word *murder* seemed to float above her, uninvited and wholly out of place in the suddenly airless space.

What her mother was saying was impossible. *Impossible!*

Joshua was incapable of killing. He despised cruelty. Hated injustice. Detested abuse against the body and soul. Every infraction that put him behind bars and in front of a judge was related to wanting to ease suffering, save lives, and help the poorest and most helpless people, mostly destitute women and children. Above all, he was a walking monument to the sixth commandment. He was living testimony to all ten.

Since the time he was old enough to attend Sunday school, Joshua had been a modern-day prophet of God Almighty, afflicted with a

passion for the holy that annoyed Rachael as much as it inspired her.
He had the books of the Bible memorized before his own telephone
number, and his childhood prayers at the dinner table were so lengthy
their mother had to leave foil on the serving dishes when it was his
turn to pray.

Joshua had always had an innate and unexplainable awareness of
the spiritual realm, a keen sense of the divine as well as the profane
that began as soon as he knew there was God and there was evil. In his
younger years, he had often come tiptoeing into Rachael's bedroom
at night to sleep at the foot of her bed, or, even more often, to sleep
on her floor with one hand on the door so that he could slam it shut
on whatever minion of hell had chased him out of his own room and
might possibly follow. It was a long time before Rachael realized he
came to her room not for refuge, but to protect.

Her brother's hypersensitivity to the forces of darkness had always
scared Rachael, but strangely, his equally heightened awareness of the
sacred unnerved her just as much. His fascination with the Trinity
made him "other-like," put him out of reach, and obviously made him
different than the other boys in their St. Cloud neighborhood. Joshua
had few playmates as a child and spent most of his free time drawing
pictures of heaven and hell and staging elaborate battles between angels
and demons with green plastic soldiers.

It worried her parents, too—especially their mother, Eva. It was
most evident to Rachael how much their mother was troubled by her
only son's eccentric ways the Christmas he was six and Rachael was
eleven. Eva had set up her olive wood nativity set in the entry on a tall
mahogany table that boasted framed family portraits the other months
of the year. On the night of a rather elaborately planned dinner party,
Eva came downstairs to find that in addition to the three Wise Men
giving the baby Jesus audience, there was also a contingent of Star
Wars storm troopers, G.I. Joes, Teenage Mutant Ninja Turtles and
several dinosaurs—all lined up in neat rows, as if paying quiet homage
to the Infant Savior. With guests due to arrive at any minute, Eva
yelled for Joshua and ordered him to "get those toys off that table!"

But instead of rushing off to attend to last-minute details, Eva stood and watched her son dutifully but sorrowfully remove the toys with a look on her face that made Rachael, watching also, wince. Fear was in her mother's eyes, not annoyance.

Much later, when the guests were getting ready to leave, Rachael, who had been helping her mother in the kitchen, noticed that the Baby Jesus wasn't in His manger. The carefully arranged crèche was missing its Emmanuel. When she went upstairs to get ready for bed, Rachael peeked into her brother's room and saw that the holy Babe was within the stiff curl of Joshua's right fist, and clutched tightly to his chest as he slept. She never forgot how she felt when she saw her little brother clasping God to his bosom as if he would perish right there in his PJs should the Almighty be taken from him. She felt like that right now.

Afraid.

Two thoughts immediately crystallized for Rachael: first, it was unthinkable that Joshua could kill. And second, it would be her turn to protect Joshua. Her mind suddenly rushed to an image of Joshua at three, running to her in tears, arms out, afraid of a towering Hamburglar statue. They were at a McDonald's restaurant and their mother was in line to buy cheeseburgers. She felt his young arms around her neck and heard herself say to him, "It's okay. Sissy will protect you."

"Rachael!" Her mother shouted her name across time and space, bringing her back to the present.

And the only response Rachael could immediately give was the one she had no control over. Her milk let down.

TWO

Trace was now leaning far over the banister, with an art pencil in one hand, curiosity etched across his face as he stared at her. His orange-tinted hair and single diamond cross earring glistened as sunlight filtered in through the window wall.

"Did you hear what I said?" Her mother's voice was tinged with fear.

"Yes, Mom, I heard you!" Rachael snatched the burp rag off the coffee table and shoved it lengthwise into both sides of her nursing bra. "But what you're telling me is impossible. Where did you hear this?" Rachael replied with an even voice. She had to remain calm for her mother.

"Hon, what's going on?" Trace's soft baritone voice floated down. Rachael covered the mouthpiece of the cell phone.

"Josh is in trouble," she said.

Trace's head lifted slightly in at least partial understanding. He came away from the banister and began to descend the open staircase to the living room. Sunlight from a lazy Manhattan sun shone on him from curtainless windows that flanked the staircase from floor to ceiling.

"He called me from jail and told me himself, Rachael," Eva Harper continued. "He called me this morning."

"Okay, Mom. Look, start at the beginning. This isn't making any sense," Rachael requested, pressing the rag tight to her chest. Trace walked across the room to her, his bare feet making hardly a sound.

"What's with *that*?" he whispered, pointing to the burp rag with his pencil.

She tossed him a look of mild exasperation. She didn't have a clue what was with *that*.

"He called me. From the Ramsey County jail," Eva continued, her voice trembling with frustration. "He confessed to killing a man. He told me there's not going to be a trial. Rachael, he'll go to prison! Just like that! Without a trial!"

The lawyer in Rachael wanted to quickly advise her mother that people who confess to crimes aren't required to participate in a trial if they don't want one, but the daughter and sister in her refused to muddy this horrible conversation with legal procedure.

"Rachael, you've got to do something!" Eva was adamant, stretched to the limits of her ability to handle this new, unspeakable chapter in her son's life in a calm, parental way. She wanted Rachael to sweep down and take the baton.

"Mom, I can't do anything until you tell me exactly what has happened." Again Rachael struggled to remain composed. "What exactly did he confess to?"

"You've got to do something!"

"For Pete's sake! What did he *do*?" Trace asked. Rachael just looked at him, shaking her head.

"Mom, is Dad there? Let me talk to Dad." Rachael pulled the burp rag out of her shirt and tossed it on the floor.

"Rachael." Cliff Harper's voice replaced Eva's on the phone. His was steady but wrapped in worry and maybe something else. Fear? Contempt?

"Dad, tell me exactly what happened."

"He's really done it this time, Rachael." The sting of disappointment was evident behind every word, though Rachael knew it had been many years since her father had been close to Joshua. Outwardly, the unraveling of the father–son relationship began when Joshua was twelve, particularly when Joshua decided to attend a weekend of tent meetings at the nondenominational Bible church on the edge of St. Cloud. Cliff had made fun of the meetings, belittling them in Joshua's presence, but Joshua had gone anyway. At first Cliff had been annoyed that Joshua went, mostly because the family attended a traditional Methodist church that had no connections whatsoever to the little Bible church on the edge of town. But his annoyance turned to disgust and then to apprehension and then finally to anger when, by the end of that weekend, Joshua was a changed young man. He had a new sense of purpose for being on the planet—a purpose that was entirely outside any plan Cliff Harper had for his only son. It was the tent meetings that stole away any aspirations Joshua might have had of college and of a traditional life of career, marriage, and family. The relational unraveling between father and son began as soon as Cliff realized he would always play second fiddle to God in his son's life, in every aspect of it.

"Dad? Please tell me what happened."

In the background Rachael could hear her mother crying. Her father cleared his throat, borrowing a snatch of time to find the words.

"Josh called this morning. Said he wanted us to hear this from him rather than on the evening news. He went to the police last night and confessed to killing the owner of a little grocery store in a Hmong neighborhood five days ago."

Rachael sat back fully on the couch and ran her free hand through her hair. An unbidden image of an Asian man lying in a pool of blood among displays of bok choy and shitake mushrooms invaded her thoughts. Joshua was in the image too. Blood was on his hands.

Impossible.

"Dad, that just can't be true," she said. "He wouldn't do that. Why would he do that?"

"He said he was trying to help this teenager, a Hmong girl, who he said was being victimized by the grocery store owner. He was her second cousin or something, and he was letting drug dealers use his basement for not only deals but also the forced prostitution of this girl."

Rachael's breath caught in her throat. "Is it true?"

"How should I know, Rachael. I know there's been stuff in the newspapers about this kind of thing happening. And it's just the sort of thing your brother would get himself mixed up with. Always trying to save the world…"

"But Dad!" Rachael cut him short. "It isn't like Joshua to *kill* someone! You know it isn't. This just doesn't make sense. Why didn't he call the police when he found out this was happening?"

She saw Trace flinch when she said the word "kill." His eyes widened. She looked away from him.

"He said it wasn't something he planned," Cliff answered. "He had gone to the store with the girl to convince the grocer to leave her alone. He thought it actually hadn't happened yet, that the girl asked him to help before she had been abused. But he found out when he got there that he was too late. She had already been assaulted a couple weeks before. He said he went crazy when he found this out, and he shot the grocer."

Joshua the Benevolent aiming a gun at another man? Pulling the trigger? It was as unthinkable as Captain Kangaroo drawing a bead on the mailman. "Joshua doesn't even own a gun. This is insane, Dad," Rachael asserted.

"It was the shopkeeper's gun. He had it with him in the basement of the store. They got into a fight and somehow during the struggle Joshua ended up with it."

In her mind Rachael saw her brother struggling with the shopkeeper, wrestling with him among cramped shelves, their feet scuffling madly on a cement floor. Perhaps the young girl was watching. Crying.

Screaming. Joshua pried the gun away from the shopkeeper, but the shopkeeper lunged for him and Joshua aimed and fired to protect himself. To protect the girl.

"So it was self-defense?" Her voice was at once hopeful.

"No, Rachael. It wasn't self-defense."

"Why not? Why wasn't it self-defense?"

"Joshua said something in him just snapped and he…" Her father's voice melted away.

"He *what?* What did he do?" Rachael whispered, afraid to imagine it.

When Cliff spoke, his voice was prickled with emotion. "He shot the grocer in the back of the head, Rachael."

For the second time in mere minutes the air in the room was whisked away. Rachael looked up at her husband, seeking the recognizable in a moment of utter unfamiliarity. Trace's eyes met hers, and his face was awash in questions. He sat down beside her and Rachael took his hand; his art pencil fell to the wood floor with a slight clatter.

"Rachael?" Trace asked.

Rachael looked away from him and spoke into the phone instead. "Dad, you know he couldn't have done this!"

"I don't know anything anymore, Rachael. He said he did it, and the police believe him. He's being arraigned on Tuesday. That's what they told him. Murder, second degree…" Cliff Harper's voice wavered and disappeared completely. Rachael could hear her mother crying in the background.

Several long moments of silence hung between daughter and father, New York and Minnesota, the called and the caller. Finally Cliff's voice floated across the long, empty space between them.

"Can you do anything for him, Rachael?" her father pleaded.

"Rachael, please come! Please come!" Her mother's voice sounded far away and yet Rachael knew she was probably hovering just at her father's shoulder, holding onto his arm, her face streaked with tears.

"I…I don't know what I can do, Dad," she mumbled, straining to imagine what help she could possibly be for Joshua. She had an arsenal of tools to help someone wrongfully charged, though her experience in the courtroom was largely focused on defending runaways, truants, and textbook juvenile delinquents. The law firm she worked for was big enough that she could specialize in defending young offenders and decline to take on drunk drivers, spouse beaters, and child abusers, leaving these cases to the other lawyers in the firm. But Josh wasn't a kid. And Josh had already confessed. What could she do?

"There must be something….Rachael, please." Her father's voice was urgent.

"I don't know. Maybe if I talk to him. Maybe if he's covering for someone…"

"Can you come right away?" Her father interrupted her. "He's being formally charged the day after tomorrow."

Rachael sighed. She could certainly change nothing in two days. But she could talk to her brother. Maybe she could convince him to tell her what really happened. Maybe it was the young girl who had pulled the trigger, the young, hurting girl whose innocence had been stolen by someone she trusted. Rachael easily imagined that during the fight on the basement floor, the gun had been pried from the grocer's hand. She closed her eyes and pictured it skittering across the floor as Joshua wrestled to subdue the Asian man. She pictured the young girl, also in the room, picking it up and aiming at the man who had traded her body for money or protection. She fired at the back of her cousin's head while he leaned over Joshua, choking him, perhaps. The grocer then slumped over dead. Anguished, Joshua rose to his feet and gathered the sobbing girl in his arms. He probably told her he'd find a way to keep her safe, and they fled the scene. The body was discovered and then Joshua waited. When it looked like the police were suspecting the girl had committed the crime, he came forward. Took her place. Confessed he had done it.

That had to be what happened. Or something like it. No other explanation was possible.

"I'll come, Dad," she said, opening her eyes. "I'll get there as soon as I can."

"Call us when you get in," her father said, relief in his voice.

"All right."

She pressed the "off" button and looked at Trace.

"What in the world did he do this time?" Trace asked, though not in an unkind way.

"Joshua confessed to murder," Rachael replied, wincing as the word *murder* tumbled out of her mouth. "He told the police he killed a man involved in drugs and child prostitution. But I know he didn't do it, Trace. He couldn't."

Trace blinked. "So what are you going to do?" he said.

"I need to talk to him. I have to talk to him."

"And that means…"

"And that means flying out there tomorrow. Or tonight if we can arrange it."

"We?"

"I want you and McKenna to come with me, of course. I wouldn't think of traveling without her, and I don't want to go without *you*. Please, Trace?"

Trace kept hold of his wife's hand, but bent down to retrieve his art pencil with his free hand. "Well, how long do you think we'll be gone?"

Rachael took in a breath. Who could say? The little she could do might take place in one short visit to the Ramsey County Jail. If Josh refused to cooperate, it would be a short trip. If he recanted, it could mean weeks…at the very least.

"I'm not sure. Maybe a few days. Maybe a few weeks. I don't know, Trace. But you could bring your projects with you. Mom will babysit whenever she can, you know she will. I'm not asking you to back out of any of your deadlines. You'll have the time to work on your projects. I guarantee it."

"Rach."

"Please, Trace. Please come with me."

Trace sat back on the couch, thinking. He sighed but then suddenly sat forward again. "Hey. We could stay with Fig."

Rachael looked over at him. Fig—Figaro Houseman—was a classmate of Trace's from his days at the Minneapolis College of Art and Design. Rachael knew him well. He irritated her to no end.

"Fig?" she said.

"Don't pretend you didn't hear me," Trace replied, a slight smirk on his face. "Yes, I said Fig. He just bought that loft and studio overlooking the Mississippi. Remember? The one he paid *cash* for? It's right in downtown in the old warehouse district in Minneapolis. And he's got tons of room. He told me himself."

Rachael swallowed a comment about where Fig might have come up with that kind of money. Fact was, Fig was wildly talented and had sold his sculptures all over the world. But he was unconventional in almost every way. He listened to strange music, ate strange food, kept strange company, and said strange things. "I doubt he'll want a new baby staying with him," she said.

"Well, that just shows you don't know everything. He told me when McKenna was first born that we were welcome—all three of us—to come stay with him anytime we wanted."

"Really?" She didn't want to believe it. But it was highly probable Fig had said just such a thing. It was outlandish to think a single man would want a new baby crowding his apartment and wailing away the midnight hours. But outlandish was just the sort of man Fig was.

"Yes, really," Trace answered. "And I would have room to work in his studio while we're away. I'm not going to get that in a hotel or at your parents' house."

Rachael sighed. He was right. And actually the location of Fig's place would be ideal, especially if their stay stretched into more than just days. "Okay. You win. You can call him."

"I win? I didn't know we were in a contest," Trace said, reaching for the phone. She handed it to him.

"Just don't let him feed McKenna anything," she said, furrowing her brow.

She rose from the couch and headed into the room she used as an office as Trace punched in Fig's number. Rachael heard him say Fig's name and then she relaxed as Trace laughed. It was good to hear a laugh at that moment. She headed to her laptop to look for the first available flight out of JFK to Minneapolis.

THREE

Fig met Trace, Rachael, and McKenna at the Minneapolis airport a few minutes before midnight. He was wearing a multistained, chartreuse painter's smock, brown leather pants, and a black fedora. The airport had long since disgorged its daily population of thousands, leaving only a few late-evening Sunday travelers to imagine what artistic pursuit he had torn himself away from to pick up friends at the airport.

Carrying McKenna in her arms, Rachael bent toward Fig at the bottom of the stairs leading to the baggage claim and allowed him to kiss her on both cheeks.

"Hello, Fig," she said.

"Rachael, kumquat, motherhood suits you. You look almost happy to see me," Fig said in return. He turned to Trace and the volume of his voice tripled in decibels. "Aren't you *the* Tracey Flynn? Haven't I seen your work in *The New Yorker*? It's you, isn't it? You're Tracey Flynn!"

"Cool it, Fig. There's nobody here," Trace said good-naturedly, nodding toward a sea of empty baggage carousels.

"And this must be the blessed progeny." Fig suddenly turned back to Rachael and the sleeping infant in her arms. "Ah, fair one, let me look at you."

Rachael cautiously peeled back the blanket covering most of McKenna's face. Fig leaned down and touched her head. Rachael noted that his fingernails were painted Kelly green. He then whispered something over McKenna's body in a language Rachael didn't recognize.

"What was that?" she asked Fig, pulling the blanket back over McKenna's face.

"Just a little Mayan blessing," he said, and then turned back to Trace. "And a little curse upon those who would harm her."

"Fig, when did you take up painting?" Trace asked, changing the subject and pointing toward Fig's smock as they walked toward the only baggage carousel that was moving.

"I didn't," Fig replied. "I just like the smock. I splattered it myself. With an egg whisk. Blindfolded. In the nude."

Rachael threw Trace a look, and he smiled and winked at her. Trace loved Fig. Loved his crazy ways.

"I'm absolutely elated you are here, amigos," Fig continued. "We shall have a splendid time." Then he cast a quick look back at Rachael. "That is, when we are not bemoaning your most wretched circumstances, Rachael dear. Killing is messy business."

Rachael stepped ahead of Fig as McKenna's car seat tumbled out of the conveyor. "My brother didn't kill anyone," she said, her voice calm.

Autumn morning sunlight swept across Rachael as she lay in the four-poster bed that was the sole piece of furniture in Fig's guest room. *That bed is a keeper of stories,* Fig had said the night before. A seventeenth-century French courtier, who had the terrible misfortune of falling in love with the village undertaker, had slept in it. And died in it.

"The story just gets worse, so we'll leave it at that," Fig had added.

Rachael had been too tired from travel, trouble, and the time change to think much about the French maiden or anything else. She had slipped in between Fig's Egyptian cotton sheets a little after midnight, leaving Trace and his exotic friend to play catch-up while they sipped ginger tea. Despite being in a bed of stories and in a strange room, Rachael had fallen asleep in minutes. And McKenna had thankfully slept through the night in the portable crib they had brought with them from New York.

McKenna now lay in the crook of Rachael's arm, sated with breakfast. Trace was in Fig's guest bathroom shaving. Rachael was holding her cell phone, warm from the lengthy conversation she had just had with her mother. It hadn't been easy to convince Eva to let her see Joshua alone this morning. Her mother had put up quite a fight, insisting that only the two of them together could convince Joshua to give up this bizarre scheme to take the fall for something he didn't do.

But Rachael had prevailed by reminding her mother of the painful truth that Joshua had always confided in Rachael before anyone else… and usually at the exclusion of everyone else. Rachael was the only one whose room Josh had escaped to when the dark overwhelmed him. She was the only one who knew how he truly felt when their father took him deer hunting that one and only time. And only Rachael knew what really happened to him during the tent meetings when he was twelve and she was seventeen.

"Well…call me the *moment* you leave him," Eva said before she hung up.

"I promise," Rachael assured her.

She eased McKenna onto the bed and placed the bed pillows around her sleeping body. *There is no sense in putting off what I came here to do,* Rachael decided. Especially since McKenna would need to be fed again in three hours. She began to get dressed.

Rachael parked Fig's car in the visitor's lot of the Ramsey County Jail and stepped into the lingering chill of the late September morning. She had been in a jail parking lot dozens of times and couldn't remember ever feeling nervous about being there. But she was anxious now. She grabbed her briefcase from the passenger side, knowing she probably didn't need it. Joshua was her brother, not her client. But she wanted it with her just the same.

Inside, Rachael politely told the deputy sitting behind bulletproof glass that she wanted to see Joshua Harper. She showed him her business card.

"Are you his lawyer?" the deputy asked.

"If he's going to need one, then I want to help him. But right now I guess I'm just his sister."

The deputy looked at the card and then looked up at her. "You'll have to wait over there for a few minutes. Why don't you have a seat?"

The deputy pointed to a row of uncomfortable-looking chairs where a lone man waited, staring blankly ahead, deep in thought. Then the deputy stepped away to speak to another officer behind a second wall of glass. The two of them disappeared from view.

Rachael waited.

A woman in a blue suit and sensible but elegant black heels sailed into the lobby. She wore conservative but shimmering gold jewelry and enough makeup to look professional, but not theatrical. She carried a black briefcase. A lawyer, no doubt. Confident and collected. Just going about her list of things to do today. Rachael knew the life of that woman. She toyed with her wedding ring and waited and watched her. The woman glanced at her watch every few minutes.

Finally the deputy returned, and the woman hurried to the window. But the officer motioned to Rachael and the woman stepped back, casting a look of impatience her way.

"You'll need to come in and sign the log, and then you can see him," he said to Rachael. "Just open the door on your left."

A loud buzzer sounded and Rachael hurried to open the massive door. She walked through a short corridor to another door. She heard another buzzer, pushed open the door, and stepped through.

"Are you taking those in with you?" The deputy pointed to her purse and briefcase.

"I guess I don't have to," she answered. She couldn't picture herself taking notes as she visited with her brother.

"We can lock them up for you while you're inside, then."

"Sure." Rachael handed her purse and briefcase to the deputy and watched as another deputy placed them in a cabinet and locked it.

"Sign here, please." said the first deputy.

Rachael bent over a table that held a visitor's log and signed her name.

"This way, ma'am."

Rachael followed the deputy down a long hallway to a room that held nothing but a table and three chairs. The interview room. Not for a sister to visit a brother in jail, but for an attorney to visit with a client.

"Why don't you have a seat," the deputy said. "Your brother will be along in a minute or two. When he comes, you'll need to stay on your side of the table, please."

"Sure. Thanks."

The deputy left and Rachael pulled out one of the chairs. It was made of white molded plastic and made a sharp grating sound as she pulled it across the floor. She sat down.

Within minutes the door opened again and Rachael saw the jailer first. Behind him was her brother, wearing an orange jumpsuit and walking slowly with measured steps. His honey-brown hair was pulled back into a ponytail, and he was clean-shaven. There was a yellowing bruise under his right eye—evidence that something had gone wrong in his life in the past few days. He had never been a big man, but his six-foot frame seemed particularly lanky, and he looked underfed as he shuffled in. Joshua's eyes were on the floor as he crossed the threshold, but then he raised them. Rachael didn't know what she expected to see in those eyes, but she hoped to see something. Joshua's eyes were lifeless.

She stood and nearly ran to embrace him but the deputy who was leading Joshua in warned her with a glance to stay on her side of the table. The deputy turned and left the room, but when door closed behind him, Rachael could see that he stood at the window, watching them.

"Josh," she said, and her voice cracked with the weight of his name on her lips.

"Hey, Rach," he replied. The voice was his; the eyes were not.

He pulled out the other chair and took a seat. Rachael sat back down.

"It looks like we've got company," she said softly, nodding toward the little window and the deputy who stood at it.

"Oh," Josh said, glancing behind him. "I'm particularly remorseful. They don't see that a lot here. When they do, it usually means more trouble, not less. If you had smuggled in some cyanide for me, it would spoil the sentencing."

He said the words as cavalierly as if he were stating his agenda for the day. Rachael swallowed. She hadn't expected Joshua to be so detached and void of emotion.

"You want to tell me what's going on here?" she asked, masking her alarm by appearing to be peeved.

Joshua met her gaze. "What don't you know?" he asked casually.

"I don't think I know the truth, Josh," she replied, leveling her gaze back at him.

He looked away.

"So you want to tell me what's going on here?" she tried again.

Silence.

"Josh?"

Joshua turned his head back to her and simply stared at her for several long seconds. Then he looked away again. Rachael was about to plead for his cooperation when Josh opened his mouth and began to speak in slow, even tones, caressing the soft words and crunching down on the hard ones: "Woe to those who make unjust laws, to those who issue oppressive decrees, to deprive the poor of their rights and withhold justice from the oppressed of my people, making widows their prey and robbing the fatherless."

Then he turned back to her and continued. "What will you do on the day of reckoning, when disaster comes from afar? To whom will you run for help?" Josh's eyes were wide but expressionless as he suddenly fell silent.

Rachael willed herself to remain unfazed. This wasn't the first time Josh quoted Scripture for the sole purpose of messing with people.

"Jeremiah?" she asked casually.

The tiniest smirk inched its way across her brother's lips. "Isaiah 10."

"That's an interesting verse, Josh, but it doesn't explain why you're here," Rachael said coolly. The minuscule grin on her brother's face had calmed her.

"It explains everything," he said softly, looking past her to the wall, which was nothing but a plain, painted surface.

Rachael leaned forward, willing Josh to turn his attention back to her. "Josh, I *know* you didn't kill that man. I know you confessed to protect someone. You did it to shelter someone, didn't you? Someone who doesn't deserve all the terrible things life has shoved his or her way. Isn't that right, Joshua? You think you can protect that person from the torment of prison by going in his or her place!"

Josh turned his head toward her. The smirk was gone. The lifeless eyes were back.

"Go home to your baby, Rach," he said gently.

"I'm not leaving here until I get some answers!" she shot back.

Joshua didn't look away from her, but he said nothing.

"I *know* what you're trying to do, but I'm not going to let you do it, Josh," she said angrily. "What you're doing is *wrong*. Whoever killed that man will have to live with what he did every day of his life. Did you think about that? How do you think that person is going to handle that in years to come? That he or she not only killed a man, but that he let an innocent man go to prison for it? How do you think that person will feel then? Are you sure you can live with *that?*"

Joshua's expressionless eyes stared back at her. He still said nothing.

Resentment welled up within Rachael. There had to be a way to get through to him short of torturing the truth out of him. She sat back in her chair.

"I don't know the Bible like you do, Josh, but I know it's wrong to lie," she murmured. "I know God hates it. He would never ask this of you. Not God."

Joshua blinked and looked away. His eyes grew glassy with moisture, and he reached up to flick away a tear that had barely begun to form.

"Josh!" Rachael continued, and her own eyes grew heavy with developing tears. "Please! Please don't do this!"

Her brother looked down for a moment, and then he inhaled deeply as if drawing strength from an extra measure of oxygen. He raised his eyes to look at Rachael. And then in a swift motion he reached across the table for her. The jailer behind the glass took a step forward and opened the door. Rachael stretched her arm across the table and grabbed Joshua's hand.

Josh clasped her fingers around his. He caught her gaze with eyes that suddenly seemed alive again. "I'm not afraid of the dark anymore, Rachael," he said, and he brought her hand to his lips and kissed it even as the jailer closed the distance between them.

"Okay, that's it," the jailer said, reaching for Joshua's arm and pulling it from Rachael's grasp. "This visit is over. Your brother is going back to his cell. Arraignment is tomorrow at two. Wait here and someone will come for you."

The jailer pulled Joshua to his feet and ushered him to the door.

"Joshua," Rachael called one last time.

Joshua turned his head toward her as the deputy led him out of the little room.

The moment had passed.

Joshua's eyes had become empty again, like those of a dead man.

FOUR

The heavy door closed at apparent leisure behind Joshua and the jailer. Through the door's tiny window webbed with crossing wires, Rachael watched as her brother walked down the tiled hallway to his cell, the accompanying jailer obscuring everything but flashes of orange jumpsuit and the back of Joshua's head.

Her breath came in uneven waves as anger and fear swelled even as Joshua disappeared from view.

Joshua didn't kill the grocer. She was sure of it. This was Joshua's way of beating evil at its own game. His comment that he was no longer afraid of the dark was his cryptic way of telling her he had found a way to compete with wickedness and win. She had to find out whom he was protecting. The police didn't know him like she knew him. They didn't know Joshua was the kind of person to confess to something he didn't do to protect the life of a hurting soul. All they knew was there was a dead Asian man in the basement of a little grocery store and a man who said he killed him.

She had to talk to the police.

The door behind her clicked and began to swing open. Rachael rose from her chair and sailed through the now-open doorway.

"I need to talk to someone," she said to the deputy who was waiting for her on the other side. "You've got the wrong man. My brother is covering for someone."

The deputy appeared only mildly interested in her announcement. He turned to unlock the cabinet that held her purse and briefcase. "Your brother turned himself in. He confessed, you know."

"But that doesn't mean he did it!" Rachael countered.

The deputy turned back around with her belongings in his hands and extended his arms. "Well, usually it does." He said it matter-of-factly, as a man who has seen every ugly side of crime would.

"Look, you don't know my brother," Rachael continued. "He's... he's kind of *addicted* to helping people. He's obsessed with aiding people who've been dealt more than they can handle. He's just the sort of person to admit to something he didn't do if it means saving someone who's in way over his head."

The deputy's arms were still outstretched with the handles of her purse and briefcase in his closed fingers. "There aren't a whole lot of people willing to lie about having killed someone," the deputy said, his voice still kind and controlled.

Rachael took her things from his hands. "I know there aren't; I'm a lawyer," she said, slinging the straps of her purse and briefcase onto her shoulder. "But I'm also *his* sister. And I'm telling you my brother wouldn't hesitate to take the fall for someone who had been wronged if it meant he could save him or her from greater harm."

The deputy said nothing for several seconds. "I'm not the one you need to talk to about this," he finally replied.

Rachael's throat tightened. "My brother refuses to listen to reason."

The deputy shrugged. "Then you don't have a lot of options, I'm afraid, unless you have proof of his innocence. But if you truly think your brother is lying about this, you should probably talk with the county prosecutor's office. They're bringing the charges against him, and they have a pretty solid case from what I hear. A confession…and a witness who said she saw a man who fits your brother's description entering the store basement the night the grocer was shot and killed."

Her father hadn't mentioned there was a witness, but it didn't matter. Rachael had no doubt her brother was probably there when it happened. But he didn't pull the trigger. She wondered what else the witness saw. The police report of the incident and the five-day investigation would tell her. It would tell her a lot about what happened that night. She needed information to wrench the truth from Joshua, and she knew her brother wouldn't provide it.

"I'd really like to see the police report. May I talk to the officer in charge of the investigation?" she said to the deputy.

The deputy motioned to the heavy door that would lead her back to the lobby. "Well, the police station is on the other side of the parking lot. I don't know if Sgt. Pendleton is in this morning, but that's who you need to talk to."

Rachael murmured a thank you and started to walk away. The deputy pressed a button, a buzzer sounded, and the door to the lobby began to slowly swing open. She turned back around.

"I know what you must think," she said to the deputy. "You probably hear this all the time from frantic family members. But I'm telling you, you really do have the wrong man."

The deputy's countenance never changed. "Then I guess you have your work cut out for you."

Despite his candor, the deputy's voice was sympathetic, not flippant.

Rachael knew he was right. Getting to the bottom of this wasn't going to be easy.

The waiting area in the Homicide Department seemed no different to Rachael than that of a dentist's office, but she was acutely aware as she waited to talk to Sgt. Pendleton, that a contest of wills was being played out behind the walls of the desks, cubicles, and offices around her—contests between right and wrong.

Or, as Joshua always saw everything, good versus evil.

Behind the partitions men and women charged with bringing murderers to justice scurried about the so-called playing field, fully engaged in the competition. Their goal: to put killers behind bars, to avenge the life of the slain, to protect the innocent from further slaughter.

She had every right to be here.

Josh Harper was not a killer. They weren't going to win this contest.

"Ms. Flynn?"

Rachael looked up, startled.

A tall black man with muted gray at his temples and a kind face was looking down at her. He stood just a few feet away. She had no idea when he had approached her.

"Yes?"

"I'm Sgt. Will Pendleton. I understand you need to talk with me?"

Rachael stood and shook the detective's outstretched hand. His grasp was firm. Over his shoulder and wrapped across his chest was a leather shoulder holster—empty now, but she knew it was not always this way. Will Pendleton wore the holster with ease, as if it were part of his skin. In his other hand he held her business card.

"Yes. Thanks," Rachael said. "I need to speak with you about my brother, Joshua Harper."

"Yes?" He waited for her to continue.

Rachael dove in. "Look, I know he confessed to killing that grocery store owner, but I'm certain he's covering for someone."

The detective regarded her silently for a moment. Without a change in the inflection of his voice he motioned to the hallway behind him from where he had probably emerged. "Would you like to come back to my office?" He didn't sound bored, but he didn't sound terribly interested either.

"Thank you." Rachael grabbed her purse and briefcase and followed

Pendleton down the carpeted hallway. All around her the investigative machine was humming. Phones were ringing, file drawers were being opened and shut, and the clicking of computer keyboards filled the spaces in between.

They stopped in front a small partitioned office with a wall of windows that faced the hallway. Will Pendleton sauntered in and waved to the set of chairs in front of his desk. "Please have a seat."

"Thanks," Rachael said, taking the one closest to the door and looking about her. The remaining walls in Pendleton's office were covered with evidence of what he did for a living. A massive white board on one wall had been wiped clean but red, green, and blue bleed marks showed where dry-erase ink had covered it many times over. A bulletin board containing haphazardly pinned notices, reports, newspaper articles, memos, and cartoons hung next to it. On another wall were plaques, commendations, and photographs of Will Pendleton in the line of duty. His desk was strewn about with files, papers, and yellow-lined notepads. A framed 5 x 7 photo of a smiling woman, presumably his wife, flanked by two teenage boys, sat on his desk in the only space uncluttered by paper.

Sgt. Pendleton took the chair behind his desk and leaned back in it, lacing his fingers together as he rested his elbows on the armrests. "So you think your brother is innocent," he said, not unkindly, but clearly unconvinced.

"I know it," Rachael replied.

Will Pendleton's eyes widened a fraction. "Is that the lawyer in you talking or the sister?"

"Does it matter? He didn't do it. My brother is incapable of killing."

Pendleton smiled, but it wasn't one of amusement. "Ms. Flynn, I understand you're an attorney…and as an attorney, you surely must know that *anyone* is capable of taking another person's life."

Rachael leaned forward in her chair. "Detective, my brother is a very religious man. Annoyingly religious. And he's deeply concerned about people in need. He's been on a one-man crusade to save the world ever since he finished high school. It's all he does! So not only would he never kill someone, he's just the kind of person to take the fall for someone who did, someone who he's trying to help."

Pendleton unlaced his fingers and leaned forward as well. "Ms. Flynn, your brother may very well be a *religious* person, but he's not your typical law-abiding citizen." He patted a thick brown file on his desk. "This is his file—a hefty collection of records from four county law enforcement agencies. *Four*. I'm sure you know what's in here."

Rachael's heart skipped a beat. Yes, she knew what was in that file. Joshua *wasn't* the typical law-abiding citizen. He had been arrested more times than she cared to count. But just as quickly she knew how to answer the detective.

"He's not your typical criminal either," she said. "You've read it, haven't you? There's nothing in there but misdemeanors and petty offenses. Blocking entrance to an abortion clinic. Breaking into a house to get a woman's food stamps away from her abusive brother-in-law. Loitering on a street corner to keep kids he knew and cared about from buying drugs there. Hardly gateway crimes to murder."

"Granted. But Ms. Flynn, your brother's numerous arrests and offenses show that he does not respect the law. He has exhibited a continual and, I think I can say confidently, a growing disregard for the law. Moreover he confessed. If he is indeed a highly religious man, like you say, then why would he lie? It seems to me a highly religious man would be just the sort of man to confess to murder. He would be unable to live with the guilt."

Rachael shook her head. She wasn't getting through to him. "Joshua only disrespects the law when it seems law enforcement or the courts aren't doing their jobs. If a wrong needs to be made right and the police and the courts are doing nothing about it, then, yes, Josh tries to make it right on his own. I'm not excusing what he does, but he does it because of his fixation for people in need."

"I understand what you're saying, Ms. Flynn," the detective said. "And to tell you the truth, you're the second person I've talked to today who believes we've got the wrong man in custody. A woman who runs a soup kitchen on Lexington *insists* your brother is innocent even though she didn't even see your brother the day of the murder. But the fact is, your brother's over-the-top compassion for people doesn't give him a license to break laws or enforce them. Can you imagine what the world would be like if everyone insisted on his own brand of justice however and whenever he pleased?"

Rachael sat back in her chair and tried to gather her thoughts. *Calm down, calm down, calm down,* she told herself. That thick file was evidence of who Joshua *really* was—a bit of a troublemaker, yes, but not a killer. It was *good* that the detective had it. It was to Joshua's advantage that he had it. She cleared her throat.

"I'm not suggesting Joshua's past offenses be overlooked," she said. "If anything, I'm suggesting you study them. Look at them in light of what he has confessed to doing. Every infraction my brother has ever been charged with has involved some poor widow he was trying to help or some orphaned child. Every one. Why would this one be any different? He is trying to *shield* someone. Someone else pointed a gun at the back of the grocer's head. Someone else pulled the trigger. Maybe it was that teenager he was trying to help. There was a girl involved with this, wasn't there? A girl my brother said was being victimized?"

Will Pendleton's head nodded once. "There were two girls actually. Sisters."

This was news to Rachael, but she plowed ahead.

"And I bet they're orphans. They are, aren't they?"

Again Pendleton offered a single nod, but this time unease was etched across his face.

"You see? My brother honestly feels commissioned by God Almighty to defend the cause of widows and orphans. He gave his life over to it when he was twelve!"

Pendleton cocked his head. "What do you mean, 'gave his life over to it'?"

Rachael leaned forward again. "I mean, he came home from a tent meeting on the edge of town when he was twelve with this story that a preacher had laid his hands on him and spoke over him those very words from the book of James."

"The book of James."

"In the Bible."

"And what were those very words?"

Rachael knew them by heart, though she had never meant to memorize them. She had simply always been able to call them back up at a moment's notice. They fell now from her lips: "'Religion that God our Father accepts as pure and faultless is this: to look after orphans and widows in their distress and to keep oneself from being polluted by the world.'"

Pendleton said nothing for a few moments as the words of Scripture were absorbed into the room. "That doesn't mean he didn't do it," he finally said. "His way of helping these orphans may have been to kill a man he believed was harming them."

"Or his way of helping may have been to tell you he killed the grocer so that an abused orphan wouldn't be convicted of murder."

"He had motive, he had opportunity, he was at the scene, and he confessed," Pendleton said.

"He made *a vow when he was twelve,*" Rachael replied softly.

Pendleton sat back in his chair, laced his fingers again, and brought his entwined hands to rest under his chin.

"Your brother has his first court appearance tomorrow. I can't go to the county prosecutors and tell them his lawyer sister has a hunch he's lying."

"Will you allow me to look at the police report?" Rachael asked. "Let me see your investigation leading up to the day Joshua confessed. Then take me to the crime scene. Please? I know I can give you more than a hunch to go on."

Pendleton sighed and pulled his hands away from his chin. "Are you planning on defending your brother? Do you have a license to practice law in this state?"

"If I have to defend him to stop this I'll look into getting a provisional license. But until then, please let me in the loop. You don't want to send the wrong man to prison. I know you don't."

Pendleton was silent as he considered her request.

"Please?" Rachael said.

"Hold on a sec," Pendleton said. He picked up his phone and punched in some numbers. "This is Sgt. Will Pendleton. Emily Lonetree, please," he said a moment later.

He put his hand over the mouthpiece of the phone. "If the prosecutor doesn't have a problem with it, I don't," Pendleton said. "Ordinarily, I'd tell you to give the defendant's lawyer a call and let them decide to show you the reports or not. But your brother doesn't have a lawyer. And he won't be offered the opportunity to have court-appointed counsel until tomorrow."

Pendleton abruptly pulled his hand away from the mouthpiece and spoke into it. "Emily this is Will across the lot. Say, I've got the sister of Joshua Harper here in my office. She's a New York attorney. She's fairly certain her brother didn't kill the grocery store owner and that he is covering for someone, one of the girls maybe....No, she doesn't have proof, but she's got some insights into Harper's character that interest me. She wants to see the police report and the confession...She's not been asked to represent him, no....Yeah, I do....All right. Is it okay if I let her see the crime scene? No, just to look. Ten minutes, tops. Okay. Thanks."

Pendleton hung up the phone.

The detective leaned forward again. "The prosecutor will let you see the reports, but you can't make any copies and no note-taking. And she wants to meet you first. I don't have time to make you a separate copy of the report and black out the names of the juveniles, so I'm assuming that as a lawyer you will guard their identities. And I got the go-ahead to take you to the crime scene. But I'm assuming that you've come to us for help because you want justice here, not an easy way out for your brother."

"That *is* what I want," Rachael affirmed.

"Well, I have a few niggling doubts of my own, but the prosecutor needs more than a gut feeling and a Bible verse to go on." He stood up. "Come on. I'll take you to meet Emily."

"Thank you, Detective. I know this is irregular."

"It's *highly* irregular. I wouldn't have asked the prosecutor if you weren't a lawyer and I didn't have a couple reservations of my own about this case."

As Rachael rose to follow Pendleton out of his office, she sensed her cell phone vibrating inside her purse. She fished for it, figuring it was probably her mother wanting a report on her visit to Joshua.

But the number that blinked back at her was Fig's, which meant Trace was probably trying to get ahold of her. But the phone stopped pulsing as she held it. There was no indication he had left a message. She would call Trace back in a little while. Rachael changed the phone from vibrate to ring, dropped the phone back into her purse and then quickened her steps to catch up with the detective.

FIVE

Detective Pendleton walked quickly across the parking lot to the county building housing the jail, offices, and several courtrooms.

"Emily's got an appointment in five minutes, so we need to make this quick," he said as Rachael quickened her steps to keep up.

Once through the security checkpoint in the lobby, Pendleton led Rachael down a carpeted hallway to a suite of offices. A few minutes later Rachael was shaking hands with Emily Lonetree, one of Ramsey County's dozens of prosecutors.

The woman was petite, fortyish with black hair sprinkled with strands of gray. She wore a navy blue suit and a pale cream blouse. "May I see your credentials, Ms. Flynn?" the prosecutor asked politely after the introductions had been made.

"Of course," Rachael replied. She reached into her briefcase and withdrew her ID case that she kept with her. Inside she carried her identification as an attorney licensed to practice law in the state of New York.

"I went to law school right here at William Mitchell," Rachael said. "And I clerked for Hennepin County. You can check with Judge Happner or Judge Marino. Or Daniel Forrester, if he's still a prosecuting attorney there. Here's my card."

"Thanks," Emily Lonetree said, taking Rachael's business card. "So you're convinced your brother is lying."

"Yes I am, Ms. Lonetree. As I told the detective, my brother isn't the kind of man to kill someone. But he *is* the kind of man to take the blame for someone, especially an orphan girl."

Emily Lonetree studied Rachael for a moment. "I haven't met a lot of people like that, Ms. Flynn."

"Joshua isn't like a lot of people. He's different."

"Why would he confess to a murder he didn't commit?" the prosecutor asked.

"Possibly to keep an abused orphan from being convicted of murder," Rachael said confidently.

"You're assuming quite a bit about those girls," Emily Lonetree said.

Rachael paused before answering. "You're right. I don't know those girls. But I do know my brother. He couldn't have killed that man."

The prosecutor took a long breath and then let it out. "I'm going to allow you to view the reports because you're an attorney, not because you're his sister," she said. "And because Sgt. Pendleton thinks it might be helpful. I'm assuming you want to make sure we don't prosecute the wrong man. I'm also assuming you will protect the integrity of this investigation and that you will do nothing to hinder it."

"Yes. Yes, of course."

"All right. No photocopies. No notes. I've got to run. Will, please keep me informed." Emily Lonetree grabbed a stack of files off her desk, clearly in a hurry.

Rachael thanked her, and she and Pendleton walked back to the lobby, back across the parking lot and to Pendleton's office.

"I'll let you sit in the conference room to read the report," Pendleton said. "And I'll trust you not to get notepaper out of your briefcase."

"I won't, I promise."

The file that lay open on the table in front of Rachael seemed skeletal compared to the monstrous collection of paper on Pendleton's desk containing her brother's previous court records. Joshua's confession had come just five days into the murder investigation of grocery store owner Vong Thao, and while there had been just the one lead to pursue, in the end it didn't matter. A headstrong Caucasian with a flair for civil disobedience had confessed. Case closed.

Or soon would be.

Joshua would be formally charged with the second-degree murder of Vong Thao tomorrow. Within the month, he'd be sentenced. The file wouldn't get a whole lot bigger.

Rachael breathed a prayer for wisdom and clarity as she mentally prepared herself for what she was about to read. There had to be something within the pages that would clue her in to why Joshua would confess to killing the shopkeeper.

As she began reading, a picture formed in her mind of what happened when the driver of a produce truck discovered Thao's body a few minutes before seven last Wednesday morning. Nao Khan had parked his delivery truck at the back entrance to Vong Thao's grocery store, which was located in the heart of St. Paul's Frogtown. Rachael didn't recognize the street address of Thao's store, but she knew where Frogtown was. Everyone in her class at the William Mitchell College of Law knew where it was. Located just a few miles from the school, Frogtown was a study in changing demographics. Working-class immigrants of European descent had built its streets, known in days gone by as the Thomas Dale neighborhood. But the cultural landscape had begun to change in the 1970s. Now, thirty years later, an influx of new residents—Hmong from Southeast Asia, African-Americans, Native Americans, and Hispanics—had converted Frogtown into one of the most culturally diverse communities in the state. But like many inner-city communities, incomes in Frogtown were low and the crime rate high. Drugs, prostitution, and violence often kept Frogtown in the headlines. Still, Rachael knew there were hundreds of decent people in Frogtown—no doubt many of them widows and orphans who were simply trying to survive.

Just the sort of place to which Joshua would gravitate.

The police report was thorough and detailed. The truck driver, Nao Khan, had a load of vegetables to deliver to Thao, and he brought crates of onions and Chinese cabbage down the basement stairs like he usually did on these early Wednesday mornings. The door was unlocked, which was convenient for him since he had his hands full. He told the police he had been glad Thao had gotten up early to open the door for him. Nao walked in with his crates and his feet kicked something dense and solid on the floor. He peered over the crates to look at what was blocking his way.

In the semi-darkness Nao saw that what lay in front of him was Thao, the storeowner, lying in a crumpled heap, a stagnant pool of blood beneath his head. The driver had nearly tossed the vegetables onto the dead man as panic seized him. He set the crates down heavily, spilling their contents, and yelled Thao's name as onions rolled about the cement floor. Golden-skinned onions were all around the dead body in the police photographs, which Rachael quickly glanced at and then just as quickly turned away from. Nao told the police he knelt down, touched the body, and then recoiled at its lifelessness. He sprang to his feet and dashed up the interior stairs to the retail section of the store, yelling for help—but of course no one was there. He snatched up the store's telephone and punched in 911. In broken English and with his heart pounding in his chest he told the operator a man lay dead at the Thao Asian Food Store off Lexington Avenue.

It had taken only minutes for the first squad car to arrive. Nao told the officers what he had seen when he stepped into the basement, and one of the officers recorded it in a small, black notebook. Yes, he knew the deceased. Yes, the door was unlocked. No, no one else was in the store or the basement when he arrived. No, he hadn't touched anything....except the doorknob and the telephone. And the body.

The sun rose, the morning commute began, and more police arrived. The store exterior was cordoned off with yellow police tape, and a small crowd gathered. One of the police officers asked the spectators if any of them had seen anything or heard anything unusual that morning or the night before. Those who understood English shook their heads.

The coroner arrived, followed by Sgt. Pendleton and his partner, Sgt. Samantha Stowe. By then it was eight thirty and a shaken Nao pleaded to be allowed to leave. He was already an hour-and-a-half behind on his route. Pendleton spoke with him for a few minutes verifying the information Nao had already provided, and then he sent him on his way.

The cause of death was quickly ruled as that of a single gunshot wound to the head. Motive was unknown as there was no sign of a robbery. The accompanying ballistics report listed the weapon used as a standard .38 handgun. A single .38 casing was found in the basement under the open staircase when crime scene investigators scoured the room for evidence later that afternoon. No gun was found anywhere on the premises. Based on where Thao was lying, the location of the entrance wound and the traces of gunpowder residue found on the cement floor near the stairs, investigators deduced the shooter was at or on the bottom stair and had fired from a standing position. The murder had taken place sometime before midnight the night before, based on the condition of Thao's body and the color and consistency of the congealed blood.

Rachael glanced back at the police photos of the body, frowned, and then read on.

Fingerprints were all over the store and basement—some old, some recent—but none had triggered any alarms with the Bureau of Criminal Apprehension, commonly known to the Minnesota legal community as the BCA. There was also a swamp of DNA evidence to slog through, including dozens of strands of human hair and clothing fibers. Thao was not much of a housekeeper when it came to his basement. But most of the little bags of DNA evidence had not been opened yet.

Crime lab technicians had just begun to wade through them when Joshua confessed. Yet even before that, Detective Pendleton had a hunch he was getting close, even without the crime lab results.

Pendleton's own report detailed his conversation with Pa Kou Her, the woman who told police she saw two teenage girls whom she recognized and a Caucasian man that she didn't entering the store basement at about nine o'clock the previous Tuesday night. Her, who lived in the apartment above the barbershop next door to Thao's store, said she was shaking out a rug on her fire escape when she saw a beat-up compact car, orange and aging, drive up to the back entrance of Thao's Asian Food Store. A tall Caucasian male she didn't know was behind the wheel. She watched as two girls got out of the backseat and led the white man down the stairs to the basement door. Her told the detective that she had seen those girls in the neighborhood before; she knew they lived nearby. Her was sure the older one was named Choua, and that she lived with an aunt because her parents were dead. She didn't know the younger one's name.

The woman told Sgt. Pendleton that she didn't hear or see anything else.

You didn't hear a gunshot? his notes indicated he'd asked, though Pendleton wrote in his report that a shot from underground in a basement might not have attracted a lot of attention, especially in Frogtown.

"I turn up my TV loud because my neighbor's baby is always crying," Her said.

"You saw nothing else out of the ordinary?"

"No. Not that night," Her answered. "But I didn't trust that Thao. I didn't shop at his place. Men were always coming to his backdoor at night. Young men who looked like they wanted to cause trouble. Sometimes they came in really nice cars. You know who has really nice cars in Frogtown?"

"Yes," the detective said. He did.

Rachael stopped reading for a moment and closed her eyes. Joshua had been in way over his head. She was sure of that. Why hadn't he just called the police when those girls came to him for help? She was sure that's why he'd been there. To help them. Rachael's father had mentioned something on the phone about a girl being victimized by the grocer. Why didn't Joshua call the police? Why did he take those girls to the basement of that store? And at night?

Rachael was anxious to get to his confession; she knew it had to be in the file. She turned the page and kept reading.

Pendleton's report indicated he went to the local high school the day after the murder to ask about two Hmong sisters who lived with an aunt, one of whom was named Choua.

The school secretary told him there were several girls named Choua on the rolls, but only one who lived with an aunt. Choua Lee. Fifteen. And she had a sister, Bao Lee, twelve. The secretary told the detectives that the girls' father had died of untreated pneumonia when Choua and Bao were just preschoolers. Black ice and a head-on collision had claimed their mother four years later. The girls had lived with their mother's older sister, a widow herself, for the past eight years. Pendleton asked to speak to Choua and was told that neither child was in school that day.

In fact, the school was becoming concerned that Choua was headed toward being charged as a habitual truant. The school's social worker told Pendleton that Choua already had five unexcused absences for the semester—that day had made it six—and that Choua had been tardy many mornings and was failing all but one of her classes. The girl had spent four afternoons in detention since school had begun for such infractions as being tardy, mouthing off to teachers, and slugging another girl. Her sister, Bao, attended the nearby middle school, but her records were quickly called up on the high school's networked computer. The younger sister had sporadic absences in the four weeks school had been in session, wasn't a discipline problem in class, usually came to school on time, and maintained a C average. Both girls were first generation Americans and spoke English as fluently as they spoke Hmong.

Pendleton had written down the home address of Koa Liang, the girls' aunt, and he and Sgt. Stowe headed there next. When they got to the house, Pendleton sent Stowe to canvass the neighborhood and inquire about the Caucasian man with the orange car. Pendleton found the aunt at home, but he was unable to have much of a conversation with her as she spoke limited English. Pendleton's report indicated that when he showed her his badge, Liang immediately became defensive and told him Choua was taking care of Bao, who was sick. It was obvious to him Liang thought she was in trouble for letting the girls stay home from school. She was able to communicate to him that she worked nights and slept during the day. Choua had volunteered to stay home with Bao, and Liang had let her.

When Pendleton asked to speak to Choua, Liang had yelled for her. Choua had come from the back of the house. Pendleton noted that her face was pale, and she appeared to be nervous.

With Liang present, Pendleton asked Choua whether or not she knew Vong Thao, the man who owned Thao's Asian Food Store half a mile away and who had been killed the day before. In his notes, Pendleton said the girl seemed to flinch at the mention of Thao's name.

As Rachel read, the scene in the girls' home unfolded before her.

"I knew him," Choua said. "He was my second cousin."

"Your second cousin?"

"He was my mother's first cousin."

"I'm sorry. I didn't realize he had been a family member."

The girl said nothing. The aunt said something to Choua in Hmong, and Choua ignored her.

"Do you know who might have wanted to kill him?" Pendleton asked.

"No."

"Can you tell me why you and your sister were at his store Tuesday night?"

Choua paused a moment before answering. "We weren't there."

"A witness saw you there."

Again the aunt said something in Hmong. And Choua ignored her.

"We weren't there."

"Was your cousin involved in something illegal, Choua? Have you been told not to tell anyone? Because I want you to know you can trust me. I won't let any harm come to you for telling me the truth."

The girl again paused. "I don't know what he was involved with," she finally said.

"Can I talk to Bao?" Pendleton said, turning his attention back to Liang.

"She's sick!" Choua exclaimed.

"I won't be but a moment," Pendleton said to Liang.

In his notes, Pendleton wrote that an argument ensued between Liang and Choua. Pendleton didn't understand a word of it. Then Liang took Pendleton's arm and led him to the back bedroom, with Choua protesting in English and in Hmong. Liang held up her arm and pointed to the corner of the bedroom where a girl sat slumped against the wall, leaning against folded bed pillows. The girl was picking at the baseboards, prying away tiny flecks of paint. Her jet-black hair was in front of her face.

"See!" Liang said. "She say sick!"

"Bao?" Pendleton said.

"She doesn't know anything! She's just a kid!" Choua yelled.

"Bao?" Pendleton said again.

But the girl in the corner didn't look up. Pendleton walked over to her, stepping over clothes, a blanket, and school books. He bent down.

"Why you talk? She sick," Liang said calmly.

Choua, on the other hand, seemed about to explode. "Leave her alone!"

"Bao, my name is Sgt. Pendleton. I'm a policeman. Are you okay? Do you need to see a doctor?"

Bao took her time, but she finally raised her eyes to meet his. "I'm okay," she whispered.

"Can I talk to you for a minute?"

The girl shrugged.

"Did something scary happen at your cousin's store a couple days ago?" Pendleton asked. "You can trust me, Bao," he assured her.

Bao didn't answer him.

"Do you know you can trust me?"

She nodded.

"Did something scary happen at your cousin's store?"

Bao looked up at her sister. Pendleton followed her gaze, but Choua's face was expressionless.

Bao looked back him. "I don't know," she finally said, lifting her shoulders to suggest she didn't care that she didn't know.

"Nothing bad happened there?"

Bao didn't answer.

"Bao, do you know someone who drives a little orange car? Someone with white skin?"

Liang said something to Choua, and this time Choua answered her. Her young voice was hot with anger.

Bao shrugged.

Pendleton reached out to touch Bao, partly to assure her she was safe, and partly to test a theory that was growing in his mind—that Bao had perhaps been abused or threatened in some way. And that Thao had been the perpetrator. Or perhaps the perp was the white man with the beat-up car. Or maybe it was both of them.

At his touch, Bao stiffened and edged herself further into the corner.

"Leave her alone!" Choua yelled.

"Bao?" Pendleton said.

"He...he is just a friend," Bao said, not much more than a whisper.

"Who is just a friend?"

Bao paused before answering. "The man with the orange car."

"What's his name?"

Bao didn't answer.

"Bao, if someone hurt you, you don't want other girls to be hurt by that person, do you?"

Bao raised her head to look at Pendleton in one swift motion. "But he didn't hurt me! He wanted to help me."

Choua's voice rang out then, quick words in Hmong that were unintelligible to Pendleton. Bao looked at her sister and then looked away.

Pendleton's report indicated that at this point he stood up and turned to Choua.

"Look, I know you girls were at the store Tuesday evening. You were seen. Do you understand? Someone saw you and identified you. And if we dust for fingerprints, I bet we'll find yours and your sister's all over that basement."

Pendleton noted that Choua ran a shaking hand though her hair.

"So why don't you tell me why you were there," Pendleton continued. "If someone told you they'd hurt you or kill you if you talked to the police, I'm telling you that's not going to happen."

"I was buying weed," Choua answered suddenly. "Thao sold it. I bought some from him and we left."

Pendleton wrote in his notes that he didn't believe Choua was telling the truth.

"Buying weed?" he asked.

"Yes."

"You encourage your twelve-year-old sister to smoke marijuana? Does your aunt know about this? Did the man in the orange car buy it for you?"

Choua shook her head, flinging her hair away from her eyes. "Bao didn't want it, I did. And I was the only one who bought it and smoked it. And my aunt was at work. You gonna arrest me for buying weed?"

Pendleton ignored her challenge. "And the man in the orange car? What about him?"

Choua stalled for a moment. "He didn't see me buy it. He thought he was taking me there to get a paycheck. I told him I worked there."

"You went to get a paycheck. At nine o'clock at night. With your little sister."

Choua paused for only a second.

"I said I *told* him there was a paycheck there for me. I didn't actually go there to get one."

"What's his name?" Pendleton asked. "The man with the orange car."

"I don't know. He's just some guy who gave us a ride."

"Where did you meet him?"

"Around."

Pendleton wrote in his notes that Choua seemed to be adept at deception. He also noted that he wondered what Choua Lee was capable of doing to a person who hurt someone she loved.

"Choua, have you ever fired a gun?" he asked her.

Choua had blinked. "I don't have a gun."

"That's not an answer to my question. I said have you ever *fired* a gun."

She tossed her head, brushing her bangs away from her face. "It's kind of hard to shoot a gun when you don't *have* a gun."

At that point Sgt. Stowe had returned from surveying the neighborhood. Pendleton thanked Mrs. Liang for her time and nodded a farewell to Bao and Choua. "I'm sure we'll be seeing each other again," he said to the girls. "Here's my card if you want to talk." He handed the card to Choua.

"I take to doctor?" Liang said, looking back at Bao.

Pendleton glanced back at Bao. She was sitting forward now, looking at him. When their eyes met, she looked away. "Not today," Pendleton replied. "School tomorrow though, okay?"

"Yes! School. Girls go."

Then he turned around just as he was walking out the door. "You and your sister better be in school tomorrow," he said to Choua. "If I find out you're not, I'm going to come here and take you there myself."

Pendleton's report for that day ended with a note that he would wait for DNA results and the full fingerprints report before heading back to Liang's house to further question Choua Lee and her sister. He was certain the girls knew more than they were telling. He also hoped the prints would lead him to the Caucasian. Sgt. Stowe had no luck identifying him by asking the neighbors. They had seen his car, but no one knew his name.

Rachael knew his name. It was swirling in her head as she read the detective's report. *Joshua. Joshua. Joshua.*

At that same moment, her phone began to play a happy tune from inside her purse. It startled her, pulled her away from the little house, the two girls, and the detective on the hunt for the truth. She had forgotten to call Trace back. She winced as she looked at the phone's tiny LCD screen. Fig's number stared back at her.

She pressed the button to answer and immediately heard the wailing of an infant in the background. McKenna. As she squeaked out a hesitant "Hello?" she looked at her watch. She had been gone for nearly four hours.

And she felt no closer to the truth than when she'd arrived.

SIX

"Rachael, where *are* you?" Trace didn't sound frantic, but it was clear he had expected her back a long time ago. McKenna's screams in the background nearly drowned out his voice.

"Trace, I'm so sorry!" Rachael replied, folding the file closed as she stood to her feet. "I completely lost track of time."

"You mean you haven't even left the jail? You're still *there?*"

Along with McKenna's wails in the background, Rachael heard another voice. Fig's. "She's breaking up, she's breaking up! I can't hold her! I can't hold her!"

"I'm leaving now. Is that Fig? What's he doing? Does he have McKenna?"

"Yes, he has McKenna. If I was holding her while trying to talk to you, believe me, we wouldn't be able to have this conversation. She's about to detonate."

Rachael grabbed her briefcase and purse and put the file under her arm. "Didn't you give her that little bottle of breast milk? I left it in Fig's fridge."

"She won't take it!" Trace said. Behind Trace's voice Rachael also heard Fig's: "It's the Amazon war cry! She's calling down curses! She'll kill us all!"

"What's Fig *doing?*" Rachael demanded, as she headed to the door of the conference room where she'd been reading. She had to get the file back to Pendleton, but she also had to tell him she wasn't finished with it. And that she wanted to come back this afternoon and visit the crime scene.

"He's trying to keep McKenna from self-destructing, Rach. You've *got* to get back here!"

"Ahhhhh! It's too late! Run for your lives!" Fig again.

"I'm coming! I'm leaving!" Rachael said, walking briskly back down the hall toward Pendleton's office. Then in the background at Fig's house, Rachael heard another sound, faint but distinct from McKenna's cries: Fig's doorbell.

"Your mother's here," Trace said.

"My mother? You called my mother!"

"Rachael, we're dying here. McKenna's been like this for almost two hours. I tried calling you, but you didn't answer."

"I'm sorry, I'm sorry...I'll get there as soon as I can."

"I gotta go. Your mom will freak if she sees how Fig is holding her. Bye."

Trace clicked off before she could respond, leaving Rachael to imagine in what bizarre way Fig was just then holding her infant daughter.

She slipped the phone back in her purse and mentally whisked away troubling maternal thoughts as she poked her head into Sgt. Pendleton's office. He was on the phone, but he held up an index finger, motioning for her to come in.

"All right," Pendleton was saying. "That sounds doable....Yep. Talk to you later. Bye." He hung up the phone and looked at her. "All done?"

"No, actually I wasn't quite finished, but I need to leave for a little while. I want to come back later today though, if that's all right. I want to read the rest, and if you're still willing to take me to the crime scene, I want to do that too."

"Well, you can come back later and see if I'm here," Pendleton said. "I'll be in and out this afternoon. I'll tell Sgt. Stowe to let you have the file back if you get here and I'm gone."

"Thanks. I really appreciate this."

Pendleton nodded.

"I've read most of your report," Rachael continued. "You had suspicions it might have been Choua that pulled the trigger. Do you still think it could have been her?"

"Anybody *could* have done it, Ms. Flynn," he replied. "But your brother said it was him. He was there. He had motive. And he has a history of breaking the law."

"But you do have reasons to think he *didn't* do it, don't you?"

Pendleton sat back in his chair. "I don't know. Maybe."

"Then you'll help me."

"I'm after the truth, Ms. Flynn. That's what I want. My goal isn't to help you. My goal is to get the truth."

"And if they happen to be one and the same?"

Pendleton raised his open palms as if to release any hidden agenda. "So be it."

The drive back to downtown Minneapolis only took twenty minutes, but as Rachael maneuvered through the post lunch-hour traffic she was distracted by dueling thoughts of Joshua's role in this mess and a crying daughter wasting away at Fig's. Her milk let down twice on the way.

She parked Fig's Lexus in his spacious underground garage at his apartment building and opted for the stairs instead of waiting for the elevator. When she reached Fig's floor, she could hear the muted cries of an infant behind the walls. She bolted for his front door and banged on it, sweating and out of breath.

"*Bonjour!*" Fig exclaimed as he opened the door wide for her.

"I'm sorry! Really, I am!" Rachael said as she swept past him, as if *bonjour* meant *How dare you!* in French instead of *good day.* "Where is she?"

"Here we are." Her mother's voice reached her from within the living room, entwined with another voice...that of an inconsolable infant.

Rachael rounded a corner, entering the living room. Her mother was pacing back and forth with McKenna in her arms, rocking the crying infant's body back and forth to no apparent positive result. Trace was sitting at a bar stool in Fig's open kitchen with his head resting on his upturned palm.

"She slept for a few minutes after I got here, out of sheer exhaustion, I think," her mother said as she walked toward Rachael. "But she must have known you were close by. She started up again a few minutes ago."

"I'm really, *really* sorry!" Rachael exclaimed, taking McKenna from her mother, giving her mother a quick one-armed hug and then looking about for the best place to nurse McKenna. *This is no time for modesty,* Rachael decided. She sat on Fig's couch, placed McKenna on her lap and threw a receiving blanket over her shoulder to provide a modicum of privacy. Nursing McKenna in the living room wasn't going to bother her mother or Trace, and she was certain Fig would probably find the image worthy of all kinds of poetic comments. She picked up her daughter and placed her at her breast. The wails stopped. A collective sigh filled the room.

"We were about ready to break out the vodka," Trace said from his bar stool.

Eva grimaced as she sat down beside Rachael on the couch. "You can't give an infant vodka!"

Rachael looked back at her weary husband. "I think he meant for *them,* Mom."

"Oh, I don't know, Trace," Fig said. "It gave me quite a rush! All that torment and emotion from such a little package. It was like the entire universe had telescoped into one almighty need. *Feed me!* It was wild!"

"I swear, we didn't *touch* any vodka," Trace said, laughing slightly at Fig's comment and slipping off his bar stool to join the others in the living room.

Rachael knew Fig's strange comment hadn't been influenced by alcohol. He was just being Fig. Fig didn't even drink.

"You saw Joshua then? You must have had a good visit to be gone so long," Eva said, a mix of hope and apprehension evident in her voice.

"I only spent a few minutes with Josh. The rest of the time I was talking with the homicide detective in charge of the investigation. And reading the file."

"So…" her mother's voice wavered.

"Nothing has changed. Joshua wouldn't tell me anything. Most of what I've been able to piece together came from reading the police report and detective notes."

"Well, what did you find out?"

"I'm not sure I can say, Mom. I do think it's possible, highly possible, that Josh is covering for someone. Someone he was trying to help."

"Why on earth would he try to help a killer? Why would he do that? Why would anyone do that?"

Rachael shook her head. "Why does Josh do anything?" The reasons were all one and the same.

"I think the killer is someone who didn't actually plan to shoot someone; it just happened," Rachael continued. "I'm thinking the person who pulled the trigger was backed into a corner…or had been hurt so many times she just couldn't take it anymore. Maybe that grocer was a very bad man who had hurt the shooter in some way. That person wasn't acting rationally; he or she had been hurt, abused maybe. And in desperation that person killed the one who had hurt her. And Josh stepped in to take the blame."

"But then that other person gets away with murder!" Eva exclaimed.

"But to Josh, maybe it's simply that that person *gets away*. She finally gets away, Mom. Can't you see Joshua doing that? Making it possible for someone who has been dealt a really, really bad hand to *get away?*"

Eva sat back on the couch and closed her eyes, which were now rimmed with tears. "I just don't get it," she whispered. "I just don't get how he could do this. What kind of person would do this?"

"I don't understand it either, Mom," Rachael replied. "But we all know Josh doesn't like to see people get hurt."

Eva snapped her eyes open. "Doesn't he know how much this is hurting *me?* Doesn't he care that this is killing your dad? Joshua would lay his life down for people he barely knows and run a knife right through my heart at the same time. Where is the compassion in *that?*"

Rachael looked up at her mother, unable to think of anything to say in return.

Eva continued, only now it seemed to Rachael she was speaking to no one. "I don't think I've ever mattered to him," Eva said, shaking her head.

"Mom, that's not true!"

Eva blinked back the tears and a look of painful resignation passed over her, replacing the anguish. "From the moment he could speak, I knew there was something different about him. The way he talked about God and to God when he was little....It was like he was never mine. Never wanted to be mine. Never hung onto my legs in fear when I left him somewhere he had never been before."

"Mom," Rachael interjected, but Eva didn't seem to hear her.

"He was afraid of the dark and of the devil and demons, but he was never afraid of being separated from me. And he didn't run to me in the middle of the night when he was afraid. He never ran to my room."

Eva turned her head now back to Rachael.

"He always ran to your room."

"Mom."

And this time her mother said nothing. She waited for Rachael to say whatever it was she was going to say. Rachael fumbled for the words.

"None of that means he doesn't love you and doesn't care about you. I don't know why he always ran to my room instead of yours. My room was closer. And he knew I wouldn't send him back to his bed like Dad might have done. It wasn't that he was choosing me over you."

"Yes, Rachael, he was. He always preferred you over me," Eva said, strangely emotionless.

"Mom, please. That just isn't true."

"No, it is true. He has a bond with you. He trusts you. He always has."

"But that doesn't mean he doesn't also trust you, Mom."

"But you saw him this morning, didn't you? You asked to see him and then you visited with him?"

"Yes, but…"

"He wouldn't see me. I went to the jail yesterday to visit him, and he refused to see me. He wouldn't see me, Rachael," Eva repeated.

Rachael was aware that Trace and Fig sat still as stones in the two overstuffed chairs across from her. McKenna had fallen asleep at her breast. A ticking clock was the only sound in the room.

In her mind Rachael pictured her brother in his cell, wearing his orange jumpsuit. He had been there twenty-four hours. A deputy had come to stand in front of the barred door. "Your mother would like to see you," the deputy said. And Joshua, who had just confessed to killing a man by shooting him in the back of the head, shook his head. *I can't look at her,* he might have thought. *I can't see in her eyes what this will do to her. And she can't see in mine what this is doing to me. She is better off thinking I'm the headstrong rebel people have always told her I am. She might even begin to hate me a little if I refuse to see her. That will be good for her. In the long run, that will be good for her.* These were surely his thoughts. He chose the pain that would hurt her the least.

"Maybe that was his way of protecting you, Mom. It was really hard to see him this morning, knowing what he has confessed to. Maybe he was trying to shield you from that."

"And yet he saw you."

Rachael gently moved McKenna away from her breast and eased her sleeping head onto her shoulder. She rubbed McKenna's small back with her hand, making lopsided circles with her palm. "I think he saw me only because he wanted to tell me something, something he thought I would understand."

"What? What was he trying to tell you?" Eva's voice was edged with curious irritation. "What could he tell you that he couldn't tell me?"

In her head Rachael replayed Joshua's last words to her that morning: *I'm not afraid of the dark anymore.*

Joshua hadn't been talking about no longer being frightened of what lay under his bed while he slept. He was talking about something else. A victory of some kind. Or maybe a truce…

"That…that he's figured something out," Rachael said, knowing that wouldn't make a whole lot of sense to her mother.

"What? What has he figured out? How to screw up his life? How to get sent to prison? How to destroy his parents?"

Rachael looked up at her wounded mother. She was quite sure now that Joshua was counting on their mother learning to be disgusted with him. It was all part of his plan. Take the rap, save the girl, and keep his mother from feeling too much pain. Disgust was easier to live with than anguish. "I'm not sure yet, Mom. But I'm going back there this afternoon. I know there are things Josh *isn't* telling me."

"You're going *back?*" Trace spoke for the first time since coming into the living room.

"Yes," Rachael said, turning her head toward her husband. "I only got through part of the file. I haven't even read the transcription of Josh's confession yet. And Sgt. Pendleton, that's the guy who is in charge of the murder investigation, he's taking me to the crime scene this afternoon. I think he also has doubts that Josh is telling the truth, especially after I told him the kind of person Josh is."

"What kind of person *is* he?" Eva said, and her facial features softened as her anger subsided. But there was no lilt to her question. No expectation that anyone in the room could answer it.

Rachael turned to her mother and replied softly, "He's the kind of person who can't walk by a hurting widow or orphan and fail to help. He made a vow when he was twelve, Mom. I know you remember this. He made a vow that he would always do whatever was in his power for widows and orphans who needed help. He believes that is what all true religion is. That's all it is to him. Nothing else matters. The girls he was trying to help—and there are two of them—are orphans. They're *orphans*, Mom."

Eva shuddered then and her breath caught in her throat. "Maybe he really *did* kill that man!" she said, her voice raspy with emotion and urgency. "He told us on the phone a girl was being victimized by the grocer. He told us he couldn't control himself when he found out what that man had done! If the grocer was molesting those girls, maybe Joshua really did kill him. Oh, dear. What if he really did it?"

"Mom, please don't start trying to imagine what did or didn't happen!" Rachael implored. "We don't know enough. I think those girls were there when the grocer was shot, and I think the older girl knows something she's not telling the police. Please just give me a chance to figure this out. Okay?"

Eva covered her mouth with her hand, as if saying the words "What if he did it" had actually made it true. She didn't answer Rachael.

"Okay, Mom? Please?"

Eva slowly nodded her head.

Several tense seconds of silence followed where no one seemed to know what to say or do next. McKenna stirred, and Rachael prepared as discreetly as she could to nurse her on the other side.

"She's changed so much since she was born," Eva murmured in a tone of voice Rachael didn't recognize. "It's only been a few weeks since I saw her, and she already looks so different."

Rachael glanced over at Eva, troubled by the strange inflection in her mother's voice. Again the room was silent as Rachael's child nursed at her breast.

"Don't even blink, Rachael," Eva continued, looking tenderly at McKenna. "Don't even blink. You blink and she'll be gone. Just like that."

SEVEN

Afternoon sunlight filtered through a gauzy swag of linen draped across Fig's guest room window. Rachael rose from laying McKenna's blanket-wrapped body in the pool of muted sunlight bathing the portable crib.

"I'll stay with her while you're gone," Eva said, standing at Rachael's side.

"You don't have to, Mom."

"I don't mind. I think Trace would feel a little better about you going back if I do stay. And I *do* want you to go back."

"I know how you feel about Fig, Mom," Rachael whispered. "Don't stay if Fig's going to drive you nuts."

Her mother gazed down at McKenna. "I'd do anything for my granddaughter. You know that. I can spend a few hours tolerating Fig."

A tiny grin eased its way across Rachael's lips. Fig's eccentricities had always exasperated her mother, beginning when Fig showed up at Rachael and Trace's wedding five years ago in his best-man tuxedo with his hair dyed sapphire blue.

"It matches the bridesmaids' dresses!" Fig announced proudly.

"Yes, but you're not a bridesmaid!" Eva shot back.

Rachael remembered this now and the grin widened. "I'll try to get back before McKenna wakes up. But if I don't, I guess you could try the bottle again."

"They didn't even warm it up, you know," Eva said, motioning with her head to Trace and Fig in the other room. "That's why she didn't take it. By the time I got here she was too mad to consider giving it a try, warmed or not."

Rachael looked at her watch. "Well, it's almost two o'clock now. Hopefully she's so worn out from her morning tirade she'll sleep a good three hours. Can you stay until five?"

"I can stay," Eva replied as she and Rachael walked out of the room. "I'll call your dad and tell him. He really wants to see you and Trace and the baby. I told him I'd ask you over for dinner tomorrow night. Can you come?"

"Sure, Mom."

In the kitchen Fig and Trace were putting away the remains of lunch: hummus and bagel chips, circles of Provolone cheese, sliced Bosc pears, and a saucer of calamata olives—the sum total of the food in Fig's house.

"I simply must get to Byerly's," Fig commented as he closed the bagel chips bag. "We can't have hummus for supper as well as lunch. I'm sure that's taboo somewhere in the world."

"You and Trace can go get groceries," Eva said. "I'll stay with McKenna, and Rachael can use my car to go back to St. Paul. Here." She reached into her purse on the bar in the kitchen and handed Rachael her keys. "I'm across the street and up a block."

"Thanks, Mom," Rachael said, taking the keys and reaching to grab her purse and briefcase from the floor where she'd dropped them. "I plan to be back by five," she added, directing her words to Trace.

"Okay, but try to look at your watch every so often, eh?" Trace said, walking with Rachael to the front door. "McKenna's a formidable gal when she's riled."

"I like that quality in a woman!" Fig yelled from the kitchen.

Trace opened the door for her. "And be careful."

"I will, I promise."

Trace leaned into her and kissed her lightly.

"Wish me luck," she added.

He flicked away a stray honey-brown strand from across her forehead. "You and I don't believe in luck," he murmured.

Rachael looked up at Trace's orange-tinged hair and the single cross earring he wore in one ear and smiled. She had to admit she and Trace were an odd pair. Her father had actually said so when she was dating Trace and things were starting to get pretty serious. And she hadn't disagreed. She liked biographies, classical music, black-and-white photography, and cathedrals. Trace liked jazz, poetry, green tea and macaroons, and worship services held in the back rooms of coffee shops. She was analytical and rational; he was imaginative and accommodating. She endured wildly unconventional people like Fig; Trace was inspired by them.

But they shared the same view of luck.

It didn't exist.

She and Trace were convinced a powerful, yet personal God held the universe together, albeit strangely sometimes. And where luck was absent, a providential hand prevailed, especially when called upon. She knew she was going to need the hand of divine intervention if she was going to uncover what really happened in the basement of Vong Thao's store. What she really needed was something far more dependable than luck.

"Then wish for me what I believe in," she whispered back.

As he had supposed, Sgt. Pendleton was out when Rachael arrived back at the St. Paul police department and asked for him. She inquired of Sgt. Stowe instead and was soon ushered back into the hallways of the homicide division.

Tall, willowy, and sporting an almost-gruff, no-nonsense demeanor, Sgt. Stowe looked to be about Rachael's age, perhaps a little older. She wore her empty holster over her shoulder as nonchalantly as Pendleton wore his. Stowe briskly led Rachael back to the conference room.

"Will tells me you're an attorney," Sgt. Stowe said as they neared the conference room.

"Yes."

"And that you think your brother is lying," the detective said, flipping on a light switch as they entered the room.

Rachael couldn't help but notice that Stowe said the belief was Joshua was lying, not that he was innocent.

"I'm sure of it," Rachael answered. "I'm convinced he is taking the fall for somebody. Maybe one of those girls."

"Will said that." Stowe stood at the table, apparently not willing to leave the room without more details. And also not in a hurry after all.

"Look," Rachael began. "I know you probably don't see too many people confessing to a murder they didn't commit, but…"

"It's never happened while I've been here," the sergeant interrupted.

"But my brother is the kind of person who *would* do that," Rachael continued. "He's the kind of person who *would* confess to something he didn't do, if by doing so he could help someone in a desperate situation."

"How does he help someone by covering up his crime?" Stowe asked simply. "I mean, how does that really help that person?"

Rachael sighed. *How indeed?* She attempted an answer. "If one of those girls killed that man, it keeps her out of jail, out of a detention center for who knows how long, or, in the case of the older one, being tried as an adult, and sent to prison."

"Okay. And how does that help her? How does letting a person commit a crime and covering for it *help* her?"

Rachael was silent. The detective in front of her was asking the same questions Rachael was inwardly posing to herself…and for which she had troubling answers brewing. Was Joshua really doing anyone any good with this charade? Was he, in fact, actually making things worse for the person he was trying to help? Could that person walk away from this unaccountable and bear no negative effects?

"It gives them a second chance?" Rachael suggested.

"A second chance to kill," Stowe said effortlessly.

"A second chance at life," Rachael said just as swiftly.

Stowe placed the file on the table in front of them. "Well, you know what they say," she said. "Two wrongs don't make a right."

"I know," Rachael said. "I don't condone what my brother is doing. That's why I'm here."

"What your brother is doing, if he's in fact lying, is not only criminal, it's also not rational. You might want to ask his public defender to petition the court for a psych evaluation before they sentence him."

"My brother isn't crazy," Rachael interjected.

"I didn't say he was," Stowe replied gently. "I'm one cubicle over from Sgt. Pendleton when you're done."

Nodding and watching as Stowe left the room, Rachael willed her pulse to return to its normal pace. It had quickened in the moments she and Stowe had spoken together.

Joshua wasn't crazy. He was…unusual.

Rachael pulled out a chair and sat at the table. She flipped through the pages in the file she had read earlier, looking for the transcript that detailed her brother's confession. She found it near the end.

The confession began with a form penned by Sgt. Don Childs, the St. Paul policeman who took Joshua's initial confession Saturday evening. It had been about five thirty. Joshua came into the station, asked to speak to the officer in charge, and then proceeded to confess to the killing of Vong Thao.

Sgt. Childs called Pendleton at home and informed him that a man was at the police station confessing to the murder of Vong Thao. Did he want to come down? Pendleton arrived twenty minutes later.

The next several pages were the transcript of Joshua's taped confession. As she read, Rachael found herself mentally in the room, hearing the conversation as clearly as if she had been there.

I killed Vong Thao, she heard her brother say. He was probably strangely calm. Serene in a sad, detached way. Anesthetized by his compassion for a young girl in trouble.

So you want to tell me how it happened? Pendleton asked.

Joshua surely rehearsed what he was going to say. Maybe he had a couple of days to come up with a story...or maybe only hours. Perhaps he had been to Liang's house earlier that day to check on the girls, to make sure they were doing okay. He was no doubt worried for them. Especially the little one. If Bao hadn't used the gun herself, she surely saw who did, which would have been equally traumatic. When Joshua got to the house, Choua probably told him the police had been by a few days earlier. A detective told them a witness had seen the three of them at Thao's the night of his murder. Choua had at first denied it, but the detective kept asking questions, like "What was the name of the man with the orange car?" Choua probably told Joshua that she and Bao said they didn't know. But then the detective had asked her if she had ever fired a gun. And the cop said he knew that if they dusted for her and Bao's fingerprints they would find them all over Thao's basement. Before the detective left, he said he would be back to talk to them again. Choua was scared, and so was Bao. Joshua told them not to worry. He'd take care of it.

"I'll tell them I did it," he said. "You girls are just children. You shouldn't have to be going through this on top of everything else. You have your whole lives in front of you."

The girls protested.

"What happened to you, never should have happened," he continued. "We failed you. All the adults who should've looked out for you failed you. Well, that's going to stop right now. We're not going to fail you anymore."

Rachael imagined Choua being rather surprised by Joshua's offer. Bao was probably dazed.

He cooked up a lie then, in front of the girls, so that if Choua and

Bao were questioned they would all have the same story. When he was assured of their participation in the ruse, he hugged them goodbye, cried over them, prayed over them. Told them to do good and be good. Love God. Obey their aunt. Stay in school. Change the world.

Perhaps he went straight to the police station. Maybe he stopped at a local church to weep or to pray for strength or forgiveness or courage. He didn't say. In any case, when he arrived at the station to confess, his demeanor was probably calm, his fate accepted.

"I killed him. I didn't go there planning to kill him. I went there to beg him to leave a young girl named Bao Lee alone. Thao was part of a child prostitution ring, and he was trying to get Bao mixed up in it. But things got out of hand. I found out that both Bao and her older sister, Choua, were already involved. He'd already got to them. They are just children! Bao's only twelve! What Thao did was despicable and I…I just snapped. I couldn't control myself. I shot him with his own gun."

Pendleton asked Joshua how he happened to have a gun on him, and Joshua told him he hadn't had one. Thao had it. And Joshua had taken it from him.

Had he ever shot a gun before?

"I hunted once with my dad. I shot at a doe. Does that count?"

Pendleton had no doubt been compelled to ask Joshua what would have seemed to an outsider an irrelevant question, but he needed to know before the interview went any further.

"What kind of car do you drive, Mr. Harper?"

"A Ford Escort."

"What color is it?"

"Orange."

Then Pendleton told Joshua he wanted him to tell him how he became acquainted with the Lee sisters.

"I befriended Choua and Bao at an afterschool program at a church in Frogtown," Joshua answered. "A Hmong friend of mine, John Tsue, who is studying to be a youth pastor, started it up during the summer as a safe place for kids to hang out, and then he just kept it going when school started. I was helping him. He called it the "Teens in the Center." Anyway, the girls started coming to it. Choua didn't come as often as Bao did, and when she did, she only stayed for a little while. Bao, though, came often. But she was quiet and jumpy and seemed to be hurting inside. She was afraid of me at first. She was afraid of John too. And I think it was because we are men. I was worried about her. I asked her from to time to time if anything was wrong at home or at school…or was anyone hurting her in any way, but she would never answer me."

"So what happened on Tuesday?" Pendleton asked. "Why were you in that basement?"

"Bao didn't want to leave the Center that day when it was time to close up," Josh continued. "John had to leave early so it was just me, and all the kids were gone except Bao. She was trembling and seemed fearful. She kept asking me why the Center wasn't open in the evenings. She wanted to stay and was agitated that the Center wasn't open. I could tell she was scared about something.

"I took her home and Choua was there. Finally, with Choua's help, Bao told me what was bothering her. Her cousin, who is Vong Thao, was expecting her at his store that night and she didn't want to go. When Choua heard this, she became livid. I wasn't sure why, and she wouldn't tell me. She and Bao started arguing, and I couldn't understand them. I don't speak Hmong. But I knew something was terribly wrong.

"Then Bao turned to me and started weeping—crying out that she didn't want to go to the store. I told her she didn't have to. 'He'll be angry with me,' she said, and I told her I would talk to her cousin. Choua told me he didn't know enough English. And I said we could all go together and with Choua's help we could settle this. Choua said there was no way to settle it. I asked her why not, and she wouldn't say. I asked her if her cousin was into anything illegal, and she wouldn't answer that question either. I told her either we try talking to him or I was going to call the police. She begged me not to call."

"You should have called," Pendleton said.

"But what would you have done? It's not a crime to ask your cousin to come to your store."

"But you believed the girl was being threatened," Pendleton asserted.

"And I'm also a man with a record. I'm not your favorite citizen. The police think I'm a fanatic. You would've done nothing."

Rachael imagined that a moment of silence passed before Pendleton continued with the questioning.

"So then what happened?"

"We went to the store and down into the basement at the time Thao had asked Bao to show up. He was ticked that I was there and told me to leave and mind my own business or something like that. It was half-English and half-Hmong. He had a gun in his pocket, and he got it out and waved it around. He told me I was trespassing and shouted at me to leave.

"Then he and Choua got into an argument. They didn't seem to be getting anywhere. Bao backed herself into a corner as they were yelling, and finally Choua turned to me and told me the truth. Thao had massive debts and was letting men use his basement to sexually abuse her for pay. Choua told me she had been promised that if she did what Thao commanded, he would leave Bao alone. But Thao no longer liked the deal. He wanted Bao for his customers too."

"Why didn't you call the police then?" Pendleton asked.

"I seriously doubt Thao would have allowed me to use his phone to call you at that point."

"You could've taken the girls and left," Pendleton suggested.

"That's not what ran through my mind, first, Detective."

"What did?"

"That I was standing in front of a monster. I jumped Thao, startling him and he dropped his gun. I picked it up. Suddenly I realized I could stop him from hurting these young girls permanently. I didn't even think about the consequences. I just told Choua and Bao to go outside and wait for me in my car. When they were gone I told Thao to get on his knees. I walked behind him and shot him."

"Where were you standing when you shot him?"

"At the foot of the stairs."

"Where's the gun?"

"I took it with me. After I took the girls home, I threw it into the river."

"So you think you did the right thing, Mr. Harper?"

"No. No, I don't. That's why I'm here. I shouldn't have killed him. He was a monster, but I shouldn't have killed him. What I did was wrong. The girls knew what I had done. It was wrong."

"Why did you wait five days to turn yourself in?"

"I thought I could live with what I had done. But I can't. I can't live with it."

At the moment she read the last words, a drop of water unexpectedly fell onto the paper in front of her, and Rachael flinched in her chair. She had begun to cry. It was a tear from her left eye that had fallen onto Joshua's transcribed statement. Surprised, she blotted at it with the sleeve of her turtleneck.

Rachael didn't know when the tears had started or that when she closed the file, her face was shimmering with evidences of grief.

It could not have happened this way! Rachael reasoned within. She savagely wiped away the tears that threatened to convince her that it actually could have.

EIGHT

Rachael was reaching into her purse to grab a tissue when she became aware that someone had entered the conference room. She looked up. Sgt. Pendleton was standing next to her.

"You okay?" he asked.

Rachael snatched up the tissue and blotted her eyes. "Yes, I'm fine. Thanks." She didn't intend for her words to sound terse, but she knew they did.

Pendleton pulled out a chair across from her and sat down at the table. He pointed to the file. "Still think your brother's lying?"

Rachael crumpled the tissue and tossed it into her purse. "Yes." She looked up at Pendleton, attempting to appear completely in control. He held her gaze, pausing for a moment before saying anything else.

"I'd like to hear why," he said.

Something in his voice suggested that he too had doubts that Josh was telling the truth. But Rachael guessed they were tiny, niggling suspicions, not like the giant red flags waving in her head.

"I'll be the first to tell you that my brother has a flair for sticking his nose into matters best left to law enforcement," she said. "I think you'd agree with me there. You've read his file. He jumps in with both feet when someone is being abused or oppressed, regardless of the consequences. If someone has been wronged, he wants to make it right. If they're being struck, he wants to take away the hammer. If they've had something stolen from them, he wants to get it back. If they're in danger, he wants to provide shelter. He'll do what he thinks law enforcement should be doing and isn't. Do you agree?"

Pendleton nodded. "It appears that way, yes."

Rachael leaned forward. "He does what he thinks *you* should be doing."

"Okay. So?"

"What policeman would put a bullet in the head of a man involved in human trafficking? You might be disgusted with a man like that. You might even want to see him rot in prison. But what policeman would insist that man be executed?"

Pendleton shook his head. "Your brother isn't a policeman. There's no reason to assume he thinks like one. Besides, he acted impulsively. He said he knew afterward it was the wrong thing to do."

"My point exactly! He's never regretted any of his other offenses. He's been quick to justify every law he has ever broken. This is the first time he's ever shown remorse."

"Aren't you relieved that he's showing remorse?"

"If he had done it, I would be. But remorse is highly uncharacteristic of him. It suggests he didn't do it far more than that he did."

Pendleton shrugged. "I hate to sound cliché, Ms. Flynn…"

"Please call me Rachael."

"Okay. I hate to sound cliché, Rachael, but there's a first time for everything. Maybe this is the first time your brother's showing remorse because this is also the first time he went completely overboard. He went way out of bounds. Went beyond what a policeman would have done had a policeman been there."

Rachael looked down at the file in front of her. She couldn't deny that what Pendleton was suggesting was possible. It was possible Joshua's exceedingly developed sense of justice went tragically haywire. That in a split-second of a highly charged moment, Josh let go of reason and killed a man—a very bad man. It was possible.

It just didn't seem probable.

There was something amiss. Something spun in circles at the back of her mind like an annoying mosquito. Something she was supposed to see.

She crinkled her eyebrows in thought, trying to picture the scene of the crime as Joshua described it in his statement. *He said when an angry, crying Choua turned to him in the basement and declared Thao had already victimized Bao and her too, that he had snapped. He had lunged for Thao and Thao had dropped the gun he was holding. Then Joshua said when he picked it up, he suddenly realized he could stop Thao from hurting Choua and Bao anymore. Permanently. That was the moment when he "snapped." When reason left him.*

That was the moment.

Rachael pictured Joshua in that mere breath of time, holding a gun, considering his options. *What he did next had nothing to do with the gun. He told Choua and Bao to go outside and wait for him in his car. In his statement he said the girls obeyed. Their obedience was also clothed in time. How many seconds did it take for Choua and Bao to heed Joshua's command to leave the basement, climb the outside stairs, get into Joshua's car and close the car door? Thirty seconds? Twenty-five?*

Twenty-five seconds was a long time for Joshua to aim a gun.

She pictured Joshua at age fifteen, the one and only time he went deer hunting with their father. Cliff had been pestering Joshua to take gun safety classes at the community center so that they could go hunting together. But Josh kept coming up with excuses not to go. Finally Cliff had insisted Joshua come with him on his yearly weekend trip up North to hunt deer so that Josh could see for himself how enjoyable it was.

Cliff stomped into the house on Sunday, two days later, in a bad mood and without a deer. Josh had caused them to miss the only shot they could've made. Neither one wanted to talk about it at first.

Then at dinner their father had suggested they try again the following weekend. Josh had politely declined. The rest of the meal had been submerged in silence.

"What happened?" Rachael asked Joshua later in his bedroom.

"Dad wanted *me* to take the shot," he answered. "Told me the angle was perfect, that I couldn't miss. He put the rifle in my hands. Raised my arms up, whispering all the time what a nice set-up we had."

He paused and Rachael waited for him to continue.

"He was right. I knew I probably wouldn't miss. I could kill it. It was an easy shot."

Her brother had looked away from her then, choosing to stare at the borrowed blaze orange jacket he had worn that day.

"That animal had no idea we were there," he continued. "Had no idea I had a gun pointed at her. She had no idea she'd been hunted."

"You couldn't shoot her," Rachael said softly, understanding.

Joshua turned his head toward her. "What was the point? When you hunt for something, you look for it until you find it. Well, we found her. The hunt was over. What was the point of shooting her? To prove to people we had seen a deer?"

"That's what deer hunters do, Josh," Rachael had said. "You can't pretend you didn't know that."

"I never said I wanted to go deer hunting," he said, turning his head away. "I went because Dad wanted me to. I don't have anything to prove to anyone."

"He just wants you to be a part of his world, Josh. He wants to do things with you."

"No, what he wants is for me to be like him."

He said it with no disrespect, but Rachael now remembered how she bristled in defense of their father. "What's so wrong with a father wanting his son to be like him, to enjoy the things he enjoys? That's perfectly normal."

Joshua had swung his head around to look at her. "You know I can't be a part of his world. And he will never be a part of mine."

It always came back to that—that invisible mark Josh believed he carried on his body, that branding that declared he belonged to God and no one else, and that he believed he had been entrusted with a mission no one could possibly understand: defend the cause of the fatherless and the widow. There was no room for any other pursuits, certainly not deer hunting.

Contempt roiled up within her. "You missed the shot on purpose," Rachael said.

"Yeah, I did."

"Couldn't you have done this for him, Joshua? Do you have to turn everything into a colossal theological debate? Couldn't you have done this *one* thing for him?"

"I *did* do it for him. I had several long seconds to think about it, Rachael," Joshua said, sounding older than his fifteen years. "And you may think that's not long enough to make a good decision. But it's a long time when you've got a gun in your hands."

Rachael snapped her eyes open. Sgt. Pendleton was staring at her.

"It was too much time," she said, staring back at him.

"Beg your pardon?"

"He had too much time to think about it. He said he just snapped and shot Thao without thinking. But that can't be true. He had too much time."

"I don't get you."

Rachael leaned forward in her chair. "Look, Joshua said after he jumped Thao and picked up the gun he suddenly decided he was going to punish Thao for what he had done by killing him. He said that was the moment he lost it, when he 'snapped.' He told Choua and Bao to leave the basement and wait for him in his car. Well, how long do you think it took those girls to do that? Especially if they were afraid of what Josh might do? Even if they ran, and I doubt they did, it would still take at least twenty seconds for them to leave the basement, climb the stairs, get into his car, and close the door. That means he had nearly half a minute to consider what he was doing. That doesn't sound like a snap decision to me."

The look on Pendleton's face was a mix of doubt and curiosity. "A crime of passion doesn't have to take place within the span of a second to be considered a crime of passion," he said. "You brother's anger and revulsion—which I can completely understand—could have easily carried over for those twenty or thirty seconds."

"But you don't know my brother like I do," Rachael said. "You're comparing him to every other person you've investigated for murder. He isn't like anyone else."

Pendleton breathed in deeply and rubbed his face with his hand. "Ms. Flynn…"

"Rachael."

"Rachael, did Sgt. Stowe happen to tell you where she was this morning about the same time you were visiting with your brother?"

"No."

"She was at the high school talking with Choua Lee. Then she went to see Bao at the middle school."

Rachael waited.

"You know as well as I that no judge will accept a plea of guilty on a confession alone," he continued. "Corroborating facts will have to be weighed against the confession. The facts must be clear as to the guilt of the defendant as his own guilty plea."

"Yes, I'm aware of that."

"Well, both Choua and Bao gave statements to Sgt. Stowe that support your brother's confession. They were interviewed separately, each without the knowledge that the other had been questioned. Both girls' statements substantiate your brother's account of what happened, with the exception of why your brother allegedly shot Thao. Neither one said they had any recollection of having been victimized inside that basement, though both admitted it could have happened—they just couldn't remember. Both girls attested that they didn't see Joshua shoot Thao, but they each told Stowe they heard a popping sound coming from the direction of the basement stairs while waiting in your brother's car. They each said Joshua had the gun in his hands when they left the basement and that he had it pointed at Thao. Their statements are nearly identical."

"I'm sure they are. I'm sure Josh told them exactly what to say if they were questioned!" Rachael exclaimed.

"Why would these girls, who most likely *have* been abused, be so quick to lie to the police?"

"Josh told them to!"

"And why would they obey your brother? A white guy they have known for what, a month?"

Rachael couldn't control the volume of her voice. "Because they trusted him!" she bellowed.

Pendleton's eyes widened as Rachael's voice carried across the room and out into the hall.

"Don't you see?" she continued in a normal tone of voice. "They trusted him! They found someone who had genuine compassion for them and who was willing to sacrifice himself for their protection."

Pendleton absently fingered the edge of the file that lay between them. "Or they're not lying at all. Perhaps their statements are so alike because that's what really happened."

Rachael shook her head firmly from side to side, "No," she said. "I think they have already demonstrated to you that they can lie to the police if they choose to. Who doesn't remember whether or not they have been sexually assaulted? Who wouldn't remember *that?*"

"How long has it been since you've lived with your brother, if I may ask?" Pendleton said after a moment's pause.

Rachael looked up at him. She could sense where this was going. "Twelve years."

"And how long since you've lived in Minnesota?"

"Five years."

"How often do you and your brother get together?"

Rachael looked away.

"Once a year?" he continued.

"About that," she sighed.

"Do you talk to each other on the phone or email more than once a week?"

"No."

"More than once a month?"

"No."

"So your contact with your brother, especially in the past five years, has been limited?"

Rachael frowned. "Look, I can see where you are going with this. You think I really don't know what my brother is capable of doing or that I don't know him like I think I do. But you're wrong. We have a…a bond that's difficult to describe. I know that sounds trite, but it's true. I can tell that there is something wrong in all of this. It's not measuring up. We're missing something."

"You've got a gut feeling?" Pendleton said.

"Yes, something like that."

"You're a lawyer, Rachael. You know gut feelings won't cut it in a courtroom. We need something we can stick a thumbtack in."

"Then I will keep at this until I find it. I know I'm right."

"I can see how much you'd like to be."

"I *am* right."

Pendleton leaned forward. "I have to tell you, I have never met anyone—in all my years on the force—who has confessed to killing someone they didn't really kill."

A weak smile spread across Rachael's face. "I hate to sound cliché, Detective, but there is a first time for everything."

NINE

The drive from the St. Paul Police Department to the streets of Frogtown took less than ten minutes. Rachael followed behind Sgt. Pendleton in her mother's car, pulling alongside the curb of a busy side street just inside Frogtown's unmarked limits. The streets were alive with people of every race—some walking, some riding bicycles, some at the wheel of moving cars, and some standing against buildings watching the late afternoon unfold.

The Thao Asian Food Store, across from where she and Pendleton parked, was marked with yellow police tape around its brick exterior. A uniformed policeman was waiting for them at the store's east corner where an alley led to the building's basement stairs. Rachael could see that the front window boasted signs in an elegant, lacy script that she couldn't read. Huge bags of rice were resting against the shelves nearest the window though the shop was semi-dark and a "Closed" sign hung on the front door. Several heads turned as she made her way across the street a few paces behind Pendleton.

"This is Officer Pohl," Pendleton said when they reached the cop.

"How do you do," the policeman said, extending his hand.

"Hi. Rachael Flynn," Rachael said, reaching out her own hand.

"You've unlocked it?" Pendleton asked as he led them into the alley.

"Yep. You're all set," the policeman answered.

Pendleton looked back at Rachael as they walked. "I don't usually do this, you know. Take the relative of a defendant to the crime scene."

"I know."

He swung his head back around. "But you're a lawyer. And you may be on to something."

"Believe me, I am grateful."

Again Pendleton turned to her as they walked. "And you're right. I don't want to send the wrong man to prison."

They arrived at the stairs.

"I don't suppose I have to tell you not to touch anything?" Pendleton asked.

"No, you don't have to."

Rachael slowly descended the stairs, mentally calling to mind everything she remembered from the class she took in forensics at law school. She took her time on each step as she took in visually what lay all around her: empty soda pop cans, candy wrappers, wilted remains of some kind of lettuce, and stains on the cement stairs of every shape, size, and color. One blot in particular caught her attention. It had the unmistakable look of blood. She bent down to study it. Already at the bottom of the stairs, Pendleton turned to look at her.

"We've swabbed that one," he said.

"Is it human?"

Pendleton shrugged. "The lab isn't done with our samples yet. I should know soon."

Rachael rose and descended the remaining stairs.

Pendleton was standing at the basement door, which was ajar, having been unlocked by Officer Pohl.

"Have you been to a crime scene before?" Pendleton asked.

"A few. Not very many."

"There's a blood puddle in the middle of the floor that we've not

allowed Thao's survivors to clean up just yet. I just thought you should
know that."

"Okay," Rachael said, nodding. She sent a tumble of thoughts
heavenward as Pendleton pushed on the door and it swung wide. They
stepped inside.

The basement gave off a rancid smell—a mixture of rotting produce, mildew, and damp cardboard. But Rachael's first impression of
the room was not its sour odor, but deep evil lurking within its walls.
It was as if a third presence were in the room. She tried to shake off the
sensation as quickly as it fell upon her. *That's just the sort of thing Joshua
would notice*, she thought, *not me*. Joshua was the one prone to tangle
with spiritual dimensions, not her. And that kind of illogical specula-
tion wasn't going to help her get to the truth. She needed a clear head.
She willed the thought away.

Pendleton reached in with a gloved hand and flipped on a light
switch. As Rachael stepped forward around Pendleton, her foot kicked
something. An onion rolled out from her foot.

"Sorry!" she exclaimed.

Pendleton looked down as the yellow-brown onion came to rest
against a pile of newspapers. "It's okay," he said. "It's probably the
same one I kicked when I came down here the first time. This place
is a mess."

Rachael stepped away over other onions, and her eyes immediately
fell on an amoeba-shaped, burgundy stain on the cement floor in the
center of the room. A light chalk drawing indicated where the body
had been, and the stain filled the space where the head would have
been. Her breath caught in her throat as she pictured Josh in this
room when Thao was shot, when blood seeped out of his head onto
the floor.

Rachael turned from the bloodstain to study the rest of the room.
Where had Josh been standing when it happened? Where were the
girls? The forensics report stated the shooter had been at or on the
bottom stair that led to the retail level of the store. Rachael walked
over to the stairs and bent down to look at the wooden slat that was

closest to the floor. She rose, stood on the floor at the bottom step and turned toward Pendleton, who was still standing next to the chalk outline. With a hand she could not keep from shaking she raised her arm as if pointing a gun. The chalk outline lay seven feet, maybe six feet away. She remembered then that Josh had told police he ordered Thao to his knees. She lowered her arm a few inches, compensating for the reduction in height. Would Joshua have stood that far away from the man he wanted to shoot execution style? She tried to imagine herself enraged enough to point a gun at someone's head from seven feet away and then ordering that person to his knees. She took two steps forward, still holding her arm out. The distance was now more like four feet.

"It couldn't have happened there," Pendleton said. "The entry angle would have been different."

Rachael turned back to the stairs. "The stairs are too far away. Would you have put seven feet between you and a man you ordered to his knees before shooting him in the head?"

Pendleton blinked. "I would have arrested him, not shot him."

"You know what I mean," she said.

"Yes. I know what you mean. But people about to commit a crime of passion don't always do the most practical thing in the commencement of it."

"Don't you think it's kind of odd that the grocer had a gun on him when my brother and the girls arrived?" she said, still aiming the imaginary gun. "He wasn't expecting Josh to be there."

"No, I'm sure he wasn't. But lots of urban shop owners keep a gun. It was after hours that night and if your brother's and the girls' story is true, Thao was involved in human trafficking and possibly the sale of a controlled substance. A deal was about to go down. It's not so odd that he decided to keep his gun close."

Rachael dropped her arm and placed both hands on her hips, looking about the basement. Where had the girls been when all this took place? It would make sense that Thao had come down the wooden stairs from the first floor when Josh and the girls entered. He would be facing the door to the outside or at least in that general direction. He was mad at Josh for coming and shouted at him to leave. Where were the girls when Thao was yelling at Josh? Cowering behind him? Rachael picked her way to the far wall. It was lined with shelves cluttered with boxes of canned goods resting haphazardly atop each other. Perhaps Bao had backed up against the shelves, behind Josh and to his left. Bao had clearly been afraid. It was Choua who had done all the talking. And where was she? She had stepped in and confronted Thao. Where had she stood?

She turned from the shelves to Pendleton. "Did Sgt. Stowe ask the girls where they were standing when my brother supposedly jumped Thao?"

"They said they were near where you were standing. At the shelves with all the canned goods."

"Both of them?"

"Yes."

Rachael could picture Bao cowering at the shelves, but something within her cried out that Choua had not been there. Choua had been standing elsewhere. But it was nothing more than a gut feeling. She didn't mention it to Pendleton.

She walked back over to the other side of the basement, carefully dodging fallen onions and stepping over other uncared-for items. She stopped by an interior wall, to where she imagined Thao must have been standing when he argued with Josh—or at least when Josh had jumped him. Thao and Josh could have fallen against the wall and into a conglomeration of empty crates that now lay in a jumbled mess. Thao probably lost his footing. Maybe he tried to brace himself against the wall, but the crates unsteadied him. He dropped the gun. Josh fell to the ground…or maybe to his knees as the men struggled. He got to the gun first.

Rachael turned toward the stairs, backing her body up against the pile of crates as Thao might have done. She tried to imagine that she was Thao and that his own gun was now pointed at him.

Maybe Josh ordered him away from wall. And then Josh backed

up toward the stairs. He ordered Choua to take Bao out to his car. Rachael looked over to the wall where the shelves were and noticed Pendleton was following her gaze. She imagined that Choua had hesitated. "Go!" Josh might have shouted. She counted off the seconds as she imagined the girls making their way out of the basement. Seven seconds to the basement door. One to close it. Eight to climb the stairs. Six to get into Josh's car.

Josh probably had twenty-two seconds to change his mind.

Rachael looked at the stain and then walked the few feet to the edge of the chalk outline. She knelt where she imagined Thao had knelt, and as she did, she noticed a large rectangular shape on the floor next to where the body had been. She hadn't noticed it before.

It was an outline; a space of clean floor that had recently been covered. Dirt, tattered paper and stains lay all round the outlined space but not in it. The patch of cement, which looked to be about five feet by four feet, was the only clean spot in Thao's basement.

Rachael rose and walked a few paces until she was inside the outline.

She looked up at Pendleton. He nodded. He had wanted her to discover this.

"There was a rug or mat here," she said.

"Yep."

"Where is it?"

Pendleton shrugged. "Thao's two employees said they have no idea what happened to that floor mat. They hadn't noticed it was gone."

"Did you ask Josh about it?"

"Your brother said he knows nothing about the disappearance of a floor mat."

"And the girls?"

"They don't either."

Rachael looked at the clean spot of cement under her feet, so out of place compared to the chaos in the rest of the room. "How long do you figure it's been gone?" she said.

Pendleton tipped his head toward her. *What do you think?* was the unspoken question, suggesting they both believed the floor mat disappeared the same day Thao was killed.

Back on the street, Pendleton thanked Officer Pohl for assisting them and he waved once as the officer drove off. He made no move to head back to where the cars were parked.

Rachael sensed Pendleton wanted to say something to her.

He turned from where they stood on the sidewalk and looked at her.

"I'd really like to know where that floor mat is and why it got moved," he said and his tone was insistent. "We impounded your brother's car and searched his apartment looking for it, but we didn't find it."

"But you think Josh might know where it is," Rachael replied.

"Yes, I think he might."

"I don't know if he'll tell me. I don't know if he'll tell me anything."

"It can't hurt for you to try."

Rachael nodded. "All right. I'll ask him."

"The sooner we can locate it and bring it into evidence, the better off for everybody—including your brother."

Rachael wasn't sure she understood the urgency in finding the floor mat. "Why do you think it matters so much?"

"Because it's missing. Besides, if those girls were molested in that basement, pehaps it occurred on that floor mat."

A ripple of revulsion swept across Rachael. "But why…why would Josh get rid of it then?"

Pendleton shook his head. "I don't know. It's just one of a couple little things that don't quite add up. But I'll bet there's a wealth of DNA evidence on that thing, and I want it. This isn't the first time Hmong girls have been victimized here in St. Paul. It has happened often over the past few years, and we've been at our wit's end as to how to combat it. I'm afraid Choua and Bao might not have been the only girls Thao was victimizing."

Rachael felt a tightening in her throat as a fresh wave of disgust seized her. "Why do you think that?"

Pendleton crossed his arms and leaned up against a lamppost. "Because I've seen it happen time and time again with these forced prostitution rings. And the truly frustrating thing for us is that Hmong girls who get raped—even gang-raped—usually don't report it. And many times their families don't either."

"Why not?" Rachael asked, incredulous.

"Because they won't testify. They choose to live with the private horror of the rape, sometimes multiple rapes, rather than the stigmatization of the public knowing and the common knowledge that they are now undeserving of marriage."

"But it's not their fault!"

"No, it's not. But we have a terrible clash of cultures—our unsafe streets and their cultural beliefs."

"Is there no way to stop it?"

"Each year we make a little more headway, but it's been an uphill battle without extra funding and outside support. It's a problem we still struggle to get above the radar. Plus, a lot of these girls are runaways who will disappear for days and then show up again with no way of accounting for where they've been. Many times they were given alcohol or drugs to gain their cooperation or render them senseless. They often can't identify their abusers or even describe them."

"But what about their parents? Where are they in all of this?"

"I've spoken to several of them. They don't know what to do to keep their girls home and their sons out of the gangs that abuse them. The ones who speak English have told me they've lost control of their kids. And they don't have the freedom to discipline their children the way they were disciplined growing up in Thailand or Laos. There is no village here."

"No village?"

"The sense that all the neighbors in your village are looking out for your child, protecting your child, and even correcting your child—that's absent here in America, and they've not been able to compensate for it."

Rachael was overcome with a sudden longing to go back to Fig's and hold her daughter. The thoughts that were crowding her mind were terrifying. Again she felt the suffocating presence of evil. "I need to go. I have a baby girl that needs to be fed. And who I really need to hold right now." The last sentence slipped from her lips with a tremble in her voice.

"I really want that floor mat," Pendleton said gently.

Rachael looked up at him. "Do you think it will make any difference?" Her voice was weary with the weight of what she knew.

"Maybe. Maybe not. But I have to hope that it will. You know I have to."

"I'll see what I can do."

"Good."

"Thanks for bringing me here."

Pendleton nodded.

They walked across the street. When they arrived at the cars, Rachael paused, her hand on the handle of the car door. Again she was struck with the horribleness of the crimes against Choua and Bao. She turned her head toward Pendleton ahead of her, who had just opened his own car door.

"Detective, the Lee girls—they'll be all right now, won't they? I mean, they aren't in any danger? Someone is looking out for them?"

The detective smiled at her. "Department of Human Services is on it. They'll be getting counseling, medical follow-up, home visits, the works."

Rachael nodded. She whispered a prayer that whoever was assigned to the girls' case was compassionate, clever, and patient.

"Coming to the arraignment tomorrow?" Pendleton said.

"What do you think?" Rachael smiled as she slid into her mother's car.

TEN

Rachael was grateful to find a parking place just across the street from Fig's building. The afternoon had taken a toll on her emotionally and physically; she felt bone tired.

She stepped out of the car, locked it, and glanced at her watch. It was only 4:45. McKenna might even still be asleep. She crossed the street to Fig's condominium complex, opened the door to the lobby, and then pressed the intercom button marked *Figaro Houseman*.

"*Hvem er det,*" a voice replied from within a small speaker. Fig. Speaking in who knew what language.

"It's me, Rachael."

"*Går inn i, vakker.*"

Rachael sighed. "English, please, Fig."

"Enter, beautiful one," Fig replied, and the beveled glass door that lead to the elevator inside buzzed as it unlocked.

At her touch the elevator doors slid open, and Rachael stepped in and pressed the button for Fig's penthouse loft. She leaned against the elevator wall as the doors slid shut. She closed her eyes as the elevator surged upward. Her head was spinning with too many facts and just as many troubling considerations. She knew infinitely more about what happened the night Vong Thao was killed than she did when she started out that morning, but she felt no closer to the truth behind Josh's decision to confess. If anything, the facts of the case implicated Josh more than they exonerated him. The goal of proving his innocence had become harder in the past few hours, not easier.

On top of that, she was bothered by the sensation she had felt earlier in the day when she stepped into Vong Thao's basement. The heavy cloak of evil that seemed to fall on her as she moved from sunlight to the dimly lit basement troubled her. She had never before had such a potent awareness of evil. It made no sense. It was just an ordinary building. A grocery store basement, for Pete's sake. Yes, a man had been shot and killed there. But that had been almost a week earlier. The body was gone. Even the stain on the cement floor no longer looked like blood. The crimson puddle had long since turned to a crusty shade of brownish-burgundy. The room smelled of forgotten vegetables and crates, not death, and yet she had felt the hairs on the back of her neck rise in alarm. She'd had to physically shake it off. Even the mere remembrance of it brought back the awareness that she had been surrounded on all sides by forces of darkness.

Rachael also couldn't account for the hunch she had that Choua hadn't been cowering at the shelves of canned goods with Bao. She was certain the crime lab report would show that Choua's prints were found elsewhere in the room. But even if they were, that wouldn't prove that Josh was innocent. So what if Choua's prints were found in other places in the basement? Choua had admitted she could have been in the basement before, that she might have been abused there. If the lab did identify a hair or two of hers on the floor or hanging on a box edge or wrapped around a shelving unit rung, that would more likely prove that she had been in that basement recently as a victim, not as a co-conspirator.

The elevator stopped and the doors parted. Rachael stepped

out and into the plush carpeted hallway. Her eyes were down at her feet.

"You look like you could use some green tea and macaroons."

She looked up to see Trace standing at Fig's open doorway, waiting for her. "That almost sounds good," she said, smiling. "But not quite."

He wrapped an arm around her as she stepped into Fig's apartment, and she caught a whiff of espresso and something sweet.

"Something smells heavenly," she murmured.

"Fig made you espresso. He knows you like it. I was only kidding about the green tea."

"Rachael kumquat, come in, come in!" Fig's voice reverberated from within the apartment's kitchen. "Look! Your mother has made you delectable circlets of sugar and spice!"

"Cookies," Trace whispered. They rounded the corner into the open kitchen and dining area, and she could see that Fig was filling two tiny cups with espresso and Eva was lifting peanut-butter cookies off a baking tray.

"Mom, you didn't have to go to all that trouble," Rachael said, slipping onto a bar stool and accepting a tiny cup and saucer from Fig. "Thanks, Fig."

"Nonsense. It wasn't any trouble at all," her mother said, handing her a cookie. "I don't know how they will taste though. I've never seen peanut butter like the kind Fig has in his cupboard."

Rachael bit into the still-warm cookie. There was the strangest hint that something other than Jif had found its way into the dough. "They're great, Mom. Thanks. How's McKenna?"

"The bambino still sleeps," Fig said, offering espresso to Eva. Rachael's mother shook her head with disdain. Fig shrugged and brought the little cup instead to his own lips.

"Good. I was hoping I would get home before she woke up again," Rachael replied.

Trace slid onto the bar stool beside her. "So how did it go?"

Eva set down the spatula and looked at her. "Yes. What happened? What did you find out?"

Rachael took a sip of the espresso. Its pungent, earthy taste instantly warmed her from within. "The detective took me to the grocery store."

"He did?" Eva sounded afraid.

Rachael looked up at her. "There was really nothing to see, Mom. I just wanted to be able to picture it the way Joshua said it happened."

"Well, how did he say it happened? Did you read his confession? What did he say?"

"It's pretty much what he told you on the phone when he called you yesterday morning from jail, Mom. He said he was trying to help two girls he believed were being threatened with forced prostitution. When he went to Thao's store Tuesday night, he found out they already *were* being victimized. He claimed he had a meltdown of some kind and he exploded into a rage. Apparently the grocery store owner had a gun on him, and when Josh jumped the guy, the gun fell to the ground and Josh picked it up. He said that's when he got the crazy idea to kill him. He sent the girls outside and then shot Vong Thao. Then he left. That's what he said happened."

"That's insane!" Eva's eyes were wide. "Joshua could never point a gun at someone, let alone fire it!"

"The girls involved were questioned by the police, and their statements support his story. The girls didn't see him pull the trigger, but they said he was pointing the gun at Thao when he told them to wait for him in his car."

"I still can't believe it," Eva said, tossing her head and wiping her hands on a dish towel.

"I don't either, Mom, but what *we* believe about Josh doesn't matter. It's what the facts point to. The police have a confession. They have a witness who saw someone fitting Joshua's description enter the basement the evening Thao was shot, and they have two young girls who saw Josh aiming a gun at Thao's head. That's what we're up against."

"You're not giving up on him, are you?" Eva asked, worry creasing her face.

"No, Mom, I'm not. There are several little things that don't make sense. Even the detective in charge of this case feels like there's something amiss. I'm just saying it's not going to be easy to uncover the truth as long as Joshua sticks to his bogus story."

"So this hearing tomorrow. It's still taking place? They're still going to have it?"

Rachael nodded.

"And what will happen?"

Rachael breathed in deeply, gathering inner strength. "He will probably be charged with murder two, intentional."

"What does that mean?" Eva asked abruptly, shaking her head and screwing her eyes shut.

"Murder two is murder in the second degree. It means they believe Josh had intent to kill at the moment he killed, but that it wasn't premeditated. First-degree murder is much worse, Mom. It carries a mandatory life sentence."

Eva kept her eyes tightly closed as if to keep herself from picturing what lay ahead for her only son. "Just like that, they will charge him?"

"They have to charge him or let him go. That's the law. And he confessed."

Eva opened her eyes, glassy now with moisture. "Is that all that will happen?"

"Well, Joshua might be asked to enter a plea."

Eva looked resignedly at her daughter. "He will say he's guilty, won't he?" It was spoken barely above a whisper.

Rachael felt her throat tighten as she looked at her mother. "Unless he changes his mind between now and tomorrow afternoon, yes, he probably will."

"So that's it then. You came for nothing. It was all for nothing." Eva began to sob. Fig, standing next to her, put an arm protectively around her.

"No, that's not *it*, Mom. Listen to me," Rachael said, leaning forward on her stool. "The judge won't accept a plea of guilty based on a confession alone. He's going to want factual evidence that substantiates the confession. Do you hear what I am saying? The judge won't accept his plea of guilty tomorrow. He won't. I guarantee it."

Eva looked up, her face a mix of anguish and confusion. "He won't?"

Trace piped up too. "He won't?"

"No."

"Well, what will happen then?" Trace asked.

"The court will set a date for an omnibus hearing. That won't take place for at least three or four weeks. Between now and then the state will continue its investigation to make sure the confession bears up under the weight of the facts. 'Omnibus' means looking at all things all at once. The judge won't just look at the confession. He will look at everything. Okay? Okay, Mom?"

Eva shuddered as her sobs subsided. "Are you saying we still have some time?"

"Yes."

Her mother wiped the tears away and became aware of Fig's arm around her. A tiny grin formed on her mouth. "Thanks, Figaro," she said. "I'm sorry…"

"No apologies, please."

Fig dropped his arm and Eva looked away, reaching up to wipe away the streaks of tears.

A muted cry from the direction of the guest room broke the awkwardness of the moment.

Rachael rose off her stool. "I think I hear someone."

"Rachael, wait. Let me say goodbye to her before I head for home," Eva said, nearly bolting from behind the island countertop where she had been standing.

"Sure, Mom."

The two women made their way into the guest room. McKenna had kicked off her blankets and was waving fists of protest as she cried.

Eva scooped her up and brought the wriggling, angry infant close to her still-moist face, nuzzling her. "Goodbye, precious! Grandma will see you tomorrow." She handed the baby to Rachael. "You're not bringing her to the hearing, are you?"

Rachael shook her head. "Trace will stay with her."

Eva nodded. "Think it will be done by suppertime?"

"This first appearance will be extremely short, Mom. It may only take five minutes, maybe ten. If Joshua's case is one of the first ones to be heard, we could be done before two thirty."

"I see. So we can have supper at six?"

"Probably."

Eva nodded and smoothed a tiny stray lock in McKenna's whisper-thin hair. "I don't want it to be longer than five minutes, but it seems like it should be."

"I know, Mom."

McKenna's cries became insistent.

"I think I'll just stretch out on the bed to feed her," Rachael said, walking over to the French maiden's bed.

"All right. I can see myself out."

"Thanks for loaning me your car, Mom. Your keys are just inside my purse, and the car is right outside across the street."

"You're welcome." Eva turned to go and then swung her head back around. "I'm so glad you are here, Rachael. I don't know what I'd do if you weren't." She walked out of the room. Rachael heard her mother's goodbyes to Trace and Fig and the front door opening and closing.

Rachael climbed up on the bed, grabbed throw pillows to support her back and untucked her sweater. Within seconds McKenna's cries were silenced. Rachael laid her head back against a bed pillow and began to stroke her infant daughter's head, amazed anew at how much having a child changed how she looked at just about everything. Her life's pursuits had seemed very noble and important until she had McKenna. When she held her child in her arms for the first time eight weeks ago, everything else tarnished into utter unimportance. All that mattered to her now, when it really came down to it, was Trace and McKenna.

And if she were being perfectly honest, McKenna needed her more than Trace did. Trace could survive without her, though she was comforted in knowing he wouldn't want to.

But McKenna? She looked down on her daughter. Tiny. Helpless. Vulnerable. Dependent. McKenna needed her desperately. Her thoughts flew unbidden to Choua and Bao, sisters whose faces she wouldn't recognize if she saw them in the street, but who had nevertheless worked their way into her newly discovered mother-heart.

How could anyone rob those young girls of so much and think so little of it? How could anyone do such a thing? No wonder Joshua had intervened on their behalf.

No wonder. . .

Despite the sips of espresso and the heaviness of the thoughts that consumed her, Rachael's eyes slowly fluttered closed. As McKenna nursed at her breast, sleep claimed Rachael.

ELEVEN

The sensation of falling headlong into a dark chasm ripped Rachael from sleep, and she instinctively spread out her arms to grab McKenna and draw her child to her chest.

But her fingers felt only air. McKenna was gone.

Snapping her eyes open, Rachael sat up, her pulse surging into overdrive.

"McKenna!"

Her voice was cloaked with the aftereffects of sleep and sounded husky and foreign in her ears.

Trace's head appeared at the semi-open doorway of Fig's guest room.

"I've got her," he said casually, but he stepped into the room when his eyes met Rachael's. "Honey, are you okay?"

"Where's McKenna?" she croaked, swinging her legs to the side of the bed and stumbling to her feet. Trace quickly closed the distance between them and reached out to steady her.

"I said I have her. She's in the kitchen with Fig and me. We're making pot-stickers for supper. McKenna's slicing the scallions."

Rachael sat back on the bed. "What?"

"I was just kidding, Rach—about the scallions." Trace sat down next to her, keeping his arm around her waist. "Fig told me to tell you that….Are you sure you're awake?"

"I…I was dreaming, I guess. Oh my goodness! I fell asleep while feeding McKenna! What time is it? Why didn't you wake me?"

"Slow down, slow down. Yes, you fell asleep. McKenna is fine. I came in to check on you after your mother left and saw that you were sleeping. McKenna was quite happy with herself. She had eaten her fill and was cooing and flirting with the bedspread. So I took her and let you have a little rest."

"At five o'clock in the afternoon?"

"You were tired. You needed it."

"What time is it?" Rachael asked again, bending her arm to look at her wristwatch.

"Just a little after six. I wouldn't have let you sleep much longer. Honestly."

Rachael shook her head, willing away the lingering effects of having felt unable to protect McKenna from harm. She reached up under her sweater to fix her nursing bra. "I feel so dazed."

"Want me to have Fig warm up your espresso?"

"I don't know. Maybe." She rose from the bed and ran a hand through her hair. Trace stood too.

"Um, Rachael? Fig invited a few friends over tonight."

Rachael looked back at him. "Really? Tonight?" She swallowed a complaint that lay poised on her lips. This was Fig's house. They were his guests. He could invite over whomever he wanted.

"Just Brick and Sidney. I haven't seen them since last Christmas. And they want to see the baby," Trace said.

Rachael relaxed a bit. At least these were people she knew. And who knew her. Alphonse Brick and Sidney Gordon, together with Fig, made up the quartet of friends that shared a house with Trace while they were all students at the Minneapolis College of Art and Design. Brick, dark-eyed and with olive-tone skin, now taught high school art in a Minneapolis suburb, but it was just to pay the bills. He longed to open his own studio. Sidney, married to a Northwest Airlines flight attendant and the father of a two-year-old, was a cartoonist at the Minneapolis *Star Tribune*.

Rachael didn't exactly mind Brick and Sidney's company; neither one was as bizarre as Fig could be. And they had known Trace longer than she had. In fact, it was a friend of Brick's who'd introduced her to Trace at a party her last year of grad school. Today she felt mentally unprepared for houseguests. Especially artists. It would no doubt be a late night, and tomorrow was going to be a long day.

"And they want to see you too," Trace said, interrupting her thoughts.

"They just want to see how many Monty Python lines they can quote that I don't know," Rachael said, stretching and then slipping her shoes back on. "Or understand."

"Ah, but look how you've improved in five years of marriage," Trace countered good-naturedly. "You know more than the average big city lawyer."

"Hurray for me."

"And there will be someone else too. Fig's invited his girlfriend."

Rachael stood up straight. "Not that woman who talks to rocks!" she interjected in a whisper laced with apprehension.

"No. No, he broke up with her a long time ago, remember?" Trace said assuredly. "And it wasn't rocks. It was crystals. She talked to crystals."

Rachael tipped an eyebrow. "My mistake."

"Her name is Jillian something. She's a fabric designer. Fig met her online."

"Great."

"Rach."

"I'll be polite, I promise. Where's McKenna?"

"She's in her car seat on the counter in the kitchen. She loves Fig, you know. His crazy voices make her smile."

Trace and Rachael headed to the kitchen where they found Fig displaying a bottle of sesame oil in front of McKenna, game-show style, and wearing her receiving blanket around his head like a turban.

Fig's doorbell rang a few minutes before eight, just as Rachael was finishing a diaper change for McKenna.

"Brick and Sidney are here," Trace said, appearing at the doorway to the guest room.

"Yep, we're coming."

Trace came into the room and held his arms out. "Let me take McKenna out. I want to show her off."

"Okay, papa."

Rachael handed over their daughter and followed Trace out to the living room.

Sidney was the first to greet Rachael with a warm embrace and a sly smile. "Rachael, if Molly saw you, she'd pretend she didn't know you!" he exclaimed. "You don't look like you've just had a baby. Other women hate that, you know."

His curly red hair tickled her ear and she laughed. "Then don't tell her."

"Rachael," Brick said, coming to her and towering over her while he also gave her a hug.

"Hello, Brick."

"She's a beauty," Sidney said, peering down at the baby in Trace's arms.

"Yes, we think so," Trace said proudly.

"Named her after your mother, eh, Trace? What a good lad you are," Sidney continued.

"Really?" Brick said. "I thought your mother's name was Elisabeth."

"Her maiden name was McKenna," Trace replied.

"It's a lovely name. I'm sure your mother would approve."

"No doubt she would."

The doorbell rang again and when Fig opened it, a young woman, Kate-Moss-skinny in tattered jeans and a pale pink-jeweled top, stepped into the apartment holding a white paper sack.

"Jills, you made it," Fig said, kissing her on the cheek. "Trace and Rachael, this is Jillian Partou."

Jillian thrust her arm forward, making the huge hoops in her ears dance on her shoulders. "How nice to meet you."

"Wonderful to meet you too," Trace said.

Rachael nodded, smiled, and said hello. She noticed Jillian had one brown eye and one blue one.

"And there's their little heiress, McKenna," Fig continued, motioning to the baby in Trace's arms.

"Cute little thing," Jillian replied, looking at McKenna. Then she abruptly turned toward Fig and held up the little white bag. "Baklava from the bakery on my street, Fig. The best."

Fig clapped his hands together. "Well, what shall we have with it? Cappuccino? Sangria? Sherry? Fruit of the vine?"

Everyone headed to the kitchen to get drinks. Rachael slid onto a bar stool to watch the "artists" reconnect and fawn over McKenna. Moments later Sidney was on the stool next to her.

"I'm really sorry about all this trouble with your brother, Rachael."

"So am I." Rachael sighed…not sure she wanted to go into it all again.

"I read about it in the newsroom. Man! So he told the police he shot the guy."

Rachael stiffened. "Yes, that's what he told the police. But that doesn't mean he did it."

"Fig told me you don't think he did it."

"He didn't."

Sidney shifted his weight on the stool. "How do you know he

didn't? I mean, it sounds like the guy that got killed was a sleaze bag. How do you know Joshua didn't do it?"

"Because I know my brother."

"I have to say I agree with Rachael on that," Trace interjected as he placed McKenna back in her carrier on the floor. "Joshua's the kind of guy who'd give you the shirt off his back in the middle of a blizzard."

"Who are we talking about?" Jillian asked as she arranged brown, diamond-shaped baklava on a plate.

"Rachael's brother confessed to killing a guy in Frogtown," Fig said.

"But I know he didn't do it," Rachael repeated.

Brick turned to Rachael and leaned over the counter, holding a tumbler of club soda and lime in his hands. "Who do you think did it then?"

Rachael shrugged. "Someone who wanted the guy dead. That grocer had been victimizing young girls. He was involved in forced prostitution and probably illegal drugs. I'm sure he had lots of enemies."

"And your brother couldn't have been one of them?" Sidney asked gently.

Rachael turned to him. "My brother barely knew him. He only met him that night. If his story is true, he knew the guy for less than ten minutes before he shot him. It doesn't add up."

Sidney reached out to accept a glass of merlot from Fig. "I'm not a lawyer, but it seems to me that's not much to go on."

"I know it's not," Rachael replied. "But there's a lot of things that don't seem quite right."

"Like what, hon?" Trace asked. "Can you tell us?"

"Well, these two sisters refuse to say whether or not they had been abused in the basement, and there's a floor mat missing and…"

"A floor mat," Sidney said.

"Yes, I said a floor mat. It's missing from the basement. Why is it missing? Josh said he doesn't know why. But it was obviously removed quite recently. Josh also said the grocer had a gun on him when he brought the girls by. Why was the grocer carrying a gun? He didn't know Josh was coming. And how could my brother, who at fifteen couldn't shoot a doe with a hunting rifle, wait twenty-two seconds for the girls to leave before putting a bullet into an unarmed man? He said he acted impulsively. That he snapped." Rachael snapped her fingers. "*That* is snapping. *That* is not twenty-two seconds."

"Hey! Let's count it," Fig said, walking over to his stove. He set the timer for twenty-two seconds and turned toward his friends. The room became silent as the numbers on the LCD screen ticked off. When the buzzer sounded, he wordlessly pressed it off.

"That seemed like a long time," Jillian said.

"Sure did," Trace said.

"I think so too. And there's something else," Rachael said almost reluctantly. "I had this...feeling when I walked into that basement today that..."

"That what?" Trace asked.

Rachael shook her head. "You'll think I'm nuts."

Fig leaned toward her. "Kumquat, we're the left-brained oddballs. You think *we're* nuts, remember?"

Rachael couldn't help but smile.

"What did you feel?" Brick asked.

"I felt...evil."

Five sets of eyes stared at her, waiting for her to continue.

"It was a tangible thing; something I could have touched if I had reached out my hand," Rachael said. "There was a heaviness in the room, like in the summer when it's so hot and humid that the air feels like, feels like..."

"It wants to suffocate you," Jillian said, nodding.

"Yes," Rachael affirmed, looking up at her. "It was like that."

Trace was staring at her. She could see worry in his eyes. This was not like her, and she knew it.

"And then what?" Sidney said, prompting her to continue.

"Well, I shook it off. I pretended like it was nothing. The rest of my time there was pretty unremarkable except for when I asked the detective where the two sisters had been standing when Josh supposedly jumped the grocer. They claimed they had been standing by some shelves. But for some reason I just couldn't picture the older one there. Instinct told me she was standing somewhere else. But I can't explain how I know that. And if I can't figure out why that matters, then I can't help my brother."

"So you think there was a fifth person in the room? Someone else pulled the trigger?" Sidney asked.

"It's more likely, at least in my mind, that it was one of the girls," Rachael replied.

"Well, why would that person wait until that moment to kill him? With Josh there, I mean. He'd be a witness," Brick said.

"I don't think it was planned. It happened in the heat of an argument, in a moment of passion. If Josh lunged at the grocer, and the grocer dropped the gun, either of the two girls could have picked it up."

"How old are they?" Jillian asked.

Rachael sighed. "The older one is fifteen; the younger one is twelve."

The room was silent except the sound of fizz in Brick's glass and a gurgle of happiness coming from the direction of McKenna's car seat.

"You really think a twelve-year-old could do that?" Sidney asked.

"I've seen a lot of tragic circumstances in the five years I've been a defense lawyer," Rachael said. "You'd be surprised what a child can do when she's been neglected or abused. If those girls had been sold into forced prostitution like my brother says they were, then yes, I think either one of them could've done it."

"So you think your brother is taking the blame for something one of the girls did?" Brick said.

"Yes, I do."

"To save them from what though?" Sidney queried just before taking a sip from his wine glass. "I mean, what court would send a kid to prison for the rest of her life for shooting a man who abused her? They're just juveniles, right? And wouldn't they be seen as victims more than perpetrators? What's the worst that could happen? A few years in juvy?"

"I'm quite sure that in my brother's mind those *few years* would be horrible, Sidney. If Josh had not confessed, the investigation would have eventually led police to those girls. They were already getting close. There would have been charges and maybe a trial. Eventually the truth would come out about the sexual assaults against them—the very thing those girls would give anything to keep secret. If you knew my brother like I do, you'd know he would sacrifice himself to save those girls from paying with the rest of their childhood for the crimes of a monster."

Again the room was silent.

"What are you going to do?" Brick finally asked.

Rachael shook her head. "I don't know. I can't go to the prosecutor with just my gut feelings and a few inconsistencies. I have to find a way to piece this together and come up with facts that are indisputable."

"And how do you do that?" Brick again.

Rachael shrugged. "I have to fill in the missing holes. There are things that just don't measure up. I've got to find out why they don't. I need to figure out what really happened in that basement."

For a moment no one said a word. Then Trace split the silence, causing Rachael to flinch on her stool.

"Hey!" he exclaimed, but he said nothing else. Instead he took off for Fig's guest room, returning a moment later with one of his large sketchpads and a handful of artist pencils. He slapped them down on the island countertop.

Four heads turned to him. Trace leaned over the countertop, looked at his friends, and then locked eyes on his wife.

"I've got an idea," he said.

TWELVE

Rachael couldn't imagine what kind of idea Trace had suddenly come up with. When he had "an idea," it usually had nothing at all to do with extended family matters or criminal law. Usually it had to with his illustration contracts or where to eat out. As a rule, Trace let Rachael handle situations that involved Josh or her career by herself.

Mostly because she preferred it that way.

Trace now picked up an artist pencil, used it as a wand to motion to his friends and looked at her. "What if we put our collective minds together and sketched out the different scenarios? You know, you tell us what you think happened, and what Josh says happened; we draw it, and then we compare the drawings. Maybe as we interpret what you tell us, something will emerge. Maybe we can help you fill in the holes."

"That's a splendid idea, Tracer," Fig said, picking up a pencil. "I love drawing."

"Don't you have any hexagonal barrels?" Brick said, poking at the little pile of pencils.

"Well, I haven't sketched anything but textiles in I don't know how long," Jillian chimed in.

Rachael didn't know how she felt about Trace's idea. It seemed a very unscientific way to arrive at the truth. But the fact was, she simply had to find a way to see beyond what Josh was telling her, and past what was in the police report, because neither one was going to lead her to the truth. She was certain of it.

"I guess it can't hurt," she agreed.

Fig whipped his head around to her. "Of course it can't hurt!" he said. "How could it hurt? Ideas don't hurt people."

"No, it's people who hurt people." Brick grimaced and selected a pale gray pencil with a smooth barrel.

"So true, so true. There is such pain in life, isn't there?" Sidney added, reaching into his shirt pocket and pulling out his own mechanical pencil.

"Life *is* pain, Highness!" Brick bellowed.

"Okay, no Monty Python lines!" Rachael exclaimed, peering over the counter to make sure McKenna was still content in her car seat.

"That one was *Princess Bride,* love," Trace said. "Okay, here we go." He flipped to an empty page in his sketchbook.

"I want my own page," Fig said, wrinkling his nose.

"Me too," Brick and Sidney said in unison.

"Fine, fine," Trace replied, tearing off large pages of white linen paper and handing them to his friends. "You want one too?" he said to Jillian.

Jillian shrugged. "I'll just help Figgy out with the clothes and curtains."

"There are no curtains in a basement," Sidney said, clicking his pencil.

"Well, how do you know? Maybe there are!" Jillian quipped.

"Let's let Rachael tell us what the basement looks like, okay?" Trace intervened. "Then how about this? I'll draw it like Joshua said it happened. Brick, you draw it like it was the older girl who shot the guy, and Sidney, you draw it like was the younger one. Fig and Jillian, you draw it like it was someone else entirely."

"Ah, the inexplicable fifth person!" Fig said, nodding. "Good, good. Move the baklava, Jills."

"Okay, now first tell us what the room looks like," Trace said, smoothing out the page in front of him and turning to Rachael.

"Well," Rachael began, "the door to the outside is on the east side. The east wall is the only exterior wall. The room is square. All the walls are made of gray cinderblock, and there are no windows."

"No curtains then," Sidney interrupted, winking at Jillian. She stuck her tongue out at him.

"Along the wall with the door are trash bins and brooms and snow shovels. Everything is messy and kind of thrown together," Rachael continued. "The floor is cement, and it's heavily stained. There are boxes everywhere. There were onions all over the floor when I was there. The guy who found Thao spilled them when he came into the basement and saw the body. On the south wall are metal shelves for canned goods—and they're a mess. The boxes are teetering all over the place. That's where the girls said they were when Thao was yelling at Josh and when Josh jumped him.

"The west wall is where the wooden staircase is to the grocery store itself. There's a furnace along that wall and a water heater and some other bins of stuff. On the north wall is what might have been a stack of crates and pallets. It's a just big jumble there now. Just a few feet from the pile of crates is…is where the body was found. Josh said he and Thao fell against the crates and Thao dropped the gun. Josh supposedly picked it up and then told the girls to go wait for him in his car. He confessed that he stood by the stairs, told Thao to kneel and then he shot him in the back of the head. From a distance of about six or seven feet."

"And how big would you say this basement is?" Sidney asked, as he poised his pencil over his paper.

"I'd guess twenty-by-twenty. Maybe a little bigger."

"And where would the mysterious floor mat have been if it had been there?" Trace asked.

"Well, it would have been just a few feet from the body."

"How big?" Sidney again.

"Five feet by four."

"Facing which direction?"

"There was somewhat of a path through the mess to the wall where the shelves were. The longer part of the mat faced that wall."

"So what did Josh say happened?" Sidney asked as he sketched a matrix of eight squares on his sheet of drawing paper.

McKenna cried out from her car seat, and Rachael left the stool, came around the island, and scooped her up. "He said he brought the girls to the store at about nine o'clock. That's when the younger one said she was supposed to come. I can't tell you the girls' names. They're juveniles. One is fifteen and one is twelve. Anyway, the younger one told Josh earlier in the day that she had been instructed to come that night to her cousin's store. She was terrified of going but she wouldn't tell him why."

"How did your brother meet these kids?" Jillian asked.

"At a youth center in Frogtown. A friend of my brother's started it, and Josh was helping him. These two sisters went to it sometimes."

"Okay, so then what happened?" Brick asked.

"Well, according to Josh, Thao was in the basement waiting for the younger sister. When Josh showed up with her and the older sister Thao got mad and told him to leave. When Josh wouldn't, the grocery store owner fished a gun out of his pocket and told Josh he was trespassing and to get off his property."

"So we're assuming Josh walks in with the girls and there's the grocer in front of him. So Josh is at the east wall," Trace said.

"Yes, I think so. Or maybe he came further in and was closer to the south wall. And the grocer is probably by the stairs or at least near the north wall where all the crates are."

"And the girls are also at the south wall?"

"Yes. But then the older girl begins to argue with the grocer. After they shout at each other for a few minutes, she turns to Josh, so he says, and tells him the grocer has gambling debts and is paying them off by forcing her and now her little sister to participate in a prostitution ring. She is crying and says she was told that if she did everything the grocer asked of her, he would leave her little sister alone, but now she has found out her forced compliance didn't make any difference at all. Josh too thought he had intervened early enough to save the little one from that kind of abuse, but at that moment he found it was too late. She had been victimized already."

Rachael paused and smoothed her daughter's hair, marveling for a second at its softness. "That's when Josh said he lost it. He said he lunged at the guy. They struggled. The grocer dropped the gun. Josh said he picked it up, ordered the girls outside, shot the guy, and left."

"Taking the floor mat with him?" Brick asked quizzically.

"Josh says he doesn't know anything about a floor mat. I don't know how it figures in to any of this," Rachael said. "The police are interested in it because it's missing. And because they think the girls were abused on it. I don't see how it could prove Josh is lying about who shot the grocer, but you have to wonder why it's gone."

"Okay. Is there anything else we should know?" Trace prodded, as he sketched in four smooth ovals in the top left corner of his paper. Four faces.

"I guess that's it," Rachael said as McKenna began to whimper. "I'm going to give McKenna a bath, feed her, and put her to bed," she continued.

"Okay. Good. That will give us masterminds time to create."

As Rachael walked toward the guest room she heard Sidney yell genially, "Hey, no looking at my paper, Brick!"

When Rachael returned to the kitchen forty minutes later, the five artists were still hard at work, the baklava was half gone and a bag of microwave popcorn was popping away inside Fig's microwave oven.

"Don't look at mine, I'm not done yet," Fig said to her as she entered the kitchen.

"Don't look at mine either," Brick echoed, covering his with his hand.

"Okay, I won't," Rachael replied. She looked at Trace and he smiled, motioning her over with his head.

He wrapped an arm around her when she sidled up to him. "What do you think?" he asked.

Rachael's eyes fell to his drawing. Trace was very good at detail; it was one of the reasons he was in demand as an illustrator. Among his many talents was his ability to draw perfectly the human body and any small part of it. What drew her to his picture more than anything else—as was always the case when she looked at his work—were the facial expressions.

He had drawn three separate scenes, each separated by the airy whiteness of the paper. In the first Josh was arguing with Thao. Josh was standing just a few feet from the grocer, near the spot where the floor mat would have been. Choua was just to his left by a hastily drawn set of stairs and near the water heater. She was parallel to Josh, and they were both facing Thao. Thao had his back to the wall of crates, and Bao was behind Josh. Not at the shelves just yet. Closer to the door. Bao's lovely Asian facial features were riddled with alarm and fear. Her fists were clenched. Choua had her arms crossed over her chest. Her facial features suggested defiance and disgust. Her mouth was closed, and her jaw set. Josh's face was alive with concern, but not loathing, not rage. He wasn't aware of the truth yet. Thao was pointing the gun in Josh's general direction. The grocer's face was a mask of anger and something else…fear, maybe. He appeared to be afraid of Josh, even though Josh was obviously unarmed.

In the second sketch, Choua had stepped forward to stand closer to Thao while she argued with him. Her facial features were now a mix of dread and wrath. Tears were coursing down her face. Her hands were raised as if to hurl stones at Thao. Thao still looked angry, but the gun hung at a weird angle in his hand, as if he had forgotten he had it. His head was cocked as he shouted back at Choua. Josh, just a few feet away, was wide-eyed with unease, suggesting he didn't know what was being said but he knew it must be something terrible. He was reaching back to Bao with his left hand but had not taken his eyes off Choua. Behind him, Bao had backed up to the shelves. Terror was written across the quickly drawn lines of her face. Her arms were crossed over her chest as if to protect her heart from exploding in two.

Rachael found herself breathing heavily as she took in the last sketch at the bottom right-hand corner of the page. In it, Josh and Thao had fallen into the pile of crates. Josh was on his knees, reaching for the gun lying at Thao's splayed feet. Her brother's face was awash in rage, his eyes wide and focused. His mouth was open, and he was yelling something. Choua was now at Bao's side, holding her sobbing sister back while pushing her toward the basement door. Choua's face was void of defiance now. All that was there was bewilderment.

"I couldn't draw the part where he says he shot him," Trace said. "I ran out of room. And courage."

"Shhh. No talking 'til the rest of us are done," Sidney said.

Rachael leaned in to Trace and rested her head in the crook of his neck and shoulder. "Why do you have the older sister standing next to Josh when Thao is yelling at him?" she whispered.

"Well, you said you thought she had to be somewhere other than by the younger one," he whispered back. "If she argued with Thao, I doubt she would've stood over by the door or by the wall where the crates are. That just doesn't seem logical to me. Any other place seems too far away to carry on an argument."

Rachael nodded. "And why does Thao look afraid?"

Trace shrugged. "I don't know. I guess he had to be afraid of something to wave a gun at Josh of all people. Like maybe he thought Josh had called the police. No offense, but Josh isn't much of a threat. He's tall and all that, but he's kind of skinny and well, unimposing."

"All right, I'm done," Sidney declared.

"I am too," Brick said.

"Let's lay them out all facing the same way so we can look at them," Fig said, turning his drawing around.

Within seconds the drawings were all facing the stools where Sidney was sitting. Rachael took the stool where she had been sitting before and began to study Brick's drawing first. The others came to stand by her.

Brick's art tended to be impressionistic so it took a little bit of skill to interpret what he had drawn. In his sketch, Josh and Thao were tangled on the cement floor. Thao had a fist raised and aimed at Josh's face. A young girl representing Bao was at the shelves wailing. Her liquid eyes were excessively overdrawn and resembled the insides of halved avocadoes. Brick's version of Choua, standing at a staircase that appeared spiral and unending, was pointing the gun at the back of Thao's head as the grocer leaned over Josh with his punching arm raised. Josh was looking at Choua and yelling "Noooo!" or something like it. His lopsided eyes were beseeching Choua to reconsider.

"If it happened this way, then it can't be that your brother was in any real danger," Brick said, pointing to Josh and the mere fist that was raised above him. "A fist wouldn't have killed him. If the grocer had a knife or was strangling your brother, then the girl could get off by saying she was only trying to save your brother's life. But since you think Josh is covering for her, he must think she meant to kill him. It wasn't in self-defense or to save Josh's life."

Rachael nodded and moved on to the next drawing. Sidney's was an eight-panel comic strip, macabre in its mock-juvenile look. The first frame showed a rough cartoon drawing of Josh and the girls stepping inside a messy basement. In the next frame, an astonished Thao with a gun in his hand was yelling at Josh to leave. The third showed Josh trying to reason with him. Then Choua stepped forward in the fourth to take on Thao, and the fifth frame showed them in a heated argument with Choua now to the right of Josh. In the sixth frame, Choua had turned to Josh, and her face was crippled with anguish as she pointed to Bao behind him. In the seventh frame, Josh was rushing at Thao, accidentally knocking over Choua in his fury. The last frame showed Bao at the stairs pointing a gun at Thao. Thao, on his knees, had his back to her. Josh and Choua, also on the ground, were turning around to look at Bao, shock and panic in their faces.

"So how did the little sister get to the stairs?" Brick said.

"How should I know?" Sidney shot back. "Rachael said the shot came from the stairs. If the little kid really did it, she had to be at the stairs. Maybe that's the direction the gun went when it flew out of the grocer's hand."

Rachael moved on to Fig's drawing. A cloaked figure in a flowing, dark robe stood at the bottom of a staircase, holding a smoking gun. A crumpled figure lay ahead of the figure. To the right, a trio of huddled people cowered together by a shelf of overturned cans—a man with his arms protectively around two girls.

"Who is that supposed to be?" Rachael said, pointing to the cloaked figure.

"The personification of evil," Fig said proudly.

"In an exceptionally nice-looking robe, if you ask me," Jillian added.

"Fig, you don't really expect me to take this one seriously, do you?" Rachael asked.

Fig took a sip of his cappuccino. "Of course not, Kumquat. But you don't seriously think there was a fifth person, do you?"

Rachael smiled. "No, not really."

Fig saluted her with his cappuccino.

"So what do you think?" Trace waved his hand toward the drawings. "Does this help?"

Rachael glanced over all the drawings: Trace's emotionally charged facial expressions, Brick's harrowing depiction of Choua pulling the trigger in front of her little sister, and Sidney's version with Bao deciding at the age of twelve to execute the man who had robbed her of her future. Which was the most probable scenario?

Which one?

The answer came to her almost from another source, another place. From inside her. Or maybe from outside. But the words that were now swirling in her head were unmistakable, regardless of where they came from.

None of the scenarios was right.

She was still missing something. Something big.

And she was slowly becoming more and more certain that it had to do with the missing floor mat and those twenty-two seconds.

"Yes…and no." she finally answered. "But I think you guys are onto something. When I know more I'd like to do this again, if you don't mind."

"Of course not!" Fig said cheerfully. "Next time, though, we do it my way. In clay."

THIRTEEN

Morning sunlight glistened on Fig's black-lacquered dining room table as Rachael sipped a mug of dark roast Moroccan coffee. At her feet, on a plush Oriental rug of crimson and tan, McKenna lay kicking her legs and marveling at rattling sounds coming from tiny, stuffed panda-heads looped around her ankles.

The loft was quiet. Trace and Fig were still asleep after presumably staying up late the night before. Rachael had gone to bed before Brick, Sidney, and Jillian left. The artists must have retreated to the floor below, to Fig's studio, when she turned in. She hadn't heard a sound after she turned out the light in the guest room.

McKenna had awakened a little before seven that morning. Rachael had brought her out to Fig's living room to nurse her, and then the young mother rummaged around in Fig's kitchen until she found a bag of imported coffee. When enough had brewed to fill a mug, she filled one, grabbed the drawings off the island countertop and headed to the dining room. It was as she was spreading them out on the table that she realized there was a new drawing, and that it was Trace's.

It was this latest sketch that now held her gaze as she brought the mug to her lips. Once. Twice. Three times. She couldn't pull her eyes from it. Trace had sketched the scene he hadn't been able to draw before she went to bed the night before: Josh pulling the trigger.

He had taken his time with this one.

The facial features he was so good at capturing were obviously drawn with care and no sense of urgency. And it struck her that there were only two faces in the drawing: Josh's and Thao's. Neither one was drawn differently from the other sketches Trace had done, but they were different nonetheless. These were more…complete. And that fact alone weighed on Rachael as she sipped her coffee. These last two faces seemed complete. Finished. Done.

In the drawing, Josh was standing at the bottom of the wooden stairs in Thao's basement. To his left Trace had drawn an overturned pile of crates and pallets. In front of Josh was Thao, on his knees and slightly bent to the right at the waist. The perspective of the drawing was from the door of the basement, looking straight ahead at the two men; one in front of the other—one on his knees with a gun pointed at his head, and one standing behind him, fully visible from the waist up, aiming the gun. The girls weren't in the picture. The two men were alone in the basement.

Josh's face was contorted by anger and revulsion. He held his arms straight out in front of him; one hand gripped the gun and the other embraced the hand that would pull the trigger. Thao's eyes were closed and his forehead was crinkled with apprehension and hopelessness. Trace had drawn Thao's mouth open. Had Thao actually said something? Had he begged for his life? Is that how Josh filled those twenty-two seconds? Listening to a monster bargaining for his life?

Did each second spent waiting for the girls to leave the basement make it easier or harder for Josh to pull the trigger, assuming he did?

It was obvious by the absence of the girls that Josh was only a second or two away from pulling the trigger. He had time to change his mind. But in the drawing there was no evidence of hesitation or shame in Josh's features. Only determination…and utter hatred.

As she sat there staring at the drawing, conflicting emotions brewed inside her. Part of her wanted to go into the guest room, wake her husband, and demand an explanation. What exactly was he suggesting with this drawing? That Josh was telling the truth after all? That Josh had purposefully killed a man in absolute defiance of the laws of man and God? Another part of her knew Trace had simply drawn what he said he would draw: the scenario that supported Josh's story.

And another part of her whispered in her ear that perhaps it was indeed possible Josh had executed an evil man who had sold young girls into prostitution. *Wouldn't that suit your own inner sense of justice?* the voice whispered. *Wouldn't you like to send a man like that straight to hell where he belongs? Can't you see your absurd little brother acting out what any civilized person would like to do if the law allowed it? Can't you?*

As she shook these last thoughts away, Rachael became aware that someone had walked up behind her. She looked up as Trace placed his hand on her shoulder.

"I see you found it," he said sheepishly.

She nodded and looked back down at the drawing.

"Rachael," he began, taking the chair next to her.

"You're up early," she interrupted, reaching across to put the drawings in a pile.

"Rachael," Trace said again, touching her hand.

She stopped fiddling with the drawings. "What?"

"I didn't *like* drawing that last one. I just felt that if I were going to help you at all with this, I had to draw the last scene. Otherwise this whole drawing experiment would have been meaningless."

A few seconds of silence passed before Rachael responded. "You really took your time with it," she said softly.

"Because I had the time," Trace replied. "You were asleep. The others were gone. Fig and I were sitting around talking."

"Were you talking about this?"

"Well, yes."

Another lengthy stretch of silence fell between them.

"Does Fig think Josh did it?" Rachael finally asked.

"Fig doesn't know Josh. He's only met him—what, two or three times?"

"That's not an answer."

Trace sighed. "Okay. Fig doesn't exactly *think* Josh did it, but he does understand passion, Rachael. Most artists do. He understands how a person of passion could do what Josh has confessed to doing. What happened to those girls in that basement is barbaric."

Rachael turned to face her husband. "Do you think Josh did it?"

Trace looked down at his latest drawing now on top of the loosely arranged pile of sketches. "Honestly, Rachael, I think we have to assume it's possible."

Rachael brought a hand up to massage her temple. "Possible and probable are not the same thing," she said.

Trace reached over and stroked the back of her head. "I know they're not."

For a moment both were silent.

"Fig wants to take us out for a late breakfast," Trace finally said, his tone suggesting he hoped he hadn't changed the subject too abruptly. "There's this place on Nicollet Mall he found that he wants to show off."

"I don't know, Trace. It's going to be a long day. And I think I should try to see Josh before the hearing today. Maybe if he'd let me represent him I could get him to hold off pleading guilty."

"But the hearing's not until two; you've got plenty of time. And you have to eat, Rachael."

Rachael sighed and ran a hand absently through her hair. "I guess that would be all right."

"That's my girl."

Trace reached down to pick up McKenna as Rachael pushed her chair back and picked up her coffee mug.

"Rachael," Trace said. "I'm sorry if that drawing offended you. I…I almost threw it away last night."

"It didn't really offend me…but it was hard to look at. I'm glad you didn't throw it away. I don't like the drawing, but I have to figure out what we're missing. And that means looking at everything, no matter how unpleasant."

"You're sure you're missing something?" Trace asked quietly, looking down at the baby in his arms.

"Yes, I'm sure." Rachael's tone was confident.

Trace looked up at her. "How do you know?"

Rachael was silent as she considered how to explain herself. Her silence only lasted a moment. There was no way to explain the intuition building inside her that there was a big piece of the puzzle missing. She also couldn't explain the overwhelming sense of evil she had felt in Thao's basement or the hunch that Choua had not been standing at the shelves with Bao, or the gut feeling that Josh was lying.

There was no way to explain any of it.

"I just do," she said. She turned toward the kitchen to refill her coffee cup.

The parking lot at the Ramsey County Jail was just starting to fill up as the lunch hour ended and Rachael and Trace pulled into it.

Rachael unbuckled her seat belt and shook her head. "I still can't believe I let you and Fig talk me into leaving McKenna with him. I must be insane."

"She'll be fine, Rach. She'll probably sleep the whole time. You expressed a whole bottle of breast milk. And he can call Sidney if things really do get crazy."

"Sidney! What can Sidney do?" Rachael exclaimed.

"Well, he has a kid. He's been through this before."

"What was I thinking?" Rachael said, closing her eyes and gripping the steering wheel in front of her.

"You were thinking how nice it would be to have your husband go with you to your brother's hearing."

Rachael opened her eyes and stared at the government building in front of her. "I left McKenna with Fig," she whispered.

"Want me to go back there? I'm sure your parents will give you a ride back." A slight layer of irritation was evident in Trace's voice.

Rachael turned to her husband. She really wanted him with her. Fig had been right in reading her when they sat at breakfast. He could tell she wished Trace could somehow come with her. Fig had insisted it would be no trouble at all to babysit. And perhaps Trace was right. Perhaps McKenna would sleep the afternoon away.

"No. No," Rachael said, turning to Trace. "I want you here. I don't want you to go back to Fig's."

"Okay then. Ready to go inside?"

Trace and Rachael got out of Fig's car, walked across the parking lot, and stepped inside the building. Seconds later, after walking through the reception area and the scanning machines, they turned right and made their way to the lock-up portion of the building. When they got to the waiting area, Trace took a chair and pulled an art magazine out of his back pocket. Rachael looked at her watch. It was just a few minutes before one o'clock. She wouldn't have much time with Josh. She guessed between now and the next thirty or forty minutes Josh would be led upstairs with other detainees scheduled for court today. She went up to the bulletproof glass, showed her card, and asked for ten minutes with Joshua Harper.

Josh looked no different than he did the previous day except he seemed surprised to see Rachael in the interview room. He hadn't been surprised yesterday. He hadn't *been* anything yesterday. Yesterday he looked dead. *Today*, Rachael thought, *he looks sad*. As much as it hurt to see him that way, Rachael thought it was an improvement. A dead man can't be reasoned with. A sad man can be.

Joshua, still in his orange jumpsuit, took the chair opposite her without saying a word. The jailer who brought him took his place just outside the door.

Rachael dove in. She knew she had only minutes to get Josh to let her help him.

"Josh, please let me represent you in the courtroom today. Please?"

He looked up at her and blinked. "Why are you still here, Rachael?"

Rachael knew he was asking why she hadn't flown back to New York where she belonged.

She ignored his question. "Josh, I think I can help you. But I need you to let me represent you, okay? Please?"

Joshua slowly shook his head. "I don't need a lawyer."

"Oh yes you do. You're going to be charged with second-degree murder. Believe me, you *need* a lawyer."

"I confessed. What do I need a lawyer for?"

"It takes more than a confession to convict a man of murder. Did anyone tell you that, Josh?"

Her brother shrugged and said nothing.

"Josh, please let me help you."

Silence.

"Josh?"

Joshua turned his head away from her. "Who may ascend the hill of the Lord?" he said softly. "Who may stand in his holy place? He who has clean hands and a pure heart."

Rachael stared at her brother. He wasn't quoting Scripture to annoy her as he had yesterday. He was mumbling it to himself as if he were the only one in the room. She knew there was no way he would cooperate with her if she couldn't find a way to connect with him as she had when they were kids. He trusted her then. Confided in her. Ran to her room when he was afraid. Told his secrets to her.

Rachael had only minutes to tell him she knew more than he thought she did. She had read the police reports. She had talked with Sgt. Pendleton. She had visited the crime scene.

The moment her mind pictured the basement, she remembered

what she felt when she had stepped inside it. And she immediately knew she had only one card to play against the ticking clock.

"Josh!" Rachael exclaimed, and he slowly brought his head back to face her. "I want you to listen to me very carefully. I read the police report. I talked with Sgt. Pendleton. He took me to that basement, Josh. I was inside it yesterday. I *felt* it. I felt the evil in that place. I know what you were up against."

Joshua's eyes shimmered for a moment. "What did you say?" he whispered.

Rachael leaned forward, encouraged by his sudden interest. "I said, I was in that basement and I felt the evil as surely as if it were another person in the room."

"Another person in the room?" Joshua echoed, his voice still not much more than a whisper.

"Yes, Josh. I know how awful it was for you. And for those girls."

At the mention of Choua and Bao, Josh screwed his eyes shut and grimaced.

"Josh, listen! I want to help those girls as much as you do. Did you know they're getting help now from the county? Did you know that a counselor is seeing them? And they're getting home visits? *They're going to be all right.* No one's going to hurt them like that anymore. In the long run, everything's going to be okay. You don't want to make things worse for them by forcing them to live a lie the rest of their lives. Don't they deserve better than that, Josh?"

Josh kept his eyes closed and said nothing.

"Josh, you didn't do this, did you." It was a statement, not a question.

Silence.

Rachael leaned forward, beseeching her brother with her eyes and voice. "Josh, I know in your heart, you want what's best for those girls!"

He opened his eyes. For a moment Josh said nothing.

Then he leaned forward too, though not as far. He locked his eyes onto hers and breathed in slowly. He opened his mouth.

"In my heart?" he said, challenging her. "The heart is deceitful above all things, Rachael, and beyond cure. Who can understand?"

"Josh."

"Jeremiah 17:9."

"Josh!"

"We're finished here," her brother said, and he slowly turned his head toward the jailer at the window. He started to rise from his chair.

"Josh, *please!* Please don't do this. Please let me represent you!"

Joshua turned back to her from a standing position. The corners of his mouth turned as if to offer the smallest of smiles. "Don't worry about me, Rachael. Please? I don't want you to. Everything is turning out just as it should."

He turned from her, and the jailer opened the door. Joshua stepped out of the room and into the hallway beyond, to places where Rachael had never been and would never see.

FOURTEEN

Rachael and Trace left the lock-up area and were headed to the west side of the building to the courtrooms when Trace broke the silence and asked her about the meeting with her brother.

"He refuses to cooperate with me," Rachael said angrily, moving her briefcase from one shoulder to the other. "He's lying to me! I know he is!"

"About everything?" Trace asked.

Rachael turned her head around. "What do you mean everything?"

"Well, part of what he's saying must be true. I mean, he was in the basement, he did take the girls there, he did argue with Thao, and he did bring the girls home that night. Right?"

"Yes."

"So then you think he's only lying to you about who pulled the trigger."

Rachael stopped walking as a revelation suddenly washed over her: Josh had never lied to her before. Never.

He wasn't actually lying to her now.

"What is it?" Trace had stopped too.

"It's not that he's lying to me," Rachael said, first looking past Trace and then straight into his eyes. "He has *never* lied to me, Trace."

"So…"

"He is keeping the truth from me—that's what he's doing!"

"And that's different than lying?" Trace said, a bit bewildered.

"Well, sure it is. There are offenses of commission and offenses of *omission*. He's not lying to me. He's withholding the truth."

"But he confessed to killing a man…" Trace began.

"But not to me!" Rachael interjected. "He said that to the police. He didn't say that *to me*."

"What did he say to you exactly?"

"Well, he said…" but Rachael's voice fell away. What *had* Josh said? She'd spent a total of maybe twelve minutes with him in the last two days. And she had done most of the talking.

"What? What did he say?" Trace repeated his question.

Rachael thought back to the two conversations. Yesterday's was a bit of a blur. She remembered Josh telling her to go home to her baby. Then he had quoted some obscure Scripture. He had told her he wasn't afraid of the dark anymore. But she couldn't remember anything else.

And today? *Why are you still here? I don't need a lawyer. I confessed,* she remembered. Then he cited a scripture verse about the deplorable condition of the human heart. And then, *Don't worry about me, Rachael. Please? I don't want you to. Everything is turning out just as it should.*

"Everything is turning out just as it should," Rachael murmured more to herself than to Trace.

"What? He said what?"

"Everything is turning out just as it should," Rachael said again, now looking at her husband.

"What the heck does that mean?"

Rachael turned and slowly began to resume their trek to the courtroom. "I don't know. But it means *something*. Josh wouldn't lie to me." They walked the rest of the way in silence.

By twenty minutes to two, the courtroom reserved for felony first-appearances and omnibus hearings had begun to fill. At the front of the wedge-shaped room, two law clerks placed file folders the color of old pennies on the prosecutor's table; the stacks collectively representing the day's agenda. Rachael knew one of those watery brown folders bore Joshua's name. She also knew that the law clerks, one woman and one man, were actually law students certified to represent the state while they completed their graduate work. Six years ago she had been engrossed in the same responsibilities in neighboring Hennepin County. Seated at the table by the law clerks was Emily Lonetree, reading from a file.

A raised platform of honey-brown wood stretched across the front of the room behind the law clerks like a crescent moon. In its center was the empty judge's chair. Court administrators sat behind computer screens preparing for the judge's arrival and the day's business. Rachael and Trace took a seat near the back so that Rachael could keep an eye out for her parents. Cliff and Eva Harper arrived ten minutes after Rachael and Trace sat down.

Eva, in a pantsuit of soft coral, slipped into the cushioned bench next to Rachael. Her eyes nervously scanned the room. Cliff—tall, graying, and wearing a blue sport coat and tan pants—sat down next to his wife. He too took in the crowded room and then turned to Rachael.

"Why are all these people here?" he whispered. He sounded perturbed. Rachael recognized the tone. Her father didn't like to be taken by surprise, and the number of strangers in the room had done just that. Her parents had sat in the gallery before when Josh had landed himself in trouble, but those appearances had always been for minor infractions. Not like this one. Rachael could guess why the unexpected crowd bothered her father. It unnerved him to be in a situation where he wasn't in control. Cliff Harper wasn't what Rachael would call a control freak. In fact, she had never thought of him as domineering. He was just a man who didn't like bolts from the blue. He didn't like not being in command. Deep down she knew it was because he loved his family more than anything, and he believed a powerless man would be unable to protect the people he loves.

Rachael leaned across her mother to answer him. "The felony court room is open to the public, Dad. Anyone can sit in on these hearings."

"Who *are* all these people?" Eva whispered.

"Some are family members like us, and some are here because this is their first appearance too, just like Josh," Rachael whispered back. "Some are here for their omnibus hearing. Others might be here to tell the judge that since they saw him last, they've done whatever the court asked of them to get their lives back on track."

"Well, why isn't Josh in here then?" Eva looked about the room for her son.

"He's in the room off that door," Rachael said, pointing to a door on the far front wall that opened to a Plexiglas cubicle that faced the bench.

"Why is he back there if all these people are out here?" Eva asked, crinkling her brows.

"Because he's...he's in jail, Mom. He's been detained. These other people haven't been arrested or detained for what they've been charged with."

"So all these people will be in the room with us when Josh is charged with *murder*." Her father's jaw was clenched. Rachael wished she had thought to tell her parents earlier that Josh's first appearance for a second-degree murder charge would be just one of many hearings that afternoon in a room filled with people they didn't know.

"Yes, well, the ones who've had their cases heard before Josh will probably leave. Rachael smoothed out the copy of the day's agenda that she had been given and showed it to her parents. "See, there are a number of other cases being heard today. Joshua's is number five."

Eva and Cliff peered at the sheet of paper.

"So we'll listen in on other people's felony charges?" Eva's tone betrayed her shock.

"And they will listen to Joshua's," Cliff grumbled. Rachael sensed her father was not only wrestling with astonishment but also growing humiliation.

At that moment, Rachael saw Sgt. Pendleton enter the room with Sgt. Stowe. They were talking to each other and didn't see her. She followed them with her eyes as they headed to the back wall and stood against it. Apparently they weren't planning on staying very long. Rachael kept her eyes trained on them, hoping to catch their gaze, but they were looking at a group of Asians seated in the fourth row. Rachael had the distinct feeling they were Thao's family members. Looking at the backs of their heads, Rachael saw that there were two men, an older woman with silvery black hair and a young woman, perhaps in her late twenties. Pendleton was studying them as she was. When he looked away from the group, he cast a glance toward her side of the courtroom gallery. Their eyes met and Pendleton nodded a silent greeting. Then he turned his head to discuss something with Stowe. He didn't look her way again.

The room grew quiet as a video explaining court procedure began to play on a large flat screen on the wall behind the court clerks. Rachael tuned it out. She knew exactly what would happen next.

Moments later, a command to rise was given by one of the clerks. As everyone stood, the judge entered the room. He was introduced as the Honorable Bryce Dauber. Rachael didn't know this judge. Judge Dauber was dressed in a robe of black that hung loosely across his slightly overweight, medium-build body. He wore rimless glasses, sported a tiny moustache and his thinning hair had been gelled into submission. Rachael's first impression was that he looked like her Uncle Warren, her dad's brother.

The first case was called to the bench, followed by the second and third. Each one took less than five minutes. The fourth involved a man charged with selling a controlled substance to a minor as well as stealing a car. He came through the door at the front of the room, behind the crescent-shaped platform, and stood inside the cubicle with Plexiglas sides. The orange jumpsuit he wore stood in sharp contrast to the yellow-beige wall behind him.

"That man has to wear jail clothes?" Eva whispered, aghast, to Rachael. "Why isn't he in street clothes?"

Rachael winced. Another detail she forgot to share with her mother.

"Mom, Josh will be wearing a jumpsuit, too."

"But that's not how it is on television!" Eva snapped.

"This isn't a trial where we have to worry what a jury might think," Rachael whispered back.

"But what will the judge think? Don't we have to worry what the judge might think?"

"Mom, please don't let that bother you. It's not going to change what the judge thinks. Honestly."

Eva sat back in her seat glowering.

The man had pled not guilty, and now his attorney, standing opposite his client, was asking for a reduction in bail. One of the law students leaned into the microphone on the prosecutor's side and stated there was no practical reason to decrease the bail. Judge Dauber agreed. A date was set for the next hearing, and the man went back through the same door he came in.

The whole process for the man in the jumpsuit had taken about seven minutes.

The court clerk announcing the cases then read off Joshua's name. The door opened and Josh stepped into the Plexiglas cubicle. Beside her, Rachael heard her mother gasp.

A woman in a dark green suit and fading auburn hair walked up to the defense podium. Rachael didn't recognize her, but she appeared to be ready to take up Josh's defense.

Judge Dauber calmly read off the charges as if they were no more serious than throwing a rock at a neighbor's window. Rachael hoped that the judge's composed demeanor would calm her mother into believing the judge wasn't prejudiced against Josh because of his jail clothes.

When asked if he understood the charges against him and his rights, Josh calmly stated that he did. Then the judge asked him why he was there without counsel. Josh said he was ready to plead guilty; he didn't need a lawyer.

The woman in the green suit spoke up then. "Maggie Fielding of the Office of the Public Defender. Your honor, I spoke with the defendant a few minutes ago to see if he qualified for indigence and to let him know that if he could not afford a lawyer, the court would appoint one, but he responded that he didn't want representation."

The judge turned to Josh. "The charges against you are very serious, Mr. Harper," he said. "This court advises you to not proceed without legal representation."

"But your honor, I did it. I'm guilty. Why do I need a lawyer?"

Even though she had expected Joshua to say it, hearing those words threw Rachael for a loop. She closed her eyes and counted to ten as her pulse raced. Josh was setting in motion a horrible chain of likely events. His confession had started it, his unrequested plea was giving it added momentum. The race to the truth had just been upped a hefty notch. She sensed her mother crying quietly beside her. It was hard to concentrate on what the judge was telling Joshua about the seriousness of what he was saying and that his voluntary confession did not confirm his guilt.

Judge Dauber then turned to the prosecution and questioned the clerks about the facts of the case and possible dates for the omnibus hearing. The public defender asked the judge if it might be prudent for a Rule 20 mental status examination to be completed on the defendant, that if her office were to be assigned the case, it would certainly be requested. The judge calmly granted the order for the evaluation.

Josh leaned into his microphone. "Your honor, I don't want a psychiatric evaluation. I'm not crazy, sir."

The judge was writing something down. He didn't look up as he spoke to Josh.

"Mr. Harper, you will indeed participate in the psych evaluation. And while I appreciate your forthrightness in coming to the police to confess, I am not accepting your plea of guilty today. At your next appearance three weeks from now this court will consider your plea in light of the facts. Until then you are to be detained. We're done for today."

"But Your Honor!" Josh pleaded.

Judge Dauber looked up at Josh. "We're done for today, Mr. Harper. I am expecting you to have another chat with Ms. Fielding before I see you again in my courtroom. Bailiff?"

A uniformed policeman took Joshua's arm and led him back through the door. The door closed.

Eight minutes had passed.

Before Rachael could catch her breath, the court clerk announced the next case. Pendleton and Stowe were already on their way out. She watched as they left, wondering if they would turn to acknowledge her. As the doors closed behind them she knew they weren't being rude. What was there to say in a room full of other people? Rachael turned to look at her parents. Her mother's dazed expression complemented the stray tears that lay unchecked on her eyelashes. Eight minutes had not been enough time to deal with the scope of what had just happened. Rachael decided it was impossible to read her father at that moment. He was staring at a speck of lint on the carpet by his shoes.

From the other side of the courtroom Thao's family members rose as a group and began to make their way outside. Rachael looked down as they neared the double doors that led to the outside corridor. She didn't want to lock eyes with any of them. When they had left, she waited a full thirty seconds before raising her eyes again to scan the room for Maggie Fielding. The defense attorney was gathering her things to leave. Rachael stood up and whispered to Trace and her parents, "Let's go. I want to talk to that defense lawyer."

The four of them stood and walked out of the courtroom behind Fielding.

Rachael hoped the public defender could spare just a few minutes. If Josh wouldn't let her represent him, the next best thing she could do was work as closely as she could with Fielding, assuming Josh would agree to take her.

Besides, while she understood Maggie Fielding's suspicion that Josh had a screw loose somewhere, Rachael doubted very much that Joshua was mentally incompetent. He had at least been truthful about one thing while on the stand today: He wasn't crazy. He knew exactly what he was doing.

FIFTEEN

As the door closed behind them, Rachael could see that Maggie Fielding was walking briskly toward the exit to the parking lot. Rachael guessed she would probably only have a few minutes to talk with her. She appeared to be in a hurry.

"Ms. Fielding?" Rachael called out.

The public defender turned toward Rachael's voice but kept walking.

Rachael quickened her steps to catch up.

"Ms. Fielding, my name is Rachael Harper Flynn. I'm Joshua Harper's sister."

"Oh hello." Maggie Fielding stopped and stuck out her hand. Rachael shook it.

"These are my parents, Cliff and Eva Harper, and my husband, Trace."

"How do you do?" Maggie Fielding said politely but slightly rushed.

"Look, I can see you're in a hurry, but I was wondering if I could have just a few minutes of your time?" Rachael asked.

Maggie Fielding looked at her watch. "Well, you can walk with me out to my car. I have to be somewhere else in twenty minutes."

"Thanks. I really appreciate it."

They resumed walking but at a somewhat slower pace.

"You live here in the Twin Cities?" Maggie Fielding asked.

"No. Actually I'm a defense lawyer. I practice in New York."

"Really? Spend most of your time on civil cases or criminal?"

"Mostly on juvenile court matters."

"I'm surprised your brother didn't ask you to take his case."

"Well, the thing is, Ms. Fielding..." Rachael began.

"Please call me Maggie."

"Thanks, Maggie. That's why I wanted to talk with you. I offered to take it. I begged him this morning to let me represent him. He refused."

"Oh. You two don't get along, is that it?"

"No, that's not it at all. Joshua and I have always been close. He and I are very different in terms of personality and passions, but we've always gotten along great."

They had reached the row of glass doors leading outside. Seconds later the group was standing in the late September sunshine on a sidewalk leading to the parking lot.

"So what's the deal then?" Maggie said.

"I know you haven't spent much time with Josh. I know you don't know him like I do. But Maggie, he couldn't have done what he said he's done. If you look at his past record you'll see that he's never been prone to violence. He's been in legal hot water before, but it's always been for petty offenses, and usually it's because he's overstepped his bounds trying to be a Good Samaritan. He just takes his kindnesses too far. But shooting a man in the back of the head? This isn't like him. I think he's refusing to let me represent him because he knows that *I* know he's innocent. That he's covering for someone else. Probably one of those girls he was trying help."

"It's true," Eva chimed in. "My son is not a violent man."

Maggie glanced at her watch. "I agree that Joshua doesn't seem like a violent man, but to be honest with you, he does come across a little unhinged. That's why I asked for that psych eval. And because I have few other options to offer a guy who confesses to murder and then practically pleads guilty at his first court appearance."

"Josh has always been rather unconventional," Rachael said. "He's different. Very different. But I really don't think he's crazy."

"Well, since neither one of us is a psychologist, I think the best thing we can do is let a professional rule that out. And if your brother did confess to a crime he didn't commit, well, that's not usually something a rational person does. Especially when it's murder."

"I know, but…"

"Listen, I can see that you have genuine concern for your brother and that you sincerely believe he didn't kill this man. The trouble is Josh confessed. He told a judge he did it. The police haven't found anything hard and fast to suggest someone else did it. All I can do, if he'll let me, is try and get your brother a reduced sentence. If he's found to have some mental deficits, it will be a heck of a lot easier for me to do that."

"Maybe she's right, Rachael," Eva said, touching Rachael's arm. "Maybe we should just wait and see what the psychologist says."

Eva's voice was soft, yet insistent. Rachael could sense that her mother had just now realized it would be easier to be the mother of a sick son than a violent one. Her father was silent beside her. He wanted neither.

"May I come and observe when the psychologist interviews him?" Rachael asked.

Maggie hesitated. "I don't think that's a good idea."

"Look, I won't tell him I'm coming, and you don't have to tell him I'm there. I can stand behind the two-way mirror. He doesn't have to know."

"And you're saying he won't ask me if you're there? 'Cause I am not going to lie to him and tell him you're not there if you are. I don't lie to my clients. That's sometimes the only thing that keeps them from lying to me."

Rachael didn't know if Josh would wonder who was behind the glass. But then again, why wouldn't he?

"If your brother, who you say you are close to, doesn't want you as his lawyer, and you say it's because you know he's lying, that doesn't sound like a recipe for a good psych eval if he knows you're behind the glass," Maggie continued. "And honestly, since you're not his lawyer, you don't really have a right to be there anyway."

Rachael knew she was right. On all counts. "All right. But may I watch the tape of the interview when it's done?"

Maggie raised an eyebrow.

"You're going to need my help to prove Josh is lying," Rachael continued. "I know things about Josh that you don't know and he won't tell you. And I've been to the crime scene, Maggie. I know things about that basement that he won't tell you either."

"I heard Pendleton took you there. You must have had a pretty convincing story to get him to agree to that."

Rachael stiffened. "It's not that I have a convincing story. It's that things don't add up. And I think he agrees with me."

"What things?"

"Like why did the grocer have a gun on him when Josh and the girls got there? And why is that floor mat missing? And how in the world could Josh point a gun at a man for twenty-two seconds before shooting him?"

"Twenty-two seconds?"

"That's how long I figure it took for the girls to leave the basement and get into my brother's car."

"Okay. And what's with that?"

"Who could hold a gun to someone's head that long and still claim that they just *snapped*? He had half a minute to unsnap. That's too long."

Maggie sighed. "Not for someone who's suffering from mental illness."

Rachael was rendered temporarily speechless. Maggie Fielding really did think Josh might be delusional. "Josh isn't crazy," she finally said.

"Look, I *really* have to go," Maggie said. "Give me your cell phone number, and I'll call you when I get the psych eval done. I'm going to try and get it squeezed in the week after next. Okay?"

"All right," Rachael said. She withdrew a business card from her briefcase and handed it to Maggie. "That's my cell phone number."

"Here's my card," Maggie said. "Now I really do have to run." She turned to go.

"Thanks," Rachael said.

"Yes, thank you so much!" Eva called as Maggie half-sprinted across the parking lot to her car.

"I think I like her," Eva said as they watched Maggie get into a silver compact car and zoom away. "I'm not sure. What do you think, Rachael?"

"She's probably a very good lawyer. But she can't make Joshua tell the truth. None of us can. He has to want to. And she seems terribly busy. I don't know if she has the time it's going to take to get Josh out of this mess."

"Perry Mason couldn't get your brother out of this mess," Cliff murmured brusquely.

For a second no one said anything. Then Eva snapped her head around to face Rachael.

"Good heavens, Rachael! Where's McKenna?"

Rachael had forgotten she would have to explain to her mother in whose care she had left McKenna. Trace was looking off toward downtown. Or maybe at nothing in particular. He wasn't going to answer for her, that was certain.

"She's with Fig, Mom." Rachael replied in mock self-assurance.

"Oh Rachael. You can't be serious."

"Mom, it's her nap time. She has probably slept the whole time." Rachael fished out her cell phone, which was still set to silent. There were no indications of new messages on the screen. "Look," she continued, showing her mother her phone. "No messages. I'm sure she's fine. Now what time do you want us to come for dinner?"

Eva looked dubious. "Six thirty, I guess."

"Okay. Six thirty it is. Can I bring something?"

"No. Just bring yourselves."

Rachael and Trace took a step toward the parking lot. "Aren't you leaving now?" Rachael queried, turning back to her parents. They hadn't moved.

"I want to see him," Eva said plainly.

Rachael paused in midstep. "Okay. Sure. Well then, I guess we'll see you tonight." She turned back and gave her mother a quick hug.

Trace thrust his hand out to his father-in-law. "See you later, Cliff."

"Yes," Cliff said quietly.

"Bye, Dad." Rachael stood on tiptoe to kiss her dad's cheek. To her surprise, his arms came around her and Rachael felt the subtle layers of tension rippling in his embrace. Despite the strength in his arms, his body gave the impression that he might fall apart at any moment. Like a house of cards bearing the weight of 300 pounds of bricks. He let her go, turned away, and headed toward the building.

Eva turned to follow him.

Rachael sent a prayer heavenward that Joshua wouldn't refuse to see them.

They were just minutes away from Fig's apartment when Trace turned to Rachael and asked her if he could change the subject for a moment. They had been talking about Josh's court appearance, Maggie Fielding, and whether or not Joshua was psychologically unbalanced.

"I haven't done any work in three days, Rach," he said. "I've got to get some work done tomorrow, okay?"

Rachael had nearly forgotten Trace was working on three commissioned projects that were due at the end of October.

"I'm sorry, Trace. Of course it's okay. I won't ask you to come with me anywhere tomorrow, I promise."

"Well, it's McKenna too. I can't work in Fig's studio downstairs if you're out somewhere and I'm home alone with her. And Fig has his own work to do."

"No, I understand, Trace. I do."

"So what exactly are you going to do tomorrow?"

Rachael thought for a moment. "I'm not sure, but at some point I need to talk to Sgt. Pendleton again. And I want to talk to the prosecutor. I saw her there today at the table up front. She was the one supervising the law students."

"Well, just give me plenty of warning, okay?"

"I promise."

They reached Fig's building, parked his car underground, and took the elevator to his loft on the ninth floor. The hallway to his front door was quiet, which Rachael took to be a good sign. McKenna wasn't screaming.

Trace used the spare key Fig had given him that morning, and they walked into the apartment. Fig was in the kitchen making a smoothie.

"Ah, amigos! You're back!" he said cheerfully. He had changed out of the designer jeans and silk shirt he had worn at breakfast and was now wearing a clay-spattered T-shirt and flannel sweats with holes at the knees and ankles.

"Nice outfit, Fig Newton," Trace said, pointing to Fig's clothes.

"What, this old thing? You're too kind."

"McKenna's okay?" Rachael asked.

"Oh yes. She's sleeping."

"Still?"

"Well, no. Not still. More like *now*. She woke up just after you left. I don't know why. I warmed up the bottle just like you said. At first she didn't want it. She seemed bored so I laid down on the floor with her and sang all the songs off the Beatles' *White Album*."

"Fig, I'm so sorry! I really thought she would sleep the whole time we were gone," Rachael responded.

"It's quite all right, really. After awhile, she got bored of my singing too. So then we played a few games, did the bottle thing, and then she fell asleep. Maybe half an hour ago."

"Well done, Fig," Trace said, clapping his friend on the back.

"It was nothing! But now that you're home, I'm going to head downstairs to my studio and get dirty. Want to come, Tracer?"

"Yeah, sure. For a little while."

"Here. Plenty of papaya smoothies for everyone." Fig handed Trace a tall glass and then pushed another toward Rachael. He grabbed a third glass.

"Shall we?"

Trace and Fig headed to the front door and the stairs that led to Fig's rented studio on the floor below. Rachael grabbed her glass, slipped off her shoes, and walked across the smooth wood floor to peek in on McKenna.

Her daughter lay on her side in the portable crib, propped up from rolling onto her stomach with a folded baby blanket. *Pretty smart of Fig,* Rachael thought. A little hand was poking out of the blanket and something about it caught Rachael's attention. She moved forward, gasped, and then pulled the loose blanket off her daughter's body.

Fig had painted McKenna's tiny fingernails and toenails a shimmering shade of aquamarine.

SIXTEEN

Traffic on I-94 was already starting to snarl when Trace, Rachael, and McKenna set out in Fig's Lexus for the sixty-mile trip to the Harper family home in St. Cloud. They had snaked their way out of crammed downtown Minneapolis and merged onto the freeway a little after five, but the lanes hadn't cleared.

"And I thought New York was bad," Trace mumbled as he negotiated a lane change.

"We're going to have to get a rental while we're here, Trace," Rachael said. "We can't keep borrowing Fig's car."

Trace shrugged. "He says he doesn't mind."

"That's because this is only our third day. I can't imagine he'll feel that way a week or two from now."

Trace was silent for a moment. "So you think we'll still be here then?"

Rachael turned her head to look at him. "Well, yes. I've barely scratched the surface of this, Trace. And Josh's omnibus hearing is in three weeks. I can't possibly think of leaving before then."

Her husband absently stroked the charcoal-gray leather covering on Fig's steering wheel. "But Rachael, if you can't prove he didn't do it and he doesn't change his plea, your being at the hearing won't change anything."

"I know that." Rachael replied, turning to face the congested road ahead of them. "But like I said, I'm just getting started. And even if I can't...if I can't prove Josh didn't do it, I should be there for my parents' sake."

"I guess."

Rachael turned to look at him. "I thought you loved being here with Fig."

"I do. It's been great. But I've been thinking that three weeks is a long time to be someone's houseguest. And then of course I have those deadlines. Most of what I need to be working on right now will be due right about the time of that hearing."

"But you brought everything you need to finish with you, didn't you? I mean, we sort of talked about this Sunday night when we left New York."

Trace nodded. "Yeah, I did."

"So it's okay, right? If we get the impression we're in Fig's way, we can get a hotel room downtown and you can just go to Fig's to work."

"He would never let us do that, to get a hotel room."

"Well, I know you don't want to stay with my parents. And I really don't want to be staying an hour away from St. Paul."

Trace was silent for a moment. Then he looked over at her. "Just forget I mentioned it. I'm just nervous about getting the illustrations done and transferring that anxiety onto other things. Sorry."

"You'll get them done. You always do."

He nodded and turned his head back to the road. "Yep."

Several minutes later the traffic began to ease, and Trace was able to click on the cruise control.

McKenna made a cooing sound from her car seat, and Rachael looked at her daughter in the backseat behind Trace. She caught a shimmer of greenish-blue as McKenna punched the air with a petite left hand.

"Maybe we should stop somewhere and get some nail polish remover," Rachael said.

"What would Fig think if we did that?" Trace replied, obviously astonished that she would even suggest it.

"Trace, what will my *mom* think if we don't?"

"She already thinks Fig is weird. But Fig, on the other hand, thinks we're his dearest friends."

Rachael turned back around. There would be no stopping for nail polish remover.

"I hope Joshua didn't turn my parents away today," Rachael said a few minutes later.

"Think he might have?"

"I don't know. He wouldn't see them Sunday afternoon after they drove an hour in who knows what kind of emotional state to see him."

Trace cleared his throat. "Pardon my saying so, but that seems like kind of a cruel thing for a guy like your brother to do. I wouldn't have expected him to do that."

"I know. I keep reminding myself that he must have done it because he thought it would be easier for them to digest the news of what he had done if they were mad at him."

Trace eased back in his seat. "Still, I wouldn't have expected him to do that."

Rachael didn't say it, but she was thinking there were quite a few things Josh had done in the past few days that weren't what anyone would have expected of him.

And that unnerved her more than she cared to admit.

It was a few minutes past six thirty when Rachael and Trace pulled off I-94 and headed to the south St. Cloud neighborhood where

Rachael and Josh had grown up. The evening commute had trickled down to comfortably manageable on Roosevelt Road, and they were soon turning onto a wooded, residential street.

Rachael had been home just nine months ago, at Christmastime. The streets and hillsides had been dressed in white instead of red, brown, and gold. On Christmas Eve she had announced to her parents and Josh that she and Trace were expecting. It had been such a magical time, so full of hope and mystery. Now so much had changed.

Josh was working at an office supply store then. His hours were spotty but apparently they had been enough to keep his rent paid up. He told her he didn't really care where he worked or which hours as long as he could pay his rent and have the time to do the things that really mattered to him.

"So what *are* you doing these days?" she said as the two of them sat by the fireplace and sipped cider. It was the day after Christmas, and Trace was watching a football game in the family room with Cliff. Eva was making turkey potpies in the kitchen. They were alone in the living room.

"Oh, you know. Same old, same old," Josh answered.

Josh never liked to brag about his efforts to ease the load on people who had to bear more than most. Rachael guessed he was involved in the lives of half a dozen needy people, but he wouldn't talk about any of them.

She decided to ask him about Mrs. DeLyle, a widowed St. Cloud neighbor Josh had been caring for over the years—since he first came home from that long-ago tent meeting. Even after he moved to St. Paul after high school, Josh regularly called Mrs. DeLyle and still visited her once or twice a month. He put her storm windows up every autumn, her Christmas lights up in December and her porch swing up every spring. Rachael knew he wouldn't balk at talking about Mrs. DeLyle. She was someone they both knew.

"Oh. Well, her grandson is moving her into a nursing home after the first of the year," Josh answered glumly.

"So she's been ill?"

Josh had shrugged. "She's just old. She needs a lot of help these days. Her grandson lives too far away, and I can't be here all the time…"

"And that's okay!" Rachael had exclaimed. "Josh, I'm sure she understands that you have your own life. Of course you can't be here all the time."

"Well, someone should be."

"Josh, a lot of older people live in nursing homes," she said.

"But Mrs. DeLyle doesn't need a home with a *nurse*. She's not sick. She's just old."

Rachael decided to just let it go. What became of Mrs. DeLyle really wasn't her business. Nor was it Josh's. She changed the subject.

"So how do you feel about being an uncle?" she asked, brightening her tone and hoping her brother wouldn't mind the topic shift.

He didn't.

"I think it's great! I'm so happy for you guys. You're going to make a wonderful mother, Rachael. I've always thought so."

"Thanks, Josh."

Rachael had been genuinely surprised at his reaction. And his confidence in her. The next comment had flown off her lips before she had time to really give it much thought.

"And you'll make a superb uncle. It will be good practice for you for when you have your own kids."

He flinched a little, as if he'd been poked. Rachael realized too late that she'd pricked him with subject matter he didn't like discussing with anyone. Josh had told her a long time ago, after the one and only date he went on in high school, that he didn't think he'd ever marry.

"Sorry," she quickly said.

"It's all right." But his tone was edgy, bothered.

"Really. I'm sorry, Josh. I shouldn't have said that."

He smiled. "You're the only one who understands *why* you shouldn't."

She smiled too. "Mom still bugs you about it?"

"Dad too." He sipped his cider. "But Mom makes a science out of finding new and creative ways to ask me if I'm seeing anyone. Dad just comes right out and says, "Don't you think it's time you settled down, Josh?"

She laughed. "So is Mom still trying to fix you up with her friends' daughters?"

"She's resorted to trying to fix me up with her enemies' daughters!"

They both laughed heartily.

"They just want you to be happy, Josh," she said a moment later when the laughter gave way to an easy silence.

"But I *am* happy, Rachael. I really am."

He locked his eyes onto hers, willing her to acknowledge she knew he didn't want his life to be any different than the way it was.

"I know you are," she said. "And you're using those wonderful talents that I know would make you a good father to love children who have neither mother or father. I forget that sometimes. And I'm sorry."

But Josh shooed away her apology as if it were a housefly.

Trace was pulling into the driveway as the remembered words filled her mind. "It's okay, really," Josh had said. "I'm glad at least you understand me, Rachael. I don't know if anyone else does."

And then with a start she recalled what he'd said next. And as she did, a jolt of electricity coursed though her. Trace didn't notice as he put the car into park and turned off the engine that she had stiffened in her seat. As she got out of the car, that last sentence somersaulted in her head.

Because Josh had turned to her, with his cider in his hand and said, "Everything is turning out just as it should."

SEVENTEEN

The temporary distraction of unbuckling McKenna's car seat gave Rachael a few moments to consider Joshua's choice of words earlier in the day as they now ricocheted across her mind.

Everything is turning out just as it should.

Was it just a coincidence that her brother had said the exact same words that morning when she begged to help him? Did he know he had said the same thing to her just nine months ago? Or was she just looking too hard for clues that would lead her to the truth?

"Everything all right?" Trace had grabbed the diaper bag and was standing next to her at the open car door.

"Yes, fine," she mumbled.

"Then you might want to let McKenna come in with us. You just buckled her back in."

Rachael looked down at their daughter. She had indeed unbuckled the car seat and then promptly rebuckled it.

"Oh for Pete's sake," she grumbled, pressing the release button on the seat belt for the second time.

"Here. Let's switch." Trace handed her the lightweight diaper bag. "I'll bring her in."

Rachael stepped away, grabbing the bag. "Thanks. I don't know what I was doing. Something Joshua said today suddenly threw me for a second," she said.

"What is it?"

It would take too long to explain, if she even could explain it. "It's probably nothing. Just forget I said anything," Rachael replied.

She closed the car door behind Trace and then followed him up the paved walkway to the front door. Lights shone in every window of the two-story house—even in the upstairs bedrooms where no one slept. It was one of her mother's little quirks. Eva didn't like the unwelcoming look of dark rooms. When the sun set, lights came on in every room of the Harper house. Cliff had long since given up trying to convince Eva it made no sense to illuminate rooms empty of people. And it did no good to switch off the lights because Eva always turned them back on.

"A well-lit house is a friendly house," she said on more than one occasion.

Just as Rachael reached for the doorknob her father opened the door, accompanied by Kipper, the Harpers' cocker spaniel. Cliff had on his name tag from St. Cloud Hospital where he managed environmental services. He must have gone back to work after the hearing. That surprised Rachael. It must've also meant her parents didn't get to see Josh. She doubted her dad could've managed to do both.

"Hey, Dad," Rachael said as they crossed the threshold into the entryway. Kipper danced around her, wagging his stub of a tail.

"Traffic bad?" Cliff asked as he stepped aside to let them in.

"No worse than Manhattan the week before Christmas," Trace quipped.

Cliff shut the door and motioned them to the living room.

"So you went back to work after you got back from St. Paul?" Rachael asked, nodding at her father's name tag.

"I had some things to take care of."

"Did you see Josh?" Rachael asked.

"No. It wasn't the right time for visitors, I guess. We'll try again this weekend."

Rachael sat down on the sofa as Trace placed McKenna's car seat on the floor next to her. The dog plunged its nose into McKenna's lap, and Cliff shooed him away. Rachael leaned down to lift her daughter out. "Is Mom okay?"

Cliff shrugged. "I guess. You want something to drink, Trace?"

"No thanks. I'm good," Trace answered.

Rachael stood. "I'll go see if Mom needs any help in the kitchen." She started to hand McKenna to Trace but her father held his arms out. "Let me take her."

Cliff gingerly maneuvered McKenna into his arms, supporting her neck with awkward caution. The worries of the day shone on his face. He tried unsuccessfully to hide the strain from Rachael, but it seemed to diminish a bit as he held McKenna close. Her father didn't seem to notice the mermaid hue of McKenna's tiny fingernails.

"Holler if you need me," Rachael stated as she walked away.

"We'll be fine," Cliff said softly.

Rachael made her way to the kitchen, catching a whiff of baking potatoes as she crossed from one room to another via a central hallway. Kipper followed her, and she bent down to pat him as she walked. On the counter by the breakfast nook was a small TV set tuned to *Jeopardy!* A covered pan on the stove was bubbling away noisily, and her mother was near the sink, slicing tomatoes. Eva looked up when Rachael walked over to her.

"Oh, Rachael! You're here. I didn't hear you come in."

"It's okay, Mom. We just got here. May I help you with anything?"

Eva looked toward the stove. "How about if you turn down the carrots?"

Rachael walked over to the stove and turned a knob. The bubbling sounds coming from the covered pan started to abate. "I'm sorry you didn't get to see Josh today," she said.

Eva scooped up the sliced tomatoes and placed them atop a bowl of lettuce. "Yes, so was I."

Rachael got the distinct impression her mother was jealous that Rachael had been able to see Joshua twice while she hadn't been able to see him at all. "Dad says you'll try again this weekend?"

"Yes. Saturday afternoon."

"Well, that sounds like a good plan."

"I guess." Eva sliced open a green pepper and thrust her hand inside to rip out the membrane and seeds. "Will they let me bring him anything? Cookies? Fruit?"

"I'm afraid not, Mom."

Eva tossed the innards into the sink. "Figures."

"May I do anything else for you, Mom?"

Her mother placed the green pepper on the cutting board and began to slice it. "Everything else is in the oven. Why don't you just go back into the living room with the others and relax."

Eva's voice was sincere, and Rachael could sense that her mother was hurting and wanted to be alone.

"Okay." Rachael started to walk away.

"Rachael," her mother said.

Rachael turned back around.

"Thanks for offering." The way she said it suggested she was genuinely appreciative of Rachael's efforts—and not just her offer of help in the kitchen. But also that she needed an interval of solitude.

"Sure, Mom." Rachael left the kitchen via the dining room. She heard Trace and her father talking in the living room and apparently McKenna was content. Rachael didn't feel like joining them, and the dining room table was already set so she couldn't offer to do that. On impulse, she turned toward the stairs that led to the second-story bedrooms.

The carpeted steps muffled her footfalls, and she lingered on several, studying the gallery of photographs that were flung across the wall like windows to the past. Joshua looked back at her from several framed portraits. Her favorite had always been the one at three years old, in which Joshua, wearing a ball cap backwards, held a baseball in his hands. It would prove to be an awkward pose as the years went by because Josh never developed a passion or even a fondness for sports. But she'd always thought that the way Josh was holding the ball made it appear as though he was holding the world in his hands. Ten chubby fingers were wrapped around it, and Josh held it extended upward and a few inches from his body as if he had just been given it from on high. She had been in the photography studio that day, watching from the side. She remembered how the photographer wanted Josh to throw the ball to his assistant in some kind of toddler-cute pitch. But Josh had just held the ball encircled in his fists as if he were meant to hold it forever.

There were photos of Rachael and Josh together, studio portraits that had been stuffed into Harper Christmas cards over the years. And there were extended family portraits too, though not very many. Cliff had only one brother, Warren, who had never married. Eva had been an only child, so there were no group shots of all the cousins because there were no cousins. There was a portrait of Grandma and Grandpa Harper at their fiftieth wedding anniversary reception in Michigan some years ago, though Grandma Harper had since passed away and Grandpa now lived in a senior living complex.

And there was Rachael's favorite photo of Eva's mother, whom Josh and she called Nana, and who had died when Rachael was a freshman in college. Grandpa Reichert, her mother's father, had been a cattle farmer near Sioux Falls, South Dakota. He died at the age of sixty-two of a massive heart attack when Rachael was only seven. Rachael barely remembered him. Her memories of Nana, however, were vivid. She and Josh spent a month with her on the farm every summer. Nana was as optimistic as she was stubborn and intuitive. She kept the farm going with hired help for several years after Grandpa Reichert's death, to the surprise and objections of just about everyone. In addition to her resilience and tenacity, Nana also seemed to understand Joshua's heart for God and actually encouraged his rather atypical ways. "God has His hand on you," she would say to Josh from time to time.

On one occasion, Joshua had asked Nana if God didn't also have His hand on Rachael. Nana had smiled, winked at Rachael and said, "God holds our Rachael, Joshua. Don't you worry about that!" Rachael, ten at the time, had thought it odd that Nana hadn't actually said that God had His hand on her, too, but that God *held* her. A subtle difference in words, but even as an adolescent, Rachael thought there was a huge difference in application. Over the next few years, Rachael had wanted to ask Nana what it meant for God to have His hand on someone, but she was afraid to hear what Nana knew about Josh and how she knew it.

The fact was, Nana was a deeply spiritual person, like Josh. There were many times Rachael would awaken in the middle of the night at the farmhouse and hear Nana whispering at her bedside—or at Joshua's—as she leaned over them in prayer. Nana never told anyone she did that, and Rachael never let on that she knew. It seemed a private thing between Nana and God. And frankly, Rachael was a bit unsettled by Nana's secret communications with God on her behalf.

Nana reminded her of Joshua. Or maybe it was the other way around. Rachael had wondered—and still did as she stood there staring at the photo—what her mother's relationship with Nana had been like. They had not seemed particularly close. Cordial, but not close. Rachael couldn't help but think Nana was part of the reason Josh grew up as he did—a good boy, but an unusual one.

Rachael climbed the rest of the stairs to the second floor, past the high school graduation photos, a wedding portrait of her and Trace, and the last one, a 5 x 7 of McKenna at three weeks. She turned at the top of the staircase and stood for only a moment at the doorway to her old room. She had been gone from home for more than a decade, and there were just traces of what the room had been like when it was hers. A lamp, the wastebasket and a small, framed lithograph of Paris were the only things in the room that had been there when she slept in it.

Josh's room, however, hadn't changed much in the seven years he had been on his own. Standing at the doorway to his old room, Rachael saw that the bedspread was the same, the prints of the Grand

Canyon and the Smoky Mountains were the same and the curtains were the same deep crimson. It was almost as if her parents hoped Joshua might decide to come back and finish growing up.

She walked into Josh's room and instantly memories both good and bad tugged at her. *The bad ones aren't really bad*, she thought. *They just remind me how much Mom and Dad wanted things to turn out differently for Josh.*

Rachael walked over to Josh's bed and eased herself down onto it, remembering the conversations she had with him while he sat at one end of the bed and she at the other. It was on the bed that he had told her about the hunting fiasco. It was also where he gave her the details, during one of her spring breaks, regarding the one and only date he went on in high school—an evening he neither particularly enjoyed nor disliked. He had told her he was indifferent to the call of romance. He could see that it was important to most people, but it wasn't to him, and he was fine with that.

She fingered the quilt pattern as she recalled it was while sitting cross-legged on the bed that twelve-year-old Josh told her about the tent meeting and what the traveling evangelist had said to him. He had biked there on that otherwise ordinary April afternoon after seeing a photocopied advertisement tacked to a signpost. The event had been billed as a "revival to bring the hearts of young and old back to God."

"He laid his hands on me, Rachael!" Josh had said, his voice still that of a boy.

"Why? What for?" she had asked.

"He told me God had spoken to him. That God told him *I* was his messenger of hope!"

She had stared back at him, wide-eyed. Speechless.

"He recited this verse from the book of James and placed his hands on my head."

"What verse? What did he say?"

Joshua's eyes had begun to shimmer. He reduced his voice to almost a whisper: "Pure and undefiled religion in the sight of our God and our Father is this: to visit orphans and widows in their distress and to keep oneself unstained by the world."

"Josh," she had said, shaking off the mesmerizing effects of his words. "What has that got to do with you?"

"Everything," Josh had answered, his voice suddenly serious and defensive.

"I don't see how."

"Nothing matters more than taking care of widows and orphans! That's what pure religion is. That's all it is."

He had said it as if he had stumbled upon his life's purpose, the sum total of all the reasons he had been born.

"Josh, you're twelve. You don't even know any widows and orphans."

He had hesitated only a moment. "There's Mrs. DeLyle."

"That's one person."

"That one person matters! And I know she's not the only widow. There are bunches at church. And there's probably bunches more out there. Orphans too."

When he said this, something had begun to well up inside her—a strange mix of pride and fear. She was proud of him, and yet she was terribly afraid. Somehow she knew something life-changing had happened to her little brother. Something that involved more than him considering how he might be able to lend a hand from time to time to widowed Mrs. DeLyle down the street.

"Josh, what exactly are you saying?" she asked.

He leaned forward on the bed. "I made a vow. I know what I'm supposed to do with my life. I know what God wants me to do."

"Josh…" she began, but he interrupted her.

"I know what God wants me to do," he said again, emphasizing every word.

"You're *twelve*," she whispered.

"King Josiah led Judah when he was only eight." He sat back on the bed like he had just rattled off an amazing football statistic.

Rachael decided at that moment to just let it go. She figured whatever it was that he had grabbed hold of he would soon let go. But as the months wore on, and then the years, Josh never did. Three years later he finally told their parents, and Rachael pretended she was hearing it for the first time, just like they were. He told them the day after the failed hunting trip that he planned to go into the ministry. And when they first heard it, her parents looked pleased. Both of them seemed to like the idea of Josh becoming a pastor. But he quickly told them he had no plans to go to seminary or even college. And he didn't want to be a pastor. His plan after high school was to search out widows and orphans and care for them in any way he could.

Rachael had been in the room when he told them. First there had been silence. But it didn't last.

Cliff had exploded in anger. "That is no way to earn a living!"

Eva had cried, "What kind of a life is that?"

Her parents hadn't been truly interested in Josh's answers. They didn't know how to be interested in his answers.

And Rachael had felt torn in two. She understood her parents' pain and disappointment. And she likewise understood Joshua's passion for his mission. She initially thought that, in time, Josh would redirect his efforts to help widows and orphans by earning a college degree in social work or counseling. When that didn't happen, she thought her parents would learn to appreciate his deeply benevolent heart, different though it was. But that didn't happen either.

As she now sat in the bedroom that had not changed, she could tell her parents were still waiting for Josh to come to his senses.

At that moment her father appeared at the doorway. "We were all wondering where you were," he commented. He stepped into the room and sat down beside her.

"I just wanted to sit in here and think," she said. "I hope you don't mind that I'm in here."

Her dad shook his head. "Of course I don't mind." Then he sighed. "I've done the same thing many times. I've come in here and sat on this bed to think."

"Dad…" she began, but he just continued as if she hadn't spoken.

"I've tried everything, Rachael. Everything I know as a father and a man, to understand my son. I want to understand him. I really do. But I just don't get it."

She said nothing. A moment later he continued.

"It's not that I want him to be like me. I know he thinks that's what I want. But I don't. He doesn't have to like what I like. Or do what I do. I just want him to take responsibility for his life. I feel like I've truly failed him in that respect. I haven't shown him how."

"Dad, that's not true," Rachael said, but again he cut her short.

"No, it *is* true. I've never been able to reach him. He's always been just beyond my grasp. Even when he was little. I tried to be a good father to him. I tried to take him fishing and to baseball games. He never wanted to do any of those things with me. I didn't know what else to try."

Tears slid down Rachael's cheeks. She reached out to touch her father's shoulder but he seemed not to notice.

"And after he graduated from high school and moved to St. Paul, I tried not to nag him about getting a real job and making a better life for himself," Cliff continued. "God knows I tried not to discourage him. But I always managed to. He would come home to visit or do something for Mrs. DeLyle and we'd get into an argument. Well, it was me mostly doing the arguing, he barely said anything. And then he'd leave, and I'd come in here and sit on the bed just like you are, and I'd ask God what else I can do."

Her father shook his head, and Rachael looked up at him. His eyes were brimming with tears.

"But I've never gotten any answers," her father said, his voice raspy. "I don't know what else I can do. I don't understand any of this."

"Dad," Rachael said and her voice was thick in her throat.

Her father stood up. "I don't understand how my son could shoot a man in the back of the head."

"But..." Rachael began.

"And I don't understand how he could say he did it, if he didn't."

Cliff turned and took two steps toward the door.

Then he turned back to her. "I'm sorry, Rachael. I didn't come up here to upset you."

She wiped her eyes and shook her head as if to clear her head. "I know you didn't."

"I came up here to tell you dinner's ready."

Her father turned back around and walked out of the room.

EIGHTEEN

The sounds of the early morning commute on the street below awoke Rachael as she lay next to Trace in the French maiden's bed. He was sound asleep, as was McKenna in her portable crib. Rachael grabbed her watch lying on the windowsill just inches away. It was a few minutes before seven. McKenna would probably be up any time now.

Rachael rose quietly from the bed, wrapped herself in Trace's robe and tiptoed out of the guest room to Fig's kitchen. He had been out when they got home the night before from dinner at her parents' house, but now there was a note taped to the coffeepot in Fig's flowing script.

Coffee's ready to go. Just press the button. Cheese blintzes in the fridge.

She pressed the button on the coffeepot and walked over to the large dining room window. Outside the nearby Mississippi River glistened as did the jewel-like matrix of headlights and taillights on the street below. Life all around her was set to "normal." She couldn't help but notice the irony of it. Minneapolis was heading to work and school—the stuff of an ordinary day.

Dinner at her parents' the previous night had been a strained affair. She knew she shouldn't really be surprised. This trip home wasn't like coming home for Christmas or the wedding of a friend or even the funeral of a loved one. Everything that defined this trip home was cold and foreign.

And unexplainable.

It seemed to her that the more time she spent pondering Josh's predicament, the messier things became and the more questions she came up with. Nothing was any clearer. She had to step outside the situation and look at it from the objective view of someone with nothing to gain or lose by Joshua's confession. She needed to approach it methodically, like she would if she were back in New York building the defense of a fourteen-year-old charged with clubbing his stepfather senseless with a baseball bat. There were always underlying reasons why a child broke the law. Always. Sometimes she had to look hard for them. But when she did, she always found them. That's what she had to do now. Start with what she knew and then pose every question possible, turn over every stone, and take every lead to where it ended.

Rachael turned from the window, grabbed a mug from the dish drainer and filled it with coffee. She grabbed her briefcase off the island countertop, the artists' drawings from the night before last, and Trace's laptop computer. She walked into the dining room and set everything down on the shiny tabletop. She pulled a yellow legal pad out of her briefcase and a pen. Uncapping the pen, Rachael wrote *Facts* at the top of the yellow pad. Then she began to list everything that was indisputable:

Joshua confessed to killing Vong Thao.
A witness saw him at the store at the time of the murder.
The two girls he was trying to help corroborate his story.
A floor mat is missing.
Josh had to wait twenty-two seconds before pulling the trigger.

Josh made a vow at the age of twelve to help widows and orphans in their distress.

The two girls are orphans.

The two girls are victims of sexual abuse.

Josh has not told me to my face that he killed Vong Thao.

Josh refuses to let me represent him.

Josh said the exact same phrase that he did at Christmastime, that everything is turning out just as it should.

I have never seen Josh lose his temper.

Josh has never lied to me.

Rachael sipped her coffee, studied her list and then wrote a new word under it: *Suppositions*. She paused for a moment and then began to list what her heart and mind were telling her but for which she had no proof.

Josh is covering up for someone else, probably one of the girls.

Josh could not have maintained his rage for twenty-two seconds.

Josh is withholding truth from me.

Josh appears to regret what he has done, and he has never before regretted actions related to helping people.

Josh disposed of the floor mat to somehow protect the girls from something or to cover their guilt.

Josh thinks he is performing the ultimate act of sacrifice by taking the blame that belongs to someone else—someone whom society and maybe the church failed.

Rachael chewed on the end of the pen for a moment before writing down the last observation.

Evil was present in that basement.

For a second she considered scribbling out the last item. It was the least logical observation she had made. But she knew this intuition she had—and didn't understand—linked her to Josh somehow. It was probably the only thing that did. She suddenly wished Nana were alive. Nana probably would've understood this strange feeling she had about that basement. Nana would have known what to do about it. Nana would've also probably had insights into what Josh thought had really happened to him that day the traveling evangelist laid his hands on him. She might have been able to help Josh interpret that calling.

Had Josh told her about it? Rachael thought back to when it had happened. It was April, a few months before his thirteenth birthday. She and Josh didn't go to South Dakota that summer because Nana had sold the farm in March and moved to an apartment in Sioux Falls. And besides, Rachael had just graduated from high school. She had felt too old to spend a month at the farm; she wouldn't have gone even if Nana still had it. Nana was supposed to come out that Christmas but she died quite unexpectedly the first week in October. To her knowledge, Josh hadn't seen Nana after his experience at the tent meeting. Did he call her? Write to her?

Rachael rose from her chair to refill her cup. She wished the senior pastor of the Brooklyn church she and Trace sometimes attended knew her. She wanted to ask his advice, get his opinion on what that verse in James meant and how Josh was trying to live it out. She was sure Josh had it skewed in his mind somehow. But the fact was that none of the pastors at that Brooklyn church knew her. With a congregation of 6,000 people, it was easy to be anonymous. And that's what she was, mostly by choice. It was why Trace liked going to the rather unconventional church that met in a former ballet studio a few blocks from their apartment. It was hard to be anonymous in a group of just sixty other people. *Soli Deo* was a very intimate cluster of believers. She didn't attend as often as Trace did; that kind of intimacy intimidated her somewhat. But Calvin, the teaching leader of *Soli Deo* had been to their home on more than one occasion. He at least knew her name. Perhaps she could call him or email him? She looked over her shoulder to see if Trace was out of bed even though she'd heard no sound coming from the guest room. She wanted his opinion before she tried to contact Calvin.

She swung her head back around and opened Trace's laptop,

switched it on, and waited for the wireless network to kick in. Then she opened an Internet window and typed in the URL for a Bible search engine she liked. When the site came up, Rachael typed in James 1:27 and was about to view the verse when she realized she knew it by heart. Looking at the words online wasn't going to help her understand what they meant. Rachael needed someone knowledgeable to *tell* her what they meant. She had always thought it a little odd that religion had been defined in the New Testament as simply taking care of widows and orphans and not by attending church or tithing or spreading the gospel. But she had never asked anyone about it. What did that verse really mean? What did it mean to Joshua?

She clicked to the keyword search window and typed in two words.

Widows, orphans.

Verses began to appear. She began to read them and stopped when she recognized one from Isaiah. It was the same verse Josh had quoted to her on Monday, two days ago.

Woe to those who make unjust laws, to those who issue oppressive decrees, to deprive the poor of their rights and withhold justice from the oppressed of my people, making widows their prey and robbing the fatherless. What will you do on the day of reckoning, when disaster comes from afar? To whom will you run for help?

Joshua had not recited the verse that immediately followed. She read it now and didn't know what to make of it.

Nothing will remain but to cringe among the captives or fall among the slain. Yet for all this, his anger is not turned away, his hand is still upraised.

Fall among the slain.

Fall among the slain.

It made no sense. She closed the browser and pushed the laptop away.

"Did you lose at an early morning game of Solitaire?"

She turned to see Trace in sweat pants and a bare chest walking up behind her. He had McKenna in his arms.

"No. I'm just trying to figure out how the mind of Joshua Harper works. I'm not doing very well."

She reached for McKenna, and Trace placed her in her arms.

"He's not really your responsibility to figure out. He's a grown man, Rach. He alone is responsible for what he does. I know you know this."

"I do. Really, I do. But Trace, if I did something crazy and it was in your power to help me, you would do it, even though I'm the only one responsible."

Trace nodded. "Point well taken."

She rose from the chair and walked over to the sofa with McKenna. "Trace, would you mind emailing Calvin and asking him a question for me?"

"Calvin? Sure. What is it?"

"Can you ask him what James 1:27 means?"

Trace studied her a moment. "You mean what it means for Josh-or what it means for the rest of us?"

"Both. You can tell him everything. Tell him what Josh has done. Tell him what happened to Josh when he was twelve. Tell him I need to know how God expects people to interpret that verse. Not just Josh. All of us."

"Okay."

Trace said nothing as Rachael readied herself to nurse McKenna.

"So how is this going to help?" he asked a moment later.

Rachael looked up at him. "I have to get inside Josh's head. I've got to see this the way he sees it. When I look at this mess with my eyes or, worse, through my parents' eyes, it looks hopeless. I don't see how I can help him. I have to know what he's thinking so I can see what he's not telling me."

"But what if the way your brother sees it isn't the way anyone else sees it? What if Calvin can't tell you how your brother sees it because no one else sees it that way?"

Rachael looked away. "One road block at a time, please."

"Sorry."

Trace went into the kitchen and poured himself a cup of coffee. He came back through the living room, opened the front door, and was gone for several minutes. He came back with the morning paper in his hands.

He sat down on the sofa next to Rachael. "You look pretty hot there in my robe."

She smiled.

For a few moments there was silence in the room as McKenna nursed, Rachael toyed with her many thoughts, and Trace read a few pages of the paper.

Then he folded a page in two and turned to Rachael. "Do you want to see this?"

"What is it?" Rachael asked.

"A little news item about the guy who attempted to plead guilty to the murder of a grocery store owner in Frogtown."

Rachael closed her eyes; inwardly glad her parents didn't subscribe to a daily paper. "Does it say anything I don't already know?" she whispered, opening her eyes.

Trace glanced at the page and then looked up at her. "No."

"Then I don't want to see it."

When McKenna was finished, Rachael took her into the bedroom for a diaper change. Moments later, in the kitchen, she and Trace were joined by Fig.

"Morning, amigos!" he said cheerfully. "I see you have made the coffee but have not had the blintzes. We must remedy that right away." He reached into the fridge and brought out a white paper bag. "And how was dinner last night?"

"Oh, not too bad, I guess. Yesterday was a hard day for my mom and dad," Rachael said.

"Yes, yes." Fig opened the bag and withdrew six creamy white blintzes. "Parenthood isn't for the fainthearted, is it?"

Rachael, holding McKenna in her arms, nodded.

"I have good news!" Fig said, interrupting the solemn moment. "I have an Austin-Healy downstairs in the garage. It belongs to a friend of mine. He's off to France for a month and asked me to babysit. How could I refuse? So now you can use my car whenever you need it. No more worries there, okay muchachos?"

"Well, thanks Fig," Trace replied. "That's something we were going to try and take care of."

"So now you don't have to," Fig said, crunching up the bag and tossing it into the trash. "Now try these. They're heavenly. You'll wish you were Jewish."

The phone rang then and Fig turned to answer it.

"So you have plans for today?" Trace asked her. "Now that you have a car?"

"Well, I thought McKenna and I could go for a long walk along the river while you work on your projects, and then this afternoon while she naps, I'll go back to St. Paul."

"And do what?"

"See if I can find out what Joshua has been up to lately."

"You're going to try and see him?"

Rachael shook her head. "No. I want to meet his friend John Tsue. And I want to see the Center where he met those girls."

Trace narrowed his eyes. "You're thinking you'll run into one of them," he said.

"No. Actually if I see either one of them, I don't want them to know who I am."

"Afraid you'd learn something that the prosecution could use?"

Again Rachael shook her head. "No. The Center is a safe place for them. They need a safe place. I don't want to scare them away from it."

As soon as the words were out of her mouth she was instantly aware of her concern for those girls, and that perhaps she already knew quite a bit about what that verse meant. For Josh. For everyone.

NINETEEN

With the promise to be back in a couple hours, Rachael set out for St. Paul a few minutes before two o'clock. She didn't know exactly where John Tsue's teen center was, but she assumed it had to be near the grocery store...within walking distance anyway. And Frogtown wasn't that big. If she had to, she would stop and ask someone.

She wished she had thought to ask Josh about his friend John and what their relationship was like. Did John approve of Josh's unique way of life? Were they good friends? Did he know what really happened that night in the grocery store basement?

Rachael made her way into the heart of the cultural landscape of Frogtown, beginning with the blocks nearest the still-cordoned-off grocery store. She had driven around several blocks numerous times and was about to stop at a gas station to ask for help when she saw a faded, white church building in need of paint and landscaping on a street corner seven blocks from the grocery store. Ornate Asian script occupied the lion's share of the sign out front. In smaller script underneath were the English words: "Teens in the Center: A ministry of Hmong Christian Fellowship—Lue Khang, pastor; John Tsue, youth pastor.

She had found it.

She drove into the tiny parking lot, which was void of cars. One lone scooter was parked against the pole of a basketball hoop that was missing half its chain links. Rachael parked, got out of the car, and locked it. She walked over to the wooden double doors and tried the knob. It opened.

She found herself in the former sanctuary of a long-ago church. The pews had been removed and Foosball and Ping-Pong tables stood in their place. At the front where an altar or podium would have been were a few speakers, a trap set, and microphone and guitar stands. Above the music equipment was a modern art mural that stretched from one wall to the other. In graffiti-like letters the mural bore two messages, one in a language she could not read and the other, its likely translation: "He Died for Me—I'll Live for Him." Mismatched sofas of various sizes and condition were arranged in the far front corner like a mini-theater. A long counter with bar stools, also of various sizes and appearance, ran along the back wall where she now stood.

The large room was quiet now, but she could imagine it full of teenagers. She could imagine Josh in this room talking with them, playing Ping-Pong with them, praying with them. She moved forward and her footsteps echoed on the weathered wooden floor. At the end of the room by the sofas was a door, partly open with light on the other side.

"Hello?" she called.

The door opened fully and an Asian man poked his head out.

"Can I help you?" he said in slightly accented English.

"I am looking for John Tsue."

The man stepped into the large room and walked over to her. "I am John Tsue," he said.

"Hi. My name is Rachael Flynn," she said.

"Are you a cop?" John Tsue asked, shaking her hand. 'Cause I already talked to one today."

Pendleton was no doubt checking out Josh's story just like she was. He had to; the county prosecutor expected it.

"No, I'm not a cop," she said. "I'm Josh's sister."

"Oh, wow! Hey, man, I'm really sorry about what's happened. Really sorry. Please call me John."

"Rachael," she said.

"Have you seen him? I tried to visit him, but I was told his visitors are restricted to immediate fmily. Is he doing okay?"

"Actually John, that's why I wanted to talk to you. I don't really think he's doing okay. I think he's lying to the cops about who shot the grocery store owner."

John Tsue's eyes widened. "Uh, you want to sit down?" He motioned to the conglomeration of couches behind them.

"Thanks."

They walked over to them, and Rachael sat down on a paisley-patterned sofa whose springs groaned slightly at her descent. John sat across from her on a green love seat.

"I have to admit I have a hard time picturing Josh shooting any-body, but he *did* say he did it, right?" John said.

"Yes, I know he said he did it, but I think he's covering for someone. Maybe one of the Lee sisters."

The minute she said it, Rachael wished she hadn't. John sat up straight.

"Look, I can't talk to you like this about any of these kids," he said defensively. "I can't help you that way."

"I'm not asking you to, really," Rachael corrected. "I'm not here to discuss who *did* do it, I just want to find out what Josh was thinking. Why he might have done what he did. I'm sure he loves these kids just like you do. It would explain a lot."

"Well, what exactly do you want from me?" John said after a pause.

"Would you mind telling me when you met my brother? How long he's been your friend?"

John sat forward. "I'll tell you what I told the cops. Josh was volunteering last year at a homeless shelter not far from here and so was I. We became friends and I told him I was on staff at the Hmong Christian Fellowship three blocks from here and that I wanted to start a summer program for Asian youth. He told me if I needed any help at all, to just say the word and he'd come. Well, this old church building got donated to us and Pastor Khang said I could use it for the student center. As soon as I had the keys I asked your brother to help me get it started.

"It was both weird and interesting to the kids around here that this tall white dude was helping me. He was like a natural draw. And he could get kids to come in and help us clean out the place. I don't know how he did, but he did. And he'd play pick-up games outside with them, and. . ."

"Pick-up games? Basketball?" Rachael interrupted, unable to hide her surprise.

"Yeah. He played terrible, but the kids thought it was hilarious. They loved playing with him."

"Really?"

"Oh yeah. He helped me find all the Ping-Pong and Foosball tables. He put up fliers in all the big churches, you know, the ones with money, and asked for them. People whose kids had grown up and gone off to college wanted to get the game tables out of their garages and basements. Josh offered to pick them up for free and do one odd job as payment for them."

"That's a great idea," Rachael said.

"You bet it is. He got the couches that way too."

Rachael looked around the room. "This place must be a lot of fun."

John smiled. "It is. And the kids are out of harm's way. But the best part is, they know they are loved here, just the way they are. They find out here that's how God loves them—just the way they are."

"Was Joshua coming every day then?"

"Well, he was delivering office supplies during the morning, but he got here every day by one. And then of course when school started a few weeks ago, he was here when the kids got here."

"And the kids like him."

"They do. They call him Whitey. He loves it."

"John, do you know much about my brother?"

"I know he's a great guy. Loves kids. Loves people who don't see a lot of love."

"He never told you what happened to him when he was twelve?"

"No."

Rachael sat forward. "He went to a revival meeting. On his own. A traveling evangelist laid hands on him and told him he had a message from God for him."

"Yeah?" John's eyes were wide.

"The evangelist said Josh had been called upon by God to care for widows and orphans for the rest of his days. He laid his hands on my brother and then quoted that verse from the first chapter of James. Do you know the one I mean?"

"Yes," John said softly.

"That has been Josh's sole ambition in life. He has never looked back. At Christmas he told me that we all must live the life we're destined to live. And that's what he was doing…and he was truly happy with his life. He was completely satisfied caring for people who no one else seems to care for."

"Why are you telling me this?" John inquired quietly.

"John, I have never seen my brother lose his temper."

John said nothing.

"Have you?" she said.

John shook his head. "No. But I have only known your brother for a year."

"Can you tell me, after all the time you've spent with him, that Josh is the kind of man to shoot another man in the head while that man is on his knees and unarmed? Can you tell me you can see my brother doing that?"

John looked down at his feet. "No, I can't."

Rachael breathed in deep. She hoped John had said this to Pendleton.

"But I have heard what Vong Thao was doing. I heard what he was letting men do in the basement of his store," John continued, almost whispering it.

"What are you saying?" Rachael said, her voice matching his.

"I'm just saying I understand how your brother must have felt when he found out what Thao had done. Especially with the girls right there."

"Are you telling me you would've done the same thing?" Rachael was incredulous.

"No, I wouldn't!"

"Then how can you assume Joshua would?"

"Because he said he did."

The doors behind them opened and half a dozen kids came inside, laughing and talking all at once.

"I can't talk with you anymore," John said. "I'm sorry. The kids are out of school. It's going to get really busy in here."

Rachael stood too. "Can I give you my cell phone number?"

"I guess. What for?"

Rachael fished in her purse for a business card. She found one and handed it to John. "If you hear of anything or think of anything that could help Josh, will you call me?"

John said nothing but took the card. "If you see Josh, tell him my family and I pray for him every day." He stuffed the card in his pants pocket.

"I will. Thanks."

John nodded and walked over to the sound system on the stage. Seconds later, the vocals of Toby Mac filled the room. She walked away, aware that eyes were on her, a strange white woman. She opened the door and stepped out into the sunshine. Several kids were already shooting hoops, and a group of teen boys was standing at Fig's Lexus, eying it suspiciously.

As Rachael neared the car the boys moved away, and as they did,

Rachael saw that four black-haired teenage girls were standing on the other side of it, leaning on the driver's door and looking at a magazine.

"Ah, excuse me," she said tentatively. The girls looked up. Two of them immediately walked away. The other two stared at her, shock and surprise swept across their faces. It took Rachael a second to realize that these two girls recognized her.

"I know who you are," the older one of the two said, but the words were barely strung together. It was almost as if she had been thinking out loud.

The younger one backed away and then sprinted for the building. Rachael watched the girl dash away.

Bao.

Rachael turned back to the girl who had spoken to her. Choua.

"I saw your picture in Whitey's wallet," the girl murmured.

Rachael could only stare at her.

"I know you," Choua said.

TWENTY

The face of the girl in front of her was awash in a blend of awe, anger, and apprehension. Rachael had seen the look hundreds of times in her work defending juveniles. Choua's stare was hard, calculating. But it was also fearful and curious. The girl was of medium build, neither skinny nor fat, and she wore low-rise jeans and a sky-blue Nike hooded sweatshirt. A tiny diamond stud shone above one nostril.

Instinct told Rachael to pretend she didn't know who Choua was. Her initial gut feeling was that it would be better for Josh if she played dumb. She figured it would also work to her advantage with Pendleton to leave the Center without having spoken to Choua Lee. Plus, at the back of her mind was the nagging thought that before her stood the person she believed *had* pulled the trigger. She inwardly reminded herself that Choua was a victim first, but one quite possibly capable of retaliation.

Rachael prayed a silent and second-long prayer for protection and wisdom.

"I beg your pardon?" she said to Choua.

Choua narrowed her eyes a bit; it was the look of someone in the habit of estimating. Rachael waited.

"You Whitey's sister?" Choua finally asked.

Careful, careful, Rachael cautioned herself.

"My brother's name is Joshua."

"Joshua Harper," Choua replied. It was not a question.

"Yes."

Choua lifted up her chin. "Your brother's in jail."

Rachael paused. She had to get out of here or she wouldn't be able to keep herself from having a conversation with this girl. She had no idea if that would help Josh or if it would seal his doom. Pendleton surely wouldn't approve. And what would Maggie say? Rachael was pretty sure no one would be particularly happy with her if she had a discussion right now with Choua Lee. "Yes, he is. Excuse me, I have to go."

"Why'd you come here?" Choua's tone was accusatory.

Rachael had no desire to mention she came to talk with John; she didn't want to ruin the trust he was trying to build with the teens that came to the Center. And Choua was clearly upset that Rachael was there. The real reason for her coming would probably not sit well with her. But she wasn't a good liar either.

She switched to an authoritative tone. "Sorry, but I really have to go now."

"Did you come here looking for me? 'Cause you found me." Choua's gaze was like ice.

God, what am I supposed to say? Rachael prayed. She thought of a quick response to give her time to think. "Why would I come here looking for you?"

Choua cocked her head. "Are you saying you don't know who I am?"

God, help me.

She knew she wouldn't be able to lie outright to Choua. She couldn't tell the girl to her face that she didn't know who she was. She had never been good at deception. There didn't seem to be any way of avoiding having a conversation with her short of just getting in the car and leaving. "I think I have a pretty good idea," Rachael murmured.

There. It was out.

A layer of anger on Choua's face seemed to weaken and was quickly replaced by one of alarm. "Did Whitey tell you about me?" she said evenly.

"No, he didn't." Rachael was relieved to be able to answer truthfully that Josh had not discussed the Lee sisters with her.

Choua looked unconvinced.

"If my brother showed you my picture, then I'm sure he told you I'm a lawyer," Rachael assured her. "I read the police report. Joshua has said nothing to me about you, nothing. He cares about you and your sister very much."

At the mention of Bao, Choua's anger resurfaced. "You better leave her alone." She said each word with surprising confidence and underlying malice. Rachael recognized it for the threat it was, though she knew there wasn't a whole lot Choua could do if Rachael decided she *did* want to talk to Bao. Still, Rachael was surprised at the venom in Choua's tone. She could imagine a gun in this girl's hands. Rachael willed herself to take command of the situation.

"If I came here to find you or your sister, do you think I would be trying to leave right now?" Rachael said, feigning nonchalance. "You were the one who insisted on talking with me. Do you have something you want to tell me?"

Choua swayed back. Rachael felt she at last had the upper hand.

"Look, I know you've been through a lot," Rachael said, locking her eyes on Choua's. "I'm not here to make things any worse for you. I just want you—and your sister—to be free of this tragedy. And I mean really free of it. I don't want this to haunt you for the rest of your life. You and your sister deserve to be free of it. Do you understand what I'm saying? You don't want to live with *anything* hanging over your head. You shouldn't have to worry about this again. Ever."

Choua's breath seemed to catch in her chest and for just a second she looked young and fragile. Then she shook her head and the look disappeared. "He killed him," she said.

The three words fell too quickly from her lips. Rachael had spent enough time listening to the pleas of the guilty and the innocent alike to know that there was something lacking in what Choua said. Something didn't ring true. Rachael wasn't sure what it was. But for the first time in four days she felt a step closer to the truth instead of constantly moving away from it.

Choua, like her brother, was hiding something. Rachael was sure of it. She reached into her purse, pulled out a business card and a pen. She scratched out her New York address and the words "Attorney at Law." She extended the card toward Choua. "If you need anything or want to talk, here's my cell phone number. I'm staying with a friend in Minneapolis, so I'm nearby. I'm not giving you my number as a lawyer, but as Josh's sister."

Choua looked at the card but did not take it.

Rachael kept her arm steady in front of the girl. She decided to gamble. "I meant what I said about wanting you to be free of this, Choua. I know Josh is doing what he thinks is best for you, but I don't think he has stopped to think how hard it will be for you to live every day for the rest of your life knowing what you know."

Choua blinked. "You don't know what you're talking about," she said confidently.

"You're right. I don't. But I do know you and my brother are hiding something. I don't know what it is. But I'm going to find out."

Choua's eyes suddenly looked away, past Rachael. Rachael turned and saw that Bao was peeking at them from the open door of the Center. When the younger girl saw Rachael, she disappeared back inside. Rachael turned back around.

"You care very much about your sister, I can see that. She's lucky to have you."

"You keep her out of this," Choua said coldly.

Rachael nodded toward the building where Bao was. "But she's already in it, isn't she? I can see you want to protect her. But do you really think she should have to live with what you are hiding? Is that fair to her?"

"You listen to me!" Choua said, taking a step forward. "You leave Bao *alone!*"

Rachael felt strangely at ease as she bent down and placed her business card at Choua's feet. Then she stood up and placed her hand on the car door. "Don't worry, Choua. I'm not coming back here. You can tell your sister whatever you want about me. But you might want to think about which one of us really has her best interests in mind."

Rachael swung the door open and eased in, closing the door swiftly behind her.

She kept her eyes on Choua as she slowly backed out and drove away.

As she made her way out of Frogtown Rachael couldn't help but drum her fingers madly on the steering wheel. Her brain flew in a million directions at once.

She had to tell Pendleton what happened. He needed to hear it from her, not from the girls, not from John Tsue. She made a quick turn and headed to the St. Paul Police station, hoping Pendleton was around.

Ten minutes later she was seated in the same waiting area where she had been two days earlier. Pendleton appeared from the hallway. Rachael stood.

"I need to talk to you," she said.

"All right," Pendleton said. "Come on back."

She followed him to his office, and he motioned for her to have a seat.

"What's up?" he queried, sitting down in his own chair.

"I want you to know exactly what happened today," Rachael said. "Because part of it I planned and part of it just happened. I didn't mean for it to."

Pendleton leaned forward in his chair. "You're not confessing to a murder, are you?"

His comedic tone calmed her. A tiny grin formed at the corners of her mouth. "No. I just…See, I went to see Josh's friend John Tsue, just to talk to him. I thought he could tell me what Josh had been up to these past few weeks. He really wasn't able to tell me anything I didn't already know. So I started to leave right about the time kids began to arrive. And as I was walking to my car, Choua and her sister saw me. They recognized me. Choua said she had seen my picture in Josh's wallet. I wouldn't have known who they were, but *they* recognized *me*."

If Pendleton was annoyed or angry, he didn't show it. "So what happened?" he said.

"Well, Bao scampered inside and Choua insisted on talking with me, even though I tried to pretend like I had no idea who she was. She wanted to know why I was there, and if I had come there looking for her. She also used a rather threatening voice to tell me to leave Bao alone."

"She knew you were Joshua's sister?"

"Yes. And she seemed very perturbed that I was there. Hostile, almost."

"And that surprised you?"

"Detective, her attitude toward me was nothing I haven't seen countless times already with the kids I've worked with. I can't tell you how many times I've seen it. I know when I'm being lied to. Just like I'm sure you do too."

Pendleton had his elbow on his desk and was resting his chin in his palm. But his eyes displayed intense interest. "What did she say to you?"

Rachael knew he would ask her this. She sighed. "It wasn't what she said, it was how she said it. She said, 'Did your brother tell you about me?' Not, 'Did your brother tell you my name' or 'Did your brother tell you where to find me,' but did Joshua tell me *about* her. About her. And when I told her I thought something wasn't quite right about this whole thing, that I was sure my brother and she were hiding something, she said, 'You don't know what you're talking about.' She didn't deny it outright, she just knew I didn't know the truth."

Pendleton rubbed his chin with his hand. "Did she tell you your brother *didn't* kill Vong Thao?"

Rachael sat back. "No."

"I think it would be best if you stayed away from the Center and those girls."

"I didn't expect to run into them today. Honest. I didn't want to talk to Choua. But she insisted. And her manner toward me was so antagonistic. It wasn't what I would have expected from her. My brother supposedly avenged the wrong done to her. It was like she didn't care. Or that there was far more to it, and she doesn't want anyone to know."

"You could jeopardize this case or worse, be called upon to testify against your brother. You'd be wise not to talk to any of the witnesses. I know you know that."

"I won't go back there, I promise."

Pendleton nodded. He looked deep in thought.

"You feel it too, don't you?" Rachael said. "That something isn't quite right?"

Pendleton didn't answer her question directly. Instead he posed a question back to her. "Did you happen to ask your brother about that floor mat?"

Rachael shook her head. "I only saw him for a few minutes before court yesterday. He wasn't in a very communicative mood."

"You know we impounded your brother's car."

"Yes," Rachael said.

"The tread in his tires is full of mud and bits of twigs."

Rachael only stared back. She had no idea where the detective was going with this.

"Your brother lives in the metro, works in the metro, socializes in the metro, yet he has mud and twigs in his tire treads. Like he has been out in the middle of nowhere lately. Does your brother do that? Take trips out to the middle of nowhere? Especially just days after shooting a man?"

"What?"

"The mud isn't caked enough to have been there very long."

"I...I don't know. Did you ask him?"

Pendleton nodded. "I went and talked to your brother this morning. He said he went to a lake to think and pray before he turned himself in. I asked him which one. He said he couldn't remember."

Rachael could see Josh spending time in prayer at a lake. She couldn't see him forgetting which one it was. Yes, there were many lakes in the Twin Cities area. But they all had names. And Josh had lived in the area for eight years.

"When we searched his apartment, we confiscated his shoes. We've got a pair of Adidas with mud covering the soles. Same kind of mud."

"So?"

"So it looks like when your brother prays he jogs in mud. Does that sound like your brother?"

"Maybe he was pacing..."

"Maybe he was getting rid of the gun."

Rachael leaned back in her chair. "Josh said he threw it into the river."

"That's what he *said*."

Rachael didn't know what to think. It was highly probable Josh had gone to a quiet place to pray before he turned himself in. But why hide the name of the lake? And what difference did it make if he threw the gun in the Mississippi River or one of the dozens of lakes around the metro?

"He also claims to have been at the lake the same day he turned himself in. But the condition of the mud suggests it had been in the tread for several days, not one."

"You think there's more to this?" she said.

"I don't doubt your brother might have wanted a quiet place to think. But you're right. I usually do know when I am being lied to. He knows which lake he went to, and he didn't go there the day he confessed."

"And the confession? Do you think he is lying about that too?"

Pendleton shook his head. "I don't know. I didn't have a reason to doubt it before, but the more I look into it the less I like it. There's another piece of the puzzle that bothers me. That blood stain on the stairs outside the basement is human, but it wasn't the victim's. We don't know whose it is. Could be one of the girls'. Could be one of Thao's employees. Could be the UPS man. I don't know. But I don't like it."

"You're starting to believe my brother is innocent, aren't you?" Rachael questioned, hope rising in her voice.

"I said I didn't like it." Pendleton leaned back in his chair and tilted his head. "I never said I think your brother is innocent."

TWENTY-ONE

Rachael said goodbye to Detective Pendleton and assured him that she had no plans to go back into Frogtown. He in turn told her he was considering advising the county prosecutor of his misgivings about Joshua's story. But he was also quick to add that there was plenty of evidence to sustain Josh's confession. She shouldn't think anything had changed. Rachael left his office resolved to find a way to break through to the truth.

As she walked out to the parking lot she realized it was after five. She had told Trace she'd be home by four. She grabbed the phone to look at how many calls she had missed and groaned aloud. She hadn't even turned the phone on. Rachael pressed the button to activate the phone and was relieved there were no messages. She pressed the speed dial for Fig's loft, mentally practicing her apology as it rang. But no one picked up.

Rachael couldn't decide if that was good or bad. It meant McKenna was up and Trace was out with her. Or Trace was occupied with her and couldn't answer the phone. Either way it appeared McKenna was awake.

Not good.

As she stood there holding her phone, it began to ring. The number in the screen wasn't one she recognized. She pressed the button to answer it.

"Hello?" she said.

"Rachael, this is Maggie Fielding. I just wanted you to know the psychologist that's going to do your brother's eval had a last-minute cancellation, so she's doing it tomorrow. I'll call you if there's anything monumental. Otherwise, it takes a week or so to get her report back."

"Are you going to watch the interview?" Rachael asked.

"I don't know. They take awhile. And I have a lot of other cases that are more troublesome than this one. I'll see what I can do."

"All right." Rachael decided not to mention to the defense lawyer that she'd run into Choua. Maggie seemed in a hurry. And what was the point? Josh still hadn't agreed to having Maggie represent him. "Thanks, Maggie."

"Yep."

The phone clicked off.

Rachael got into the car and tried Fig's number again as she started the engine. No answer. She pulled out of the parking lot into the thick of five o'clock traffic.

By the time Rachael pulled into Fig's underground garage it was twenty minutes to six. She raced to the elevator, punched the floor number for Fig's loft, and paced as the elevator lumbered upward.

Fig's front door was locked, and Rachael had to rummage in her purse for the spare key he had given her. She finally got the door open and sailed inside.

"Trace?" she called out.

The loft was quiet.

She walked into the guest bedroom. McKenna's portable crib was empty. A rolled-up used diaper lay on the floor. She picked it up and took it to the kitchen, again calling Trace's name.

No answer.

Rachael tossed the diaper into the trash and noticed a half-empty can of infant formula sitting on the counter. The bottle of breast milk she'd left was in the sink empty.

Could McKenna have been that hungry? Where was everybody?

Frustrated, she turned to go into the living room, but then she saw two drawings on the fridge. She recognized the work as Fig's. The first drawing showed a wide-eyed man with a little cross earring in a state of panic. In his arms was a squalling baby wearing a tiny tiara and brandishing a scepter. Next to the first man was another man in a black fedora in a greater state of shock with an empty baby bottle in his hands. The contents of the bottle were spilled at his feet.

Rachael groaned.

Fig!

He had apparently spilled the bottle of breast milk in a valiant effort to warm it in the microwave. One of them had rushed to the store to get formula while the other paced the floor with an angry baby. Amazingly, McKenna must have taken to the formula because the next drawing showed two men smiling like Cheshire cats, walking the princess baby in a stroller into Candyland.

Fig had found an annoying, albeit creative way to let her know he and Trace were out with McKenna and that all was well.

With nothing better to do than wait for them, Rachael opened the fridge, found a bottle of Perrier and poured it into a glass. She took it to the dining room where the pile of drawings still lay. Rachael separated the drawings and arranged them in a row. For several long minutes she sipped her drink and stared at the sketches. She moved Fig's away from the others. There was no sense contemplating that one.

Trace's drawings were the hardest to look at, but she had to admit they made the most sense. Except for the fact that Joshua had to aim a gun at a man's head for nearly half a minute. Sidney's creation—the cartoon version of Bao holding the gun—was unthinkable now that she had seen Bao for herself. That timid slip of a girl could not have shot a man in the head. She pushed that drawing aside too.

Brick's abstract depiction of Choua didn't resonate with Rachael. The expression on Choua's overdrawn face was not one Rachael had seen today, and she had seen a lot of emotions pass over Choua's face. But the scenario still seemed highly possible. Rachael had sensed that day how far Choua would go to protect her sister and perhaps take revenge for her own suffering.

But Brick's drawing didn't explain the missing floor mat or the mud on Josh's tires or why he lied about which day he went to a lake. It didn't explain the dead look in Josh's eyes when she visited him or why Vong Thao had been carrying a gun.

Too many unknowns.

Her eyes drifted over to Fig's drawing of the personification of evil floating down the stairs in a death robe. That one was almost starting to look plausible.

Insane.

Rachael looked away from the table as a doorknob turned and she heard voices in the entry. She rose from her chair as Fig and Trace walked in. Fig held the collapsed stroller; Trace had McKenna in his arms.

"Trace, I'm so sorry," she said, coming to him and reaching for McKenna. "A lot happened this afternoon. I lost track of time."

"Oh, we managed, didn't we, Tracer?" Fig said jovially.

Trace handed McKenna over to her. "Yep," he said flatly. He wasn't mad, but he wasn't like Fig either.

"I don't suppose you got much work done this afternoon," she said.

"Nope."

"I'll stay home tomorrow, I promise. You can work all day, okay?"

"Sure."

"You saw my note on the fridge?" Fig's question was playful.

Rachael nodded. "I saw it…them."

"You can put them in her baby book!" he continued, now walking briskly into the kitchen. "Let's order some curry, eh? I know this great place. The guy who owns it is from New Delhi. They deliver."

Fig picked up the phone.

Rachael turned to Trace. "I really am sorry, Trace."

"I know you are."

They walked into the living room, and Rachael sat down on the sofa with McKenna. Trace stretched out next to her.

"She's quite opinionated," he said, pointing to their daughter.

Rachael smiled. "But that can be a good thing."

"If you're a dictator," Trace said wryly.

"Or a lawyer."

Trace produced a conciliatory grin and closed his eyes as he leaned back into the couch. "So what happened this afternoon?"

"Trace, I went to talk to John Tsue, that youth pastor with the teen center. When I was leaving, I saw those two girls. I saw Choua and Bao."

He looked up at her. "You did? How did you know it was them?"

"I didn't. They knew *me*. Josh had shown them my picture. They knew who I was."

"So what happened?"

"Well, Bao ran off right from the start like I was the bogeyman. Choua kept at me, even though it was obvious she was ticked off that I showed up there. She assumed I'd been snooping around. Her attitude and demeanor are the kinds of stuff I see when someone is guilty of something and is afraid of being found out."

"So what did she say?"

"Well, nothing I don't already know. And she's adamant that I not talk to Bao. Seriously, Trace, she acted like Josh had done no great favor in killing the man who had abused her. Or taking the blame for her because she did it. She acted like she has something to hide."

"So did you follow her home or something?"

"No. I went to tell Sgt. Pendleton what happened."

"Was he mad that you talked to her?"

"Not really. He was preoccupied with the mud he found on Joshua's tires and on his shoes."

"Mud?" Trace gave her the same look she knew she had given Pendleton.

"There's mud and twigs in the treads of Joshua's car tires and in a pair of his shoes. It's relatively fresh. When Pendleton asked Josh about it this morning, Josh said he had gone to a lake the day he confessed to think and pray. But he said he couldn't remember which lake it was. And the crime lab says the mud had been in the tread longer than a day."

"So?"

"So Josh is lying about when he went to the lake. Plus, it doesn't seem likely he would forget which lake he had gone to. So he's lying about that too. Pendleton thinks it's where Josh *really* got rid of the gun."

Trace sat back. "You know, this is why I enjoy being an artist. I make up my own truth."

Rachael smiled at him. McKenna kicked her little legs in Rachael's lap and made a gurgling sound of contentment.

"I'm really sorry I lost track of time today, Trace."

"Knock it off, Rach," Trace said while grinning.

She leaned into him, and Trace put an arm around her.

"Hey, I got a call from Calvin this afternoon before the dictator awoke and the civilized world capitulated to her haughty demands."

Rachael elbowed him. "Okay, okay. So he must've gotten your email. What did he say?"

"Well, he said first of all that he'll be praying for Josh and for you and for you to call him if you need anything."

"Nice guy."

"Yep. About your question, he said that throughout history God has had a special interest in the care of widows and orphans. It's not just in the book of James."

"Yes, I discovered that this morning too."

"Calvin said he thinks it's because of a couple key reasons. One being that widows and orphans, especially in biblical times, were the most vulnerable of all people. And it wasn't just that they had to worry about getting food, clothing and shelter, but they also had to battle loneliness, and survive without an inheritance. He also said since God is spoken of as our Father, and Christ, the bridegroom of the church, there are metaphorical reasons why we should take note. Orphans are fatherless and widows have no husbands. Calvin says we are just like them when we don't have God. You know, just as needy, just as vulnerable, just as broken."

"Wow. That's really good," Rachael whispered as the imagery filled her mind.

"I knew you'd like that."

"About James 1:27 then, how does that verse fit with all of this?"

"Calvin said that 'pure and faultless' means 'unmixed and clean,' you know, like a pure solution that's in a clean container. Pure water in a clean cup, for example. He said the word 'religion' is typically defined as the practice of reaching up to God. So if we want to reach up to God, we need to be unmixed and clean, I guess, and take care of the people who we are most like when we're without God."

"That's heavy," Rachael replied, shaking her head.

"Yep."

Rachael sat still for several long moments, letting the idea move across her heart and brain. This was Josh's greatest desire: to reach up to God the way God reached out to him, by loving and caring for the most defenseless of people.

"Oh and there's one more thing," Trace said. "Calvin said don't forget the instruction in James 1:27 is twofold. It's not just the care of widows and orphans that constitutes a religion that God will accept. There's the other half."

Rachael looked up at Trace as the rest of the verse filled her ears and spilled out of her mouth, "To keep oneself unpolluted by the world."

"That too."

"Unpolluted by the world…" Rachael murmured. "Trace, did Calvin say what he thought that meant?"

"Well, I didn't ask him to elaborate. To me I guess it means not getting sucked up in the whole 'live any way you please' thing."

"Like choosing to ignore the laws of God?" Rachael said as a notion began to blossom in her head.

"Well, I guess you, being a lawyer and all, could say it that way."

"I've got to find a way to get Josh to listen to me," Rachael said. "He's lying, Trace. About a number of things. He's *lying*. I don't need to tell you lying is one of the big ones. You know what that means?"

"He's ignoring the law of God?" Trace said, reciting her own words.

"That's right. He's been sold on that verse from James since he was twelve. If he's really the same guy he was when he made that vow, he can't do this."

"But he already is."

"Because no one has called him on it. He's always been kind of a loner Christian, doing his own thing, living his own way, under the authority of no one. I need to find someone who can remind him of what he promised. And that he doesn't get to make the rules."

"Where are you going to find someone like that?"

Rachael sighed. For the first time in her life she wished that traveling evangelist who had changed Josh's life forever was a close friend. Josh would listen to *that* man. "I don't know. If I thought Josh would listen to him, I'd fly Calvin out here to talk to him."

"What about that John guy at the teen center?"

Rachael shook her head. "I don't think Josh thinks of him as a spiritual leader. They're probably the same age. It needs to be someone he respects."

The intercom rang at that moment, and Trace stood to answer it because Fig was in the bathroom. The curry had arrived.

Rachael stood and held McKenna close to her, inhaling her sweet fragrance. *What to do, what to do? Who would Josh listen to?* She pondered as Trace opened the front door and yelled to Fig that their food had arrived. There was perhaps one person who might be able to help her. Nana would have been ideal, but Nana was in heaven. Perhaps the minister from the church they grew up in could assist her. She was fairly certain he was still at the church her parents attended. He had been Josh's pastor during that pivotal time in his life. Maybe Josh had confided in him. She seemed to recall Josh talking to Reverend Albers about what had happened to him under the tent on a starry April night.

It was worth a try.

The aroma of spicy Indian food wafted over to her, and she made her way into the kitchen with McKenna in her arms.

As soon as supper was over, she'd call her parents and ask them to stop by and get her after they visited Joshua on Saturday. She'd spend Saturday night with them and attend her childhood church the following morning.

Someone had to break through to Josh. Someone had to force him to see that he was actually breaking the vow he cherished more than his own life.

TWENTY-TWO

Rachael awoke Thursday morning to the sound of light drizzle outside the guest room window. Trace had worked in Fig's studio well into the night, and she wasn't sure when he'd come to bed. Now she lay quietly next to him, enjoying the coziness of the feather mattress until McKenna began to stir. Rachael arose, grabbed some clothes and her daughter, and tiptoed out of the room so Trace could sleep. After a quick diaper change on the rug in the bathroom, Rachael headed with McKenna into the kitchen.

Fig had already left the loft, to her surprise, though it was not even eight o'clock. He had made coffee and left a carton of Krispy Kreme doughnuts on the island countertop. There was a note taped to the green-and-white box: *Best if nuked a bit.*

McKenna was anxious for breakfast, so Rachael looked away from both the promise of imported coffee and the delicate sweetness of doughnuts. She slid into one of the overstuffed chairs in Fig's living room to feed her daughter.

While McKenna nursed, Rachael mentally planned what she could do that day. With regard to Josh, there was really nothing she *could* do. There was no point in going back to Frogtown. And no point in going to see Josh either. Besides, he had his psych eval today and would be busy.

On top of all that, she had promised Trace he could work all day today if he needed to. And she guessed he probably did.

The previous night Trace had suggested as he ate his *naan* that Rachael look up a college or grad school friend to spend the day with. She had immediately declined. Her closest friends hadn't stayed in the Twin Cities, and acquaintances would surely be working. And she really had no desire to discuss the reason she was in town with people she only communicated with at Christmas.

When McKenna was satisfied, Rachael placed her on a blanket and turned on the TV to the weather channel. For some reason McKenna liked the blue hues of the satellite maps and the smiling faces of the well-dressed meteorologists. She would be content to lie there and watch the screen change colors for a good thirty minutes.

Rachael returned to the kitchen, poured herself a cup of coffee, and lifted a doughnut out of the box, opting not to warm it up. She tore it in half and took a bite out of one end, wondering how her visit with Reverend Albers would go Sunday after church. When she'd called her parents the night before, they had quickly agreed to pick her up Saturday after visiting Josh. And her mother had informed her that Reverend Albers was still at the Methodist church they had attended as a family.

Eva had been curious to know why Rachael wanted to talk with him.

"I just want to talk with him about Josh," Rachael had answered.

"About why he's in jail?"

"No. I want to ask him if Josh ever talked to him about what happened when that traveling evangelist came to town."

"Oh. That." Eva's voice was flat. She changed the subject and asked Rachael what she would like to have for dinner Saturday night.

Rachael had said anything would be fine, amazed anew that her mother never liked to look back. She finished the doughnut, refilled her coffee cup and then checked to make sure McKenna was happy and safe. Rachael settled onto the sofa. Maybe she and McKenna could spend the day walking the enormous square footage of the Mall of America. She had brought no work with her, no books, and no journals—not even her address book. The next two days were going to be slow going if she didn't at least get a few books to read.

She whispered a prayer that Josh's evaluation would go well that day. But then she stopped. She had no idea how she wanted God to answer that one.

By Friday afternoon, Rachael still hadn't heard anything from Maggie Fielding.

"That probably means she learned nothing monumental," Trace said to her as he sat at Fig's dining room table and checked his email.

"Which must mean Josh is okay mentally," Rachael said as she burped McKenna.

"And that's what you've said all along," Trace replied, looking up at her.

Rachael paced with McKenna over her shoulder. "I know. I guess I hoped the psychologist would find a little chink in the armor somewhere. Something that would cast doubts on Josh's recollection of what happened."

Rachael stopped pacing. She abruptly handed McKenna to Trace. "Here. Take her a sec. I'm just going to call her myself."

She walked over to her purse, which was hanging on the back of one of the bar stools, and reached in for her cell phone and Maggie's card. A couple minutes later she was put through to the public defender.

"Maggie, it's Rachael Flynn. I'm sorry to bother you, but I was wondering how Josh's evaluation went yesterday."

"Well, I'm on my way to court so I can't talk long, but really, there isn't much to tell you. The doctor gave a clean eval with no red flags. I haven't seen the finished report, but the psychologist said your brother appeared to be well in control of his mental faculties. He was a little aloof, but some people are like that. It's not a crime or a sign of illness to be standoffish."

"Yeah, except Josh isn't normally that way. He's usually very personable, Maggie."

"That's probably because he's never killed a man before. I've got to tell you, Rachael, he's showing what I usually see as genuine remorse."

"I don't believe it." Rachael's voice was firm.

"I know you don't. But look at what we've got. On one side we've got a confession, witnesses, and a dead man. On the other side we've got your intuition and a missing floor mat. I don't need to tell which side is going to stand up in court."

"Please don't give up yet," Rachael pleaded.

"I don't give up, Rachael. But I also don't hold out hope where it doesn't seem to exist. Your brother said he killed a man. He did finally agree to let me represent him. But Rachael, he wants to waive his right to a trial. Unless you have evidence that clears him or you can get him to change his plea, we don't have a whole lot of options."

"Okay. But I'm not done with this," Rachael said.

"More power to you! Call me if you find out anything that will stand up in front of a judge. I've gotta go."

"I will. Thanks, Maggie."

"You bet."

The line went silent.

Rachael clicked it off and tossed the phone back into her purse. She walked back to Trace and lifted McKenna out of his arms.

"So?" he said.

"So Josh isn't crazy."

"You knew that already."

Rachael pulled out a chair across from Trace and sat down. McKenna began to ogle the chandelier above the table. "He's going to hang himself on this, Trace."

"If he does, it's his own doing, Rach. You're doing everything humanly possible to loosen the noose. But if he really wants to hang, I don't know that you can stop him."

"It's not over yet," she said quietly.

Trace studied her for a moment, resting his chin in his upturned hand. "May I change the subject?"

Rachael shrugged.

"I want to run an idea by you. And I want you to promise you will think it over before you respond."

"What is it?" she asked.

"Promise first."

Rachael leaned back in her chair, and McKenna gurgled at the chandelier. "Okay, I promise."

"Okay. I got an email today from my agent. You remember that proposal I sent to the Mayo Clinic?"

Rachael vaguely remembered Trace preparing a portfolio of sketches of the human body for a medical publication. It was right about the time McKenna was due. She had been a little distracted by pre-labor discomfort. "Yes," she said.

"They want me on the project, Rachael. And it's a big one. Really big."

"Really? That's great, Trace! What's there to talk about?"

"It's going to keep McKenna in diapers for a long time. I'll be working almost solely on this contract for quite a while."

"Okay."

"It would be really nice to live closer to Mayo than New York."

Rachael finally understood. Trace was suggesting they move back to Minnesota. "You want to move? To Rochester?"

Trace paused. "Not necessarily Rochester. We could live here in Minneapolis. It's only an hour's drive to Mayo from here."

Rachael didn't know how to respond. It had been Trace's idea to move to New York in the first place. She had initially resisted, but he convinced her. Five years had passed, and she had since grown very fond of Manhattan. She had a job there. They had a home. And friends.

"Wow, Trace. I can't believe you're thinking of doing this!"

"I know it's a big change, Rach, but it's not like we're obligated to live in one place and never move. We aren't tied to New York."

"But that's where my job is."

"You can be a lawyer in any state you please. And Rachael, you told me you really only want part-time hours when you go off maternity leave. You told me you're not even sure the firm will give them to you. Besides, I make more than enough for you to be able to stay home for a while with McKenna. You don't have to rush to go back. And we could sublet the apartment in Manhattan so that we can go back to New York if we don't like it here."

"I'm just so surprised," Rachael said.

"I'm thinking it might be good for your family too, Rach. No matter what happens with Josh, it's going to be a tough road ahead for your parents. I know they were a little upset with me for shuttling you off to New York, and now that they have a granddaughter, I'm sure they really wish we had stayed."

Rachael had to admit the thought of being close to home was comforting in many ways. But quitting her job? Moving? Finding a new place to live? Those were big changes.

"I don't know, Trace. It's so sudden," she said.

"We don't have to decide today. But I noticed there are available lofts in the building down the street that's being renovated. Fig told me they're getting snatched up fast. If we like them and want one, we'll want to move on it quickly."

"Down the street? So you want to live downtown?"

Trace cocked his head. "You know I'm addicted to city life, Rachael. I'd expire in the suburbs. Besides, Fig's studio downstairs is huge. I could share the rent with him and actually have an office to call my own."

"You sound like you've already talked this over with Fig," she said, narrowing her eyes.

"Fig doesn't know I got this contract," Trace said, pointing to his laptop. "But I told him it was out there and that I stood a good chance of getting it. It was his idea to share the studio. It makes sense, Rachael."

"But..."

"Look, I can check out the loft tomorrow when you're with your parents. If it's a dud, we'll put off the decision for a little while. But if it's a keeper, I want to do something about it on Monday. Does that sound okay?"

McKenna wiggled in her arms and cooed. Rachael had pushed back the thought of going back to her full-time job for weeks. The truth was, the mere thought of leaving McKenna for nine to ten hours every day prickled her. Change she could handle, hour upon hour of separation from her daughter she didn't think she could.

"Well, why don't we just go look at the building right now? Just to look?"

Trace winked at her and clicked out of his email inbox. "I'll get my shoes."

TWENTY-THREE

Eva and Cliff Harper arrived at Fig's apartment a few minutes before noon on Saturday, and Fig insisted on taking everyone out to lunch at his favorite Italian restaurant.

Over linguini and clams, Rachael announced to her parents that Trace had just landed a major contract with the Mayo Clinic and that they were thinking of moving back to Minneapolis, at least for awhile.

Eva's tears were instant and joyful. Cliff too seemed genuinely delighted.

"That's wonderful, Trace. Congratulations!" Cliff said, shaking Trace's hand. "You know there isn't a better place to raise a family than the Midwest."

"I just couldn't be happier," Eva said. "This is coming at such... such a good time. With everything else, it's so wonderful that something *good* is happening." Eva leaned down to gaze at McKenna sitting in her carrier on the chair next to her. "So wonderful."

"Well, it's not a done deal yet, we're still thinking it over," Trace cautioned. "We did look at a loft yesterday down the street from Fig's place. An old warehouse is undergoing the most marvelous restoration. The lofts there are going to be stunning."

"A loft?" Cliff said.

"A warehouse?" Eva echoed.

"Mom, they're lovely," Rachael interjected. "Just like Fig's place. Very nice. And very safe. And Trace will be able to work in Fig's studio. He's got tons of room."

"It's true," Fig said, waving a breadstick.

"So you're going to live downtown? With a baby?"

"Well, if we do this, it's not like she'll be riding her bike in the streets, Mom. It might only be for a year or two."

Eva looked thoughtful for a moment. Then she shrugged. "Well, I guess it's your decision."

"It will be fine, really, Mom," Rachael said.

"Of course," Eva said. "Of course it will. You'll be here! I can't tell you how much that means to me now that…I mean since Josh…" but she didn't finish.

A moment of awkward silence hovered over their table.

"Did you have a good visit with Josh today, Mom?" Rachael asked tentatively.

Eva stuck her fork into her pasta and toyed with the noodles. "I don't know. Was it a good visit, Cliff?" She looked up at her husband.

Cliff wiped his lips with his napkin. Then he opened his mouth as if to say something but quickly shut it. A vein in his neck wiggled under the weight of restrained emotion.

"I'm sorry," Rachael said. "We don't have to talk about this right now."

Her father looked away, and his eyes were glassy. Eva put down her fork.

"He told us he loved us. That was good," Eva said in a voice that seemed almost childlike.

"Mom, really. We don't have to talk about this now."

"He told us he never meant to hurt us. That he wanted us to know we'd been wonderful parents to him. The best." Eva laughed. It was a panicky laugh. There was nothing comical about it.

"Mom."

"No, it's okay. He said some wonderful things, didn't he, Cliff?"

Rachael turned to face her dad. He was still staring off into nowhere.

"But…" Eva stopped mid-sentence and looked down at her plate. Two tears slipped out from her eyes and fell into her pasta.

Rachael felt Trace's hand on hers under the table. "Mom, let's just talk about something else, okay?" she said.

Eva ignored her. "But when he was done saying all those nice things, he told us he wanted us to just let him go."

"Eva." Cliff did not look at his wife. He said her name but kept his eyes on the moving lunchtime bustle of the restaurant.

"He told us we didn't have to come see him anymore," Eva continued, speaking to no one in particular.

"Eva!" Cliff's tone was quiet but intense.

"He told us just to let him go. Let him go. Like he was dead."

"Eva! Stop it!" Cliff turned to face her, his face a shade of angry red.

Eva reached up to her eyes with her napkin and dabbed at them. She sighed heavily, shaking her head like she was declining something. "Okay. I've stopped." Her voice was tight, on the edge of disintegrating.

Rachael felt heat rising in her own cheeks. Several people at other tables had turned when her father yelled.

The silence that followed was fat with discomfort.

"Okay, so we've had a tense moment, and now the moment has passed," Fig said cheerfully. "Now we move on to other things. Like dessert. I, for one, never leave this place without a dish of spumoni."

Cliff placed his napkin back in his lap. "I don't care much for ice cream," he said quietly.

"Then it's tiramisu for you, Cliff. You must try it or you're paying. Waiter!" Fig exclaimed, looking for their server.

Rachael squeezed Trace's hand. Thank goodness for Fig.

It had been a long time since Rachael had been in her childhood home without Josh or Trace with her. So very long that it seemed odd, uncomfortable. She felt out of place without Trace there and incomplete without Josh. She clung to McKenna until her father begged to be able to hold her.

"I'm okay with you helping me in the kitchen today, Rachael," Eva said. "I promise I won't kick you out tonight."

Rachael laughed uneasily. "You didn't kick me out the other night!"

"Yes, I did. But I'm not going to tonight. C'mon. Let's let Grandpa have his little girl to himself for a while. You can help me peel the potatoes."

Rachael followed her mother into the kitchen and washed her hands. Eva handed her a paring knife and a russet.

They stood at the sink and began to remove the potato skins.

For some reason Rachael suddenly wondered if this was something her mother had done with Nana: stand at a sink and peel potatoes together. Nana had been on her mind a lot the last few days. She wondered if her mother's thoughts flew to Nana from time to time. She decided to ask.

"Mom, did you do this with Nana? Peel potatoes with her?"

Eva laughed. "What kind of a question is that?"

Rachael smiled sheepishly. "You know, did you help her in the kitchen?"

"What daughter doesn't? Before you know it, McKenna will be in the kitchen with you."

For several seconds there was only the sound of scraping, of flesh against metal.

"I miss Nana," Rachael said a moment later. "A lot."

"Yes. I do too." Her mother's voice sounded far away.

"Especially now with what has happened to Josh," Rachael added gently.

Eva said nothing and Rachael continued.

"She seemed to understand Josh. It was like they...*clicked*. I suppose it's because they were both so connected to God. Nothing Josh did ever surprised her. And the rest of us were always finding ourselves surprised by what Josh did."

Rachael laughed and looked at her mother. Eva's face was expressionless.

Rachael was probably saying too much, but she didn't care. She had wanted to have this conversation with her mother for a long time. The opportunity was suddenly before her. They weren't often alone like this.

"Mom, were you close to Nana?"

Eva placed a peeled potato in a bowl and grabbed another one. "You're just full of questions tonight," she said evenly.

"Yes, I guess I am."

Eva began to whack at the potato in her hand. "Nana and I didn't see eye to eye on everything, Rachael, you know that. But I loved her, if that's what you mean."

"What didn't you see eye to eye on? May I ask?"

"You just did."

Rachael waited.

"Nana was...Nana had this vision of who she wanted me to be. What she wanted me to be like. What she wanted me to do with my life. She wanted me to be a missionary and sail away to Africa when I graduated from high school. She had all these unmet dreams for herself that she wanted *me* to fulfill. Well, I wouldn't do it."

"Why did Nana have all those unmet dreams? I mean, if she had wanted to be a missionary, why didn't she become one?"

Eva turned to her. "Because she fell in love with a cattle farmer, that's why. After she married my father, she prayed to God to give her a dozen kids to send out as missionaries in her place as penance for falling in love with a man who would never step foot on an airplane."

"And they only had you," Rachael said.

"They only had me."

The two women were silent for a moment. "She never quite got over the fact that I liked a quiet life and a quiet faith," Eva finally said. "I was like my father. She wanted me to be like her."

"I'm sorry, Mom. I didn't know it was that way."

"Of course you didn't. She never told you that. She never actually said it to me. I could just sense it in everything she said to me and in everything she didn't say."

Rachael placed her potato in the bowl and took up another.

Eva continued. "But I don't want you thinking I didn't love my mother, Rachael, because I did. I was actually in awe of her and her faith in God. I really was."

"I was too," Rachael whispered. "She seemed like she was always just one step away from heaven."

"She loved you kids something fierce," Eva said. "And you're right. She did understand Joshua. And I know why she did. They were just like each other. They were both tuned in to some secret frequency reserved for people with a special 'in' with God."

Rachael knew her mother wasn't trying to be comical, but she laughed lightly.

"She used to pray over my bed when I stayed at the farmhouse," Rachael said a second later, wondering too late if she was divulging too much.

"She prayed over mine when I was little too, Rachael. Every night."

Rachael reached for the last potato. "Did she know what happened to Josh at that tent meeting?"

Eva set her peeler down and began to stuff the skins into the drain. "I told her."

"You did?"

"Yes."

"Well, what did she say?"

"She was hesitant at first because she didn't know the guy who had laid his hands on Josh." Eva overemphasized the word *hands* and shook her head. "And it had been three years since it happened. No one remembered the guy's name, not even Josh. But then she told me that if it was the real deal, if God really had touched Josh in a special way, then the passion in him would grow, not dissipate. And if it was real, then I wouldn't be able to do anything about it."

Eva switched on the faucet and flipped the switch on the garbage disposal. The peels disappeared in a grinding splash of water and power. She flipped the switch back and turned the water off.

"And mother was right," Eva continued as if there had been no lull. "The passion grew. And there was nothing I could do about it."

The two were quiet for a moment as they began to quarter the potatoes.

"Josh *did* talk to Reverend Albers about what happened, didn't he?" Rachael inquired, not looking up from the cutting board. "I mean, there is a point to my talking to him tomorrow, isn't there?"

"He talked to him. But only because I asked him to," her mother answered.

"And what did Reverend Albers say?"

Eva threw a handful of quartered potatoes into a pan of water. "I don't know. Josh never told me. And I never asked because deep down I knew it was too late. He had waited almost three years to tell us what had happened to him. He was already convinced that whatever that preacher told him was true."

Rachael said nothing more. She couldn't tell her mother she had known all along what had happened to Josh. Her brother hadn't specifically asked her to keep it a secret, but she did anyway. She had assumed if she said nothing, he would outgrow it.

McKenna began to cry in the other room.

Rachael excused herself and left.

It was obvious to Rachael that having McKenna at church on Sunday made it easier for her parents to attend. She doubted they would have come had she not been with them. News had traveled fast in a week's time. After the media coverage in the papers and on TV, there weren't many people in the church who didn't know that Joshua Harper, a former member, had confessed to killing a man in St. Paul.

There were sympathetic nods and hugs, but gossipers too. Rachael was also glad McKenna was there to provide a distraction from the whispers, the looks, and the wide-eyed stares.

She and her parents hung back after the service, partly to avoid having to discuss the situation with both the well meaning and the overly curious and partly so that Rachael could speak to Reverend Albers in private.

When she told her parents she wanted to talk to the pastor alone for a few minutes, neither her mother nor her father seemed to care. It mattered to Rachael though. She didn't know if Reverend Albers would remember the conversation he had with Josh ten years earlier, but if he did, he might know that Rachael knew about Josh's encounter with the traveling evangelist long before her parents did. She didn't want her parents to have to contend with that knowledge on top of everything else.

When the foyer was nearly empty and most of the congregation had gone out to their cars and the lure of Sunday brunch, Rachael and her parents ventured to where the reverend waited to greet his congregation on their way out. They made sure they were last.

The pastor extended his arms to them, wrapping Eva in a hug and patting Cliff on the back. "I want you to know I'm here for you," he said kindly. "Whatever I can do, I will do. I'm praying for you all."

"Thank you, Reverend," Cliff said.

"Reverend Albers, you remember our daughter, Rachael," Eva said.

"Yes, of course. How wonderful to have you here this morning, Rachael."

"Thank you."

"And this is your baby girl?"

"Yes. This is McKenna."

"Why, she's just precious."

Rachael handed McKenna to her mother. "Reverend Albers, could I have just a moment of your time?"

"Certainly."

"We'll be in the car," Cliff said, and he and Eva walked away.

"Would you like to sit down?" Reverend Albers asked, pointing to a row of chairs in the foyer.

"No, thank you," Rachael said. "I just need to ask you a question. About Josh."

Reverend Albers waited for her to continue.

"Reverend, my brother came to you ten years ago and told you that something significant happened to him," Rachael said. "Do you remember that day?"

"Well, yes. Actually I do."

"Do you remember him telling you that a traveling evangelist laid his hands on him and told him God had selected him to spend the rest of his life fleshing out James 1:27?"

"To care for orphans and widows in their distress, yes, I remember. I had never had a fifteen-year-old say something like that to me."

"Do you remember what you told him?"

"Well, I recall that I told him that verse is for everyone. That I was very happy to hear him say he wanted to obey God's Word because we all need to do that."

"And what did he say?"

"Oh, something to the effect that it was different for him. That he was to do that and *only* that. He told me he wasn't going to go to college or get married or have a family because he had been called out to care for widows and orphans."

"And you said?"

"Well, I think I told him he didn't have to give up going to college or having a wife and family in order to care for widows and orphans.

I think I said he could serve them in any number of wonderful ways with a college degree, and that a wife could serve right along with him."

Rachael waited for him to continue.

"But he said he had been given a message from God that he could not ignore. I asked him who gave him the message. And he said an evangelist did. And I said, 'How do you know the evangelist got it right? God speaks perfectly but we don't always hear perfectly. Maybe the evangelist didn't hear it right.'

"I think about then he was starting to get a little angry with me. I asked him how your parents felt about what he wanted to do, and he said they weren't too happy. I reminded him that the Bible says to honor your parents; that God gave *that* command before the one to care for widows and orphans. But he just quoted that verse from Matthew that says 'He that loves his father or mother more than me is not worthy of me.'

"I could tell we were getting nowhere, so I asked if I could pray with him and he said no and left. He avoided me after that. And of course, three years later, he left St. Cloud and this church."

Rachael sighed. It was highly unlikely Josh would listen to an admonition from this man of the cloth.

"May I ask why you're asking me this?" Reverend Albers said.

Rachael sighed. "It doesn't matter now. I'm just trying to help Josh see things clearly. I think he's covering for someone, Reverend. I don't think he shot that man. I think he's covering for the young girl who did. She's an orphan."

"Would it help if I talked to him?"

She smiled at him. The reverend was a good man. "You're sweet to offer, but I don't think it will do any good."

"You know, if I remember correctly, your brother was always extremely fond of you, Rachael. Maybe you should talk to him."

"I've tried," she said, looking down at her feet.

"Try again."

She looked up and the reverend was smiling at her. "Thanks, I will."

She started to walk away.

"Rachael," the reverend called out and she turned to face him. "Go in peace."

Rachael lingered for just a moment as the benediction fell on her and seemed to swirl about her body. Then she turned and walked out.

TWENTY-FOUR

Cliff drove Rachael back to Minneapolis after lunch but declined to come in and visit with Trace and Fig before heading back to St. Cloud. He helped her inside the lobby with McKenna's carrier, diaper bag, and her overnight suitcase.

"You can go, Dad," Rachael said as she pressed the intercom for Fig's loft. "You don't need to come up with me. You're double-parked."

A voice crackled across the intercom. "Trace here."

"It's just me and McKenna, Trace," Rachael said into the speaker.

"Welcome home."

A buzzer sounded at the double doors in front of them, and Cliff grabbed the handle, opening a door wide and bracing it with his body so Rachael could step in.

"Really, I'll be fine, Dad. I've got it."

"All right." Cliff bent down and kissed McKenna's forehead as she lay wide-eyed in her carrier. Then he leaned forward and kissed Rachael on the cheek.

"I'll call you guys later this week, okay?"

Cliff nodded. "Let us know how that loft thing turns out. Make sure you read the fine print."

"I will. Thanks for the ride."

Cliff nodded and stepped away. The door clicked shut and Rachael pressed the button for the elevator. Her father waited on the other side of the glass with his hands in his pockets until the elevator doors swished open and she stepped inside.

She waved goodbye to him and he nodded. The doors closed.

Moments later the elevator doors opened again and on the other side stood Trace. "It was getting pretty lonely around here," he said, kissing her as she stepped out of the elevator.

Trace grabbed the overnight bag and McKenna's carrier. "So how did it go?" he asked as he put his arm around Rachael and led her into the loft. He shut the door behind them and helped her take off her jacket.

"Well, my mom and I had a good talk—one that I've wanted to have for a while."

"Okay."

"But I don't think Reverend Albers will be able to help me get through to Joshua. They didn't part on the best of terms. Josh was kind of ticked at him for minimizing his encounter with that evangelist—who I sometimes wish I could strangle!"

Rachael bent down and lifted McKenna out of her carrier. Trace reached for her.

"Let me have her," he said. "I've missed my little dictator." Trace nuzzled his face into McKenna's neck, and she rewarded him with a gurgle of delight.

Rachael sank down into the couch, and Trace plopped down next to her.

"So I guess Reverend Albers isn't going to be your prophet of God then?" he said.

"No."

They were silent for a moment as McKenna kicked her legs against Trace's chest.

"Why don't *you* just tell him?" Trace said. "You said it had to be someone your brother respects. I can't think of anyone he respects more than you, Rachael."

Rachael leaned into Trace, and he placed his head against hers.

"I'm afraid it will close some kind of door if I confront him with this. If I'm the one to accuse him of failing to live out his mighty call of God, he'll probably shut me out completely."

"But you're only going to accuse him of failing *half* of it. He's done a pretty admirable job of taking care of the needy, wouldn't you say? It's just the other half he seems to be ignoring at the moment."

Rachael sighed. "It's just so weird, Trace. Josh has never been what I would call a liar. I mean, a liar is someone who lies. Josh doesn't do that. He is *lying* to the police. Even Pendleton thinks Josh is lying about some of this."

Trace was thoughtful for a moment. "I think you should just go to the jail tomorrow, sit down in front of your brother, and command him to tell you to your face that he killed that man. You told me Josh has never lied to you. Make him say it to your face. If you're right about him, Rach, he won't be able to do it."

Rachael pondered Trace's words. "Okay, so what if he says absolutely nothing in return? What if I ask him to say it to my face, and he says nothing back at all? Or what if he says something like 'You read the police report, you heard my confession.'"

"Isn't that kind of like saying he did it?"

"Not in court, it's not. I would be no better off than I am right now except Josh would tune me out for good. I wish I had just one insight that I could play against him."

"You could tell him you talked to Choua."

"No. She was absolutely no help to me at all. She's lying too. He'd probably be quite relieved to hear she's sticking to the game plan."

"You could ask him about the floor mat. Or the mud. Make him think the police are beginning to doubt his story."

"Maybe. I just wish I had something with more bite to it. I know

I'm missing something huge. I keep going back to the drawings you and Fig and the others did, and I know I'm missing something huge."

"That reminds me," Trace said, rising from the couch and placing McKenna in Rachael's arms. "Fig drew another one for you last night."

"Another what?" she said as Trace walked over to the island counter in the kitchen.

"Another personification of evil."

Trace came back with a piece of sketchpad paper in his hand. Rachael took it from him. In ink this time Fig had drawn a hooded figure hovering over the basement like a Tolkien ring wraith. Its skeletal fingers were pointed at three cowering people as if to impose its dark will on them. A fourth person lay dead at their feet. One of the bony fingers was emitting smoke from its tip, as if to suggest it had pulled the trigger.

"Ugh. This is gross!" Rachael said, tossing the drawing onto the coffee table.

"Fig was bored last night. I worked until midnight in his studio. He stopped long before me."

"Well, it's still ridiculous. And it's not going to help me."

"Don't tell him you hate it. He'll take it personally," Trace said, sitting back down next to her and taking McKenna back.

"But it doesn't help me!" Rachael reiterated. "A minion of hell didn't pull the trigger. There was no dark force controlling the events in that room! There were just four people, and two of them couldn't have done it. Thao didn't shoot himself, and I know Bao didn't do it, so that just leaves..." but Rachael's voice fell away.

"That leaves Josh and the other girl," Trace offered.

"Yes...unless..." Rachael paused for a moment. Then she sat up straight. "Oh my goodness, Trace." Rachael exclaimed, and she snatched up Fig's newest drawing. "Do you see what this is?"

Trace blinked. "It's a gross picture that can't help you?"

Rachael stared at the drawing. "It's what I've been missing all along. It's why nothing fits!" she said more to herself than to Trace.

"Okay. So now you think the Grim Reaper *did* do it?"

Rachael looked up at him, her face flush with discovery. "Trace, this implies there was a fifth person in the room. What if there *was* a fifth person?"

"Yeah, but that's a...whatever *that* is," Trace said, pointing to the specter-like creature.

Rachael looked down at the drawing again. "It wouldn't have been a demon, Trace. It would've been human. A man or a woman. Or maybe even another teenager."

Trace looked at the drawing. "Well, what would that fifth person have done? You think that fifth person killed Thao?"

"No. I don't know. Maybe."

Trace sighed. "This just makes it more complicated."

"Trace, it already is complicated! It's so complicated we're missing the truth! Where's Fig?"

"Fig?"

"Yes, where is he?"

"He's out having coffee with Jillian."

"Can you call him on his cell phone?"

"Well, sure. You change your mind about the drawing? Want to tell him you like it?"

"I want you guys to try again. I want you and Fig and Brick and Sidney to try again!"

"Try again?"

"I want you guys to do what you did before. Draw the crime scene as it could've happened. But this time I want you to pretend there was a fifth person."

"Doing what?"

Rachael stood up. "Doing whatever your artistic brains tell you. You guys are the creative minds, not me. Where's my purse?"

"Right there by the chair."

Rachael reached inside her purse for her cell phone. "Here," she said, handing it to Trace and taking McKenna. "Ask Fig if we can do that. Ask him if he can call Brick and Sidney."

Trace took the phone from her. "You're really convinced there was someone else in the room, aren't you?"

Rachael nodded. "Yes."

Trace shrugged. "How come?"

Rachael couldn't explain how she knew someone else had been in the basement. There was nothing in the police report to suggest there had been a fifth person. The witness on the fire escape hadn't seen anyone else enter the basement. But Rachael quickly reminded herself that woman had been shaking out a rug, not sitting on a deck chair enjoying the sights and sounds of Frogtown at night.

Rachael had no idea what role the fifth person played. If that person had pulled the trigger, then it was obviously someone Josh was trying to protect. If that person didn't, then he or she surely knew who did.

The plain truth was, she knew in her heart that someone else had been there.

"Rachael?" Trace said.

"I can't explain it, Trace. I just know it. There were five people."

The aroma of freshly brewed coffee filled Fig's kitchen and open dining area as the artists fanned out in the room.

"I want the floor. I want lots of room," Brick said, "And I brought my own pencils, thank you very much."

"I'm taking the countertop here," Sidney said. "I need to be close to the coffee if I'm going to be drawing imaginary people."

"Not imaginary, Sidney," Rachael scolded as she held McKenna in her arms. "There *was* someone there. I just don't know who it was."

"Well, Tracer and I can share the dining room table," Fig said. "That way we can spread out. Alright then. I've got a list of possibilities that Rachael has made."

"But I could be way off," Rachael cautioned. "It could be someone else completely."

"Or no one," Sidney intoned.

"Sid, behave," Fig commanded. "Okay, so we've got the girls' aunt. Or a third victim—which would be another teenage girl, of course—or a vengeful relative of Thao's, or a cohort of Josh's, you know, someone who has a heart like his and an itchy trigger finger."

"I didn't say that!" Rachael exclaimed.

"Well, if he shot the guy, then he did," Fig said smugly, and he turned back to the list. "Or maybe a concerned community member—a grandma or grandpa type, or maybe an enemy Thao had. So there you go."

"Let me see the list," Brick said and Fig handed it to him.

"And if you guys don't mind, there's that missing floor mat," Rachael said. "Oh, and one more thing. Josh went to a lake, walked around, got mud in his shoes, and won't tell the police which lake he was at or which day it was. But it happened after the murder and obviously before he confessed."

"What's the deal with that?" Brick said.

"She doesn't know," Fig replied before Rachael could answer. "She wants us to take a crack at it."

Sidney turned around in his stool. "Can we have the football game on?"

Three voices called out "No!"

"A little sketching music then?" he said peevishly.

Fig walked over to his stereo. "I sketch to Enya," he announced.

Sidney whipped around in his stool. "I said *sketching* music, not sleeping music!"

"How about the jazz station, eh, Fig?" Trace said.

"Oh, all right," Fig grumbled.

A few moments later the loft was awash in brassy blues.

"Go do the baby thing," Fig said to Rachael as he returned to the dining room. "We'll call you when we're done."

Forty-five minutes later, when Rachael returned from bathing, feeding, and putting McKenna to bed, Fig told her she had not yet been summoned. Trace looked up from his sketchpad and winked at her but shooed her away too.

"Go watch a DVD in my room," Fig called out to her as she headed back to the bedrooms. "I've got everything. Even the chick flicks."

Rachael curled up in a comfy armchair in Fig's bedroom, slipped *Casablanca* into the DVD player, and waited for the artists to tell her they were finished.

But when the movie ended and they still hadn't called her, she walked into the main room of the loft and poked her head into the open dining and kitchen area. The four artists were huddled at the dining table, all whispering at once. Drawings lay across the table like giant squares of confetti.

"I'm going to bed," she said.

"Go away!' Fig said, whipping his head around.

"I said, I am going to *bed*," she repeated.

Trace broke away, walked over to her, and kissed her. "Nighty-nite." He walked with her to the entrance to the hallway.

"What are you guys doing?" she whispered.

"Oh, Fig has an idea. He's really getting into this."

"Is it some outlandish thing with Grimms' fairy tales written all over it? 'Cause if it is, it's a waste of time. I need ideas that are credible."

Trace kissed her again. "It's a good idea. But it will take awhile. Go to bed."

She lingered a moment, watching as Trace returned to the dining room.

"That means starting all over!" Sidney grumbled.

Rachael turned, walked into the guest room, and closed the door.

TWENTY-FIVE

Rachael didn't hear Trace come to bed Sunday night, nor did she hear Sidney or Brick leave. When she awoke Monday morning to the muted sounds of McKenna's first protests, Trace was sound asleep beside her. It was a few minutes after seven.

She got out of bed, grabbed the diaper bag and McKenna and tiptoed out, closing the door quietly behind her. After taking care of her own needs and changing McKenna's diaper, she wandered into the dining room to see what had kept Trace, Fig, Brick, and Sidney busy into all hours of the night.

The messy pile of sketches was gone. In its place were three black artists' portfolios, arranged in a neat row. Across the tops on blue Post-it Notes Fig had written Door #1, Door #2, and Door #3. McKenna was fussing to be fed. Reluctantly Rachael walked away from the portfolios, heaved herself into a living room armchair, and fed her daughter.

She knew she had to see Josh today. She had to confront him with one last-ditch effort to give up the charade. She made a mental list of what she'd be going in with: half a dozen unanswered questions, including the twenty-two seconds and the mud in his tires; a gut instinct that there had been a fifth person in the room; and the proclamation that Josh was failing God at the core of his commission: He had allowed himself to be polluted by the world by lying to the police. It wasn't much, but what else was there? Reverend Albers couldn't help her. Her parents couldn't. Hopefully the artists' sketches would provide some insights into the role of that fifth person, assuming of course, that her instincts were right and there actually was a fifth person.

When McKenna had her fill, Rachael placed her on a blanket on Fig's sheepskin rug, flipped on the weather channel and hurried over to the dining room table. The portfolios lay before her like scandalous invitations. She pulled out a chair, sat down, and drew the one marked Door #1 close to her. She hesitated for a moment and then opened it. A single sheet of paper lay on top of a pile of half a dozen drawings. It read: "Josh Did It."

The first two drawings that followed were Trace's original drawings. The next two were Brick's handiwork and they showed Josh's face in twenty-two frames as he waited for the girls to leave the basement. Brick had drawn the evolution of Josh's face from angry to repulsed to desperate. In the last frame, as he pulled the trigger, great tears of disgust and anguish were dripping from Josh's eyes. Rachael felt her own eyes grow moist. She flipped the page over. The next was Sidney's. He had drawn Choua with the floor mat in her hands as she made her way up the stairs. A thought bubble was drawn above her head. 'No one can ever know what happened to me here.' The last was a new one by Trace. Josh had taken the floor mat and the gun to a lake and buried them both in the soft earth near the shoreline.

It could have happened this way.

A ripple of fear ran through her. It could have. Except that Josh still had to knowingly fire a revolver into another man's head with the express intention of killing him.

And she refused to believe he could do that.

She slapped the portfolio closed and pulled the one marked "Door #2" to her. On the first page were the words, "The Girl Did It." The second page was Brick's original drawing of Choua aiming the gun. Behind it was a drawing by Trace showing Josh wrapping Choua in his arms after she fired it. Choua was in anguish. The third, by Sidney, showed Choua vomiting onto the floor mat. In the fourth, Brick drew the lake scene, where again Josh is burying the floor mat and the gun.

Rachael kept the second portfolio open and reached for the third. Inside were the words "The Fifth Person Did It." Underneath, Fig had written the words "Victim." The artists had come to the conclusion that Josh would only take the fall for someone who had been hurt greatly and deserved no more pain, which meant it had to be another girl.

The first drawing was Brick's. It showed the fifth person, the unknown girl, lying on the floor mat, crying. Josh and the two other girls had come early. They had surprised Thao. He had been beating the girl and threatening her with his gun. In the next two sketches, Trace had drawn Josh helping the girl up as he yells at Thao. Then Trace had drawn two scenes showing an argument between Thao and Josh, and another with Choua rushing at Thao, Thao losing the gun, and the two of them falling to the floor. Sidney's drawings showed Josh helping Choua to her feet, while unknown to him, Bao is handing the unknown girl the gun. Next Sidney drew the unknown girl aiming the gun at Thao, while Josh looked on in horror.

Brick's final drawings were of Josh taking the floor mat—which bore the unknown girl's blood—and the gun, and leaving the basement. The last sketch was of Josh burying both at the shore of an unnamed lake.

Rachael sat there, staring at the drawings for a long time. At some point, Trace came up behind her and began to massage her neck.

She closed her eyes. "Is McKenna okay?" she said.

Trace looked back over his shoulder. "There's a nasty storm on the Atlantic seaboard. A good map. She likes it."

Rachael nodded. Trace stopped rubbing her neck and took the chair beside her.

"Not much help, is it?" Trace said, nodding to the drawings.

"I wouldn't say that," Rachael replied. "It makes sense that Josh would dispose of the floor mat at the lake, I guess. He said he threw the gun into the river, but I can see where he might have lied about where he disposed of it. He's lying about other things."

"Well, we tried to come up with different scenarios for that fifth person, but none of them worked except creating another victimized girl. That's no different than Josh taking the fall for Choua. It's just another young girl with a name we don't know."

"I suppose."

"Fig had this one idea, but none of us liked it."

"What was it?"

"Well, it was different, Rachael. Too surreal. I don't think you would've liked it either.

"What's it of?" Rachael asked.

"Well, a man. But not anyone on your list."

Rachael felt a prickle of interest move across her. "May I see it?"

Trace shrugged. "Well, I'm sure it's in the trash. We told him to pitch it."

"Think you could find it for me?"

"Really?" Trace looked doubtful.

"I just want to see it."

"Okay." Trace got up, padded over to the kitchen trash, and started tossing out crumpled pieces of sketch paper. Rachael joined him and began smoothing them out.

"Well, this is it," Trace said a moment later, as he flattened out the creased drawing. He handed it to her.

It was only half done; there was nothing else in the picture except two figures. Fig had drawn Joshua twice, one standing next to the other. One looked sad and sickened, the other looked livid. Ready to explode.

"What's this supposed to mean?" she said.

"Fig wasn't quite sure himself. He said it was like Josh's alter ego. Like a part of him stepped out of his body and…and shot Thao."

Rachael fingered the pencil lines. Something about the drawing mesmerized her. "I think I want to keep this one," she whispered.

"Really?" Trace commented as he began putting the other crumpled-up drawings back in the trash. "Fig will be happy."

Rachael walked slowly back to the dining room table, holding the strange drawing. Something about it tugged at her.

"Want some coffee?" Trace called out.

"Sure."

"Rachael, what is it?"

She looked up at him. "I don't know, Trace. I think we're getting close, but we're just not quite there."

"You're going to go see him today?"

Rachael nodded.

"Before or after we go look at the loft again?"

"After. Who knows what kind of mood I'll be in after I talk to him."

"You going to ask him what I told you to ask him?" Trace asked.

"Yes. But I don't have any bargaining chips to get him to answer me."

Trace pulled out a brown bag of coffee beans. "You can only do what you can do."

"I know. Sometimes it just doesn't seem like it's enough." She slipped Fig's drawing into the portfolio marked Door #3 and went to rescue McKenna.

Her daughter had grown bored with the storm.

Rachael sat for ten minutes alone in the interview room waiting for Josh to be brought to her. She used the time to think and pray. And calm her nerves.

She had tried to rehearse what she was going to say to him, and every time she did, she changed the words.

No approach seemed like the best. Every tactic seemed doomed to failure.

The doorknob turned and she sat up straight. Through the tiny window she could see Josh's head and the orange hue of his collar. The door opened and a jailer showed him in.

"Hi, Josh," Rachael said as calmly and brightly as she could.

Josh looked tired. "Hey."

"You doing okay?"

He shrugged and took the chair opposite her. For a moment neither said anything.

"You want to tell me why you're here, Rachael?" His voice was kind, but the intent was to get her to get to the point and leave. She was sure of it.

"Can't you guess?" she said.

"Look, Rachael, I appreciate what you're trying to do, I do. But it's painful for me to have you come here. Okay? I'd rather you didn't."

"It's painful for me to see you here."

"Then don't come."

"You know that's impossible."

Josh leaned forward. "No, it's not. You just get back on a plane and go back to New York, Rachael. It's easy. And it's what I want."

Rachael felt a surge of anger rise up within her. "This whole thing is all about what *you* want, isn't it? You want to call all the shots. And you're going to make those girls live by *your* rules the rest of their lives! Doesn't it matter to you what you're asking them to do for you? Lie for you! I can't believe it doesn't."

"I did what I had to do," Josh said calmly.

"So you admit you are asking them to lie for you?" Rachael demanded.

"I never said that."

"But you don't deny it!"

"I can't answer for what other people do or don't do, Rachael. I can only answer for me."

Rachael leaned forward and locked her eyes onto Joshua's. In the liquid blueness she saw the little boy who had clutched the wooden baby Jesus to his chest, the boy who had run to her room to chase the demons away, the boy who had come home from a tent meeting with the light of God shining in his eyes.

"Joshua, I have never lied to you about anything," she said. "And you have never lied to me. You shared with me your deepest dreams and darkest fears. You kept nothing back from me. And I kept your secrets safe for you and never tried to turn you away from what you honestly felt was God's call on your life. And I am asking you now to tell me the truth."

Her eyes felt hot with moisture and emotion. She could sense that her hands were shaking under the table. Joshua's hardened features softened as the words left her lips. He looked away from her.

"Please don't ask me to do this, Rachael," he whispered.

"Look at me, Josh, and tell me the truth!" Rachael kept her voice as steady as she could. Her hands under the table were clenched into fists.

Josh kept his eyes off her.

"Josh, you told me when you were twelve that you made a vow before God. A vow! You told me the evangelist spoke over you the words of that verse in James. I have never forgotten those words, Joshua! I know you have given your life to caring for widows and orphans. I know the good things you have done. I know the lives you have touched. But, Joshua, that's only half of the verse. You also vowed to keep yourself unpolluted by the world. Unstained by it. Do you honestly think you can live a monstrous lie the rest of your life and not be stained?"

Still Joshua would not look at her.

"I *know* you couldn't have pointed a gun at that man's head for half a minute while those girls left the basement and got into your car. I *know* you couldn't have! And I know why you told the police you can't remember which lake you went to and why you told them you went on the day you confessed when you really went the day Thao was killed."

Josh turned to look at her, surprise etched in his face.

"That's right, Josh, I've been figuring things out. I know you probably buried the floor mat there. And maybe the gun too. And there was someone else in the basement, wasn't there? There was, wasn't there!"

Josh looked away again.

"Well, then tell me to my face I'm mistaken, Joshua!" she exclaimed. "Look at me and tell me I've got it all wrong!"

Joshua brought his hands up to his face. When he took them away a second later, he seemed to have aged. He sighed deeply and slowly opened his eyes to look at her.

"Rachael." But he stopped, closed his eyes, swallowed, and then opened them again. His eyes were on her eyes. She waited.

"I don't want to hurt you..." he began.

"Then don't," she interjected. "Just tell me the truth."

He shook his head and looked away. "That's what will hurt you," he whispered.

A rivulet of fear trickled down her spine. What did he mean?

"What are you saying?" she said.

He turned his head toward her but didn't meet her gaze. "Do you remember last week when I told you I wasn't afraid of the dark anymore?"

She opened her mouth to beg Josh to come to his senses. But all that came out of her mouth was "Yes."

"I'm not afraid of the dark anymore because I'm part of it."

He was making no sense. How could the psychologist have missed this? Josh was speaking madness.

"Joshua..."

But he went on as if she hadn't spoken his name.

"I'm no different than anyone else," he said. "No better. Worse, actually."

"Joshua, listen to me. You *are* different. In the most wonderful of ways. God has always had His hand on you. I've always known it. Nana knew it!"

He raised his eyes to hers. "Nana was wrong."

"No, she wasn't! Joshua, from the time you were little you were set apart by God. It was obvious to everybody. I have always been in awe of that."

"Then you were deceived."

"Joshua, you…" But he raised his hand to silence her.

"Rachael, listen to me. I swear to you by God Almighty, that it's true."

Blood rushed to her ears as the unthinkable began to woo her.

"What?" she whispered. "What is true?"

"I killed a man," Josh said simply. "Do you understand what I'm saying? I killed a man."

She heard the words as they fell from his mouth, but her brain refused to embrace them. She had gone over this a thousand times in her head. It was impossible.

"No," she heard herself saying.

"Yes," Josh replied in a cotton-soft voice.

"No."

"Yes, Rachael, I did. Do you hear me? I *did*."

"No!"

"You should go now," Josh said and she was aware that he had stood. "Go now, Rachael, please. Please go."

But she could only sit there and shake her head. Her body felt composed of lead.

A flash of orange in her peripheral vision told her Josh had left the room. She looked up to see his retreating form in the hallway and that of the jailer through the tiny window with the criss-crossed wires.

But for many long minutes she could not move.

When power seemed to be restored to her body, Rachael stood, left the room, and signed out of the jail. She walked out to Fig's car, unlocked it, and got inside.

She closed the door and put on her seat belt. Leaning forward onto the steering wheel, she wept.

TWENTY-SIX

The drive back to Fig's loft in Minneapolis took just twenty minutes, but to Rachael it seemed both interminably long and far too short. As she put the key into the ignition, Rachael had wanted nothing more than to distance herself from the ebb and flow of the city. She wanted to be separate from the hectic hubbub of an ordinary Monday afternoon in St. Paul. She had waited in the jail parking lot until her tears had subsided and numbness replaced them. The numbness was a defense mechanism that had allowed her to drive back to Fig's; she sensed her analytical side taking this into consideration. But the tears would begin again as soon as she saw Trace—or anyone whom she loved—so she both dreaded and longed to arrive at the loft.

What she really wanted was to be alone.

A dozen different responses to Joshua's announcement were warring inside of her, all wanting to break out at once. But only two actually materialized in the last thirty minutes: sorrow and denial. Her grief poured out of her as soon as she was inside Fig's car. Denial simply allowed her to drive home. The other responses, including raw, seething anger, she didn't want to display in front of Trace or anyone else. She wished there was a place of utter solitude where she could run to and just let the explosion come; where she could hurl her grievances at the heavens, for she was as angry with God as she was with everyone else.

As she neared Fig's street, she couldn't shake the hellish notion that God had tricked her and her brother all these years; that the joke of the ages had been played on them both; Josh foremost. A dark voice seemed to whisper in her ear that she had been a fool for believing Josh had been anointed by God for a special task, and that Josh had been one too.

A fool.

And God was laughing.

In her being she knew such a thing was inconceivable, but it weighed on her nonetheless like the icy fallout from an avalanche.

Rachael pulled into Fig's underground garage and shut the car off.

"God!" she said, and in that one-word prayer was a plea for an explanation. Illumination. Mercy. But the air around her in the car and in the garage was soundless.

She closed her eyes and the stillness of the underground began to encircle her as if to suggest that a person can be buried under stone and concrete and yet breathe. As the full weight of what she now knew settled on her, the image of Josh pulling the trigger replayed in her mind over and over.

Bang.

Bang.

Bang.

What she thought impossible was true. Josh had executed a man. A bad man, but a man nonetheless. A kneeling, unarmed man. Josh had shot and killed a man, not in a split-second burst when emotion exceeded wisdom, but in a calculated expanse of time—perhaps with twenty-two seconds at his disposal to change his mind.

He could have called the police instead of shooting Thao.

The girls begged him not to.

Since when did Josh take his orders from teenage girls?

They begged him not to let the world know what had happened to them. That vile thing that had happened to them. That hideous thing.

Josh could have called the police right after shooting Thao. Why didn't he? When Vong Thao lay dead at his feet, the moment of rage surely had passed. Why didn't Josh call the police then? Surely when the fury subsided and clarity of thought returned to him, Josh knew that what he had done was wrong.

Of course he knew it was wrong. He had proceeded to throw the gun into the river. Or a lake.

He had disposed of the murder weapon. Because that's what it was. A weapon used in the act of a murder.

Murder.

Josh had committed murder.

He was a murderer.

Rachael leaned forward and rested her head on the steering wheel as a fresh wave of grief overtook her.

"You had your hand on him," she whispered to the heavens. "You had your *hand* on him."

She waited for affirmation but none came.

If God had indeed had his hand on Joshua all these years, and she couldn't believe that God hadn't, then surely he had suddenly removed it.

"Why?" Rachael groaned. "After all Josh has done for you? Why?"

No answer.

She couldn't sit in Fig's garage forever, waiting for it. Sighing, she grabbed her purse, opened the car door, and got out. When she closed the door, the sound ricocheted off the cement walls and Rachael involuntarily grimaced. She walked to the door that would lead her to the elevator, hearing each footfall as it bounced around the cave-like room. She was inordinately glad to step across the threshold to the hall that housed the elevator. The thick carpet hushed her steps and let her feel like she could pretend she was invisible for a tiny stretch of time.

Moments later she slipped Fig's spare key into the lock, opened the loft door and walked inside. Trace, sitting on the couch with McKenna, looked up at her. Fig was seated in one of the armchairs.

"What happened?" Trace's voice was coated with concern. Rachael knew he was no mind reader. Her tear-stained face was a dead giveaway that something terrible happened at the jail.

She opened her mouth…but closed it as quickly. The corners of her lips pulled down as if yanked by a puppeteer and her eyes filled with tears. Trace stood and placed McKenna in Fig's lap. Fig too was wide-eyed with sudden apprehension. Trace closed the distance between them, placing his arms on Rachael's shoulders.

"What is it, Rach?"

Her throat felt lined with steel as she opened her mouth again. The words squeaked out of her as if forced through an opening too small for them to fit.

"Trace, he did it. Josh killed that man. Josh killed Thao."

Rachael held a cup of strong coffee, flavored with amaretto, compliments of a frazzled Fig. She sat on the couch with Trace at her side. McKenna had been placed in her carrier in front of the Weather Channel with the sound muted.

"Can I get you anything else?" Fig worried. "Anything at all? Do you want to be alone? Do you want me to leave?"

Rachael shook her head. "You don't have to go, Fig."

Fig slowly sat down in the armchair across from them.

"Rachael, it doesn't mean it's the end of the world," Trace said gently. "This doesn't make Josh a serial killer. Or even a killer. He just got carried away. For all kinds of understandable reasons."

"I was just so sure he was covering for that girl. I was sure of it. That's exactly the kind of thing he would do. Not this. Not *this!*"

"Okay, so it's not what we would've expected. But, Rachael, I can imagine how incensed he must've been when he realized what had happened to those girls. And he was right there *where* it happened with the guy who made it happen."

"No offense, Trace, but you're not addicted to piety like Josh is, and even you wouldn't have done what Josh did. You can imagine his disgust, maybe even feel it, but you wouldn't have shot that man."

Trace rubbed her shoulder. "It's hard to know what you might do in a situation until you're forced to decide. I don't have to tell you that, Rachael. I know you know it already."

Rachael sipped her coffee. It was hot, strong, and aromatic. "That's what scares me."

"What scares you?"

"If that's true, than any one of us could do what Josh did. I could."

The three were silent for a moment.

"Passionate people tend to do passionate things," Fig offered.

"Passionate people get into trouble," Rachael replied glumly.

"Passionate people can change the world," Fig whispered back.

That night Rachael lay in bed unable to sleep. Moonlight bathed the guest room in pearly white—an almost haunting reminder that innocence still called out to be embraced. Trace, asleep next to her, stirred slightly as she rose from the bed. She leaned over and peered at McKenna. Her daughter was curled up in her portable crib, sucking lightly on her fist.

Rachael stood straight and gazed at the luminescent moon hanging in the autumn sky. She and Josh had imagined when they were little that the moon was God's porthole from heaven; that from it, the creator of the universe had an unlimited view of the world. They had surmised that when the paper-thin moon was visible on a sunny day, God was reminding them that even when you think he cannot see you, he can.

As she stood in the pool of moonlight Rachael reasoned that either

God did see everything—all the time—or he didn't. He either did have his hand on Josh or he didn't. Everything within her told her God was anything but capricious. Baffling, yes. Whimsical, no. She could believe Josh could crumble morally and kill a man; she had to believe it. But she couldn't believe God was a celestial prankster. To believe one rocked her world, to believe the other would obliterate it.

She reached up her hand to the window and placed her palm over the white disc of moon, covering it from her view, making it disappear. She had hidden the orb of God; the moon was gone. But all around her the bridal hue of the semi-dark room remained constant. Moonlight still bathed her daughter; still spilled onto her own skin, still lay across Trace as he slept. She closed her eyes, silently considering that the primary answer she had pleaded for every second since she had learned the truth earlier that day had come in the form of a cloudless night and full moon.

Rachael opened her eyes and pulled her hand away. The imprint of her palm lay across the moon's face as it shone through the glass.

Her heart was calmed but still she felt no pull to sleep. Rachael tiptoed out into the main area of the loft and the moonlight followed her. She poured herself a glass of water and drank it as she leaned against the sink. Across from her, the drawings Fig had done of McKenna blowing a figurative gasket and then of him, Trace, and McKenna strolling into a kid's paradise still hung on the fridge.

She gazed at the comic illustrations for several long moments. Then she put the glass down and walked into the dining room.

On the table were the three portfolios. She stared at the one marked Door #1 before opening it. She turned the first two pages over and pulled out the drawing with the twenty-two faces; the sketch in which Brick had imagined how Josh might have evolved from a man who wanted to save two orphans from abuse to a man who wanted to kill their abuser.

Rachael lingered over each frame, studying how Brick had added layer upon layer of loathing and wrath.

This is how it happened. This is how my brother killed someone.

She reached out and touched face number twenty-two—the one that belonged to a man who was pulling a trigger, sending a bullet into the brain of a kneeling grocery store owner.

The face was etched in Brick's overdrawn fashion with far too many angles and proportions that didn't match up to real life. Yet she felt Brick had captured it as accurately as anyone could.

This was her brother...and it was not. It was like something had come over him, an intense urge he couldn't control.

On impulse, Rachael reached for the portfolio marked Door #3 and opened it, removing the half-crumpled drawing Fig had done of the fifth man—Josh's alter ego.

She pulled out the chair in front of her and sat down, pulling the drawings close—Brick's twenty-two faces and Fig's sketch of Josh's darker side.

She sat for a long time that way, with the drawings in front of her, not really acknowledging that she gazed at them by no other light than that of the moon.

McKenna's cries to be fed awoke her. For a moment Rachael didn't know where she was. She was startled by the strangeness of McKenna's voice. It seemed far away.

Rachael snapped her eyes open.

She was on Fig's couch.

Rachael remembered then, finally pulling herself away from the drawings sometime after two and curling up with Trace's jacket on Fig's sofa. She sat up quickly and saw that Trace was coming toward her with their daughter.

"There you are," he commented, handing McKenna to her.

"Sorry, Trace. I didn't start out to spend the night on Fig's couch. I just couldn't sleep. I came out here to think and...I don't know. I just ended up on the couch."

"S'all right," Trace said, sitting down beside her. "I won't take it personally. Besides, you were cuddled up with my jacket. That's a good indication you aren't mad at me for something."

Rachael put McKenna to her breast and leaned back against the couch. Trace leaned back too and stretched his long legs across Fig's coffee table.

"So?" he said.

"So...I don't know, Trace. I don't know what to think. I'm not mad today, not like I was yesterday. But I still feel betrayed somehow."

"Betrayed by Josh?"

"I guess. And I'm dreading telling my parents. I can't tell you how much I'm dreading it."

Trace was quiet for a moment. "Why do *you* have to tell them? Let Josh do it. This is his doing, not yours."

"But I'm the one who's been telling my parents all this time that Josh couldn't possibly have done it. Josh never wanted them to think he was innocent. I planted that notion in their heads."

"Well, I think all along your mom has chosen to believe he couldn't have done it, Rachael. You reinforced that, but I don't think you're to blame for giving her the idea."

"I just think I owe them the truth. I wanted it so badly for myself. And I have always believed that it's truth that keeps us from disintegrating into anarchy."

"Still, I think this is Josh's truth to tell," Trace said.

"But, Trace, he's already told it," Rachael replied. "He has said from the beginning that he did it. *I'm* the one who refused to believe it."

They were silent for a moment.

"So what are you going to do?" Trace said.

"I guess I'm going to have to go see them and tell them I was wrong."

"I'll take you," Trace offered.

Rachael nodded. "But not today. I don't want to do it today. I don't want to do anything today."

The morning passed quietly.

When Fig got up, he and Trace went to work in the studio on

the floor below. Rachael played with McKenna, watched the History Channel, read a few magazines, and paced the loft.

After lunch Trace went to talk with the agency handling the sale of the new lofts down the street. Rachael opted to take McKenna for a long walk on the riverfront where she could breath deep the autumn air and pray three-word prayers like *Help me understand, watch over Josh,* and *make me brave.*

By the time Rachael put McKenna down for her afternoon nap, she was feeling an odd sense of calm. Perhaps it was more like a sense of resignation. In any case, her head no longer throbbed with the weight of knowing too much.

When McKenna was at last asleep, Rachael went into the kitchen to put water on for some chai tea. Her cell phone rang. She walked over to her purse, drew out her phone, and looked at the tiny screen. "Unknown number" was written across the top. Rachael frowned and pressed the button to answer.

"Hello?" she said.

There was muffled breathing on the other end.

"Hello," she said again, more forcefully.

"Is…is this Rachael?" a voice said. Rachael didn't recognize it. It was a young woman's voice.

"Who is this, please?" Rachael said.

"Are you Rachael?"

Something in the sound of the girl's voice registered with Rachael. She knew this voice after all.

"Yes, this is Rachael."

"This is Choua Lee. I need to talk to you."

TWENTY-SEVEN

As Rachael drove to Frogtown, the lawyer within her implored her to reconsider meeting alone with Choua Lee. Whatever it was that the girl wanted to tell her, it no doubt would figure in somehow to Joshua's case and would either help him or hurt him. It was this unknown that fueled the appeal of her rational side to turn around and go to Pendleton's office instead.

But she didn't do it.

Choua had sounded scared on the phone. It was the tension in her voice that had thrown Rachael when she first answered the phone and didn't recognize the voice. She had not sensed this kind of fear in Choua's voice when they had spoken a few days earlier. Something had changed.

The girl had obviously picked up the business card Rachael had left at her feet after she drove away from the teen center. Not only had Choua picked it up, she had kept it.

And now she had used it.

Choua asked for help. The girl hadn't elaborated on what kind of help she needed. And Rachael hadn't insisted she tell her. Instead, Rachael suggested they meet in the park across from John Tsue's teen center. It was an open place where they both could feel safe.

Choua agreed.

Now, as Rachael turned down the busy street, she could feel her pulse quickening. Trace didn't know where she was. She had left McKenna with Fig and no explanation of where she was going. She had just said she was going out.

No one knew where she was.

God, she whispered, *protect me.*

She pulled Fig's car up along the curb, across the street from the Center. The park was nothing more than a few benches, a slide, a merry-go-round, and a swing set. Two of the three swings were broken. A couple of kids were playing in a little sandbox. A few others were twirling on the merry-go-round. There wasn't a teenager in sight.

Rachael was about to get out of the car when a figure appeared at the passenger side and tapped on the glass. She flinched and turned.

It was Choua. "Roll down your window," the girl said.

Rachael lowered the window several inches.

"Let me talk to you in your car. I don't want the whole world to see me talking to you," Choua said nervously.

Okay, God, Rachael breathed. She pressed the automatic lock and Choua wrenched the door open, slid in, and shut the door. The girl sat facing forward for a moment, appearing to need to gather strength or courage.

Rachael waited.

"It's not working," Choua finally said, shaking her head. "It's not working." She raised her head to look at Rachael, obviously expecting Rachael to understand.

"What's...not working?" Rachael replied, masking her unease.

Choua looked away. "Bao can't...Bao can't do it. She's...they came and took her."

"Who?" Rachael exclaimed, panic building inside her. "Who came and got her?"

"The county people! She's...the school called them. She tried to cut her wrists. They took her to a hospital. Some psycho place. They think she's...She can't pretend anymore."

"Pretend what?"

Choua turned her head back around, and now it was clear Choua thought Rachael knew more than she did. "She can't pretend it happened the way we said it did," Choua said impatiently.

Instinct told Rachael to remain calm and act as if none of this startled her. A tiny seed of hope was starting to germinate within. Perhaps Josh had learned to lie to her after all. Perhaps he thought that if he could convince Rachael he had shot and killed a man, he could convince anyone.

"Please tell me what *really* happened, Choua. Let me help you," Rachael said.

"But I promised," Choua said and she looked away.

"Sometimes promises can't be kept, Choua. Not if they're going to hurt people."

"Bao can't pretend anymore!" Choua exclaimed, and her face suddenly appeared childish and weak. Rachael could sense the walls around Choua's resolve crumbling.

"And you can't either, can you, Choua?" she said.

Choua closed her eyes and said nothing.

"Choua, I have a little girl. A beautiful daughter named McKenna. I would lay down my life to protect her. I know what you've been through. No young girl deserves what you have suffered. What Bao has suffered. You deserve that same protection. You do. And I'm really very sorry you didn't have it when you needed it most."

A tear slipped down Choua's cheek. "I didn't...plan it. It just...it just happened."

A cool wave of relief and understanding passed over Rachael. At last, at last. Finally. The truth.

"Josh didn't kill your cousin, did he, Choua?" Rachael said.

Choua shook her head. "No. He killed the other man. I killed Vong Thao."

For a moment Rachael could not blink or even breathe. The girl next to her was wiping away a tear, oblivious to Rachael's predicament.

He killed the other man.

He killed the other man.

The fifth man.

"What...what did you say?" Rachael whispered.

"I'm the one who shot Vong," Choua groaned. "Whitey just said he did it. He said it may as well have been him, 'cause he killed that Xiang guy."

"That Xiang guy," Rachael said, willing herself to just say the words and not consider them.

"I went and got the gun from upstairs," Choua said. "I knew where my cousin kept it. By the register in this little box. Whitey told me to go call 911, but that's not what I did . . . .That's not what I did."

Choua was shaking her head, and Rachael sat as if frozen. Josh hadn't lied to her about killing a man. He had killed someone. It just wasn't Vong Thao. It was someone else entirely.

The fifth man.

"What happened?" Rachael whispered, her analytical side coming to the rescue.

"Whitey said, 'Choua, go call 911!' and I went upstairs to use the phone, but I saw that little box. I...I knew what was in it."

"Choua," Rachael said as calmly as she could. "Why did my brother tell you to call 911?"

" 'Cause that Xiang guy was lying there, and he wasn't getting up. Whitey had knocked him down to the ground when he finally figured out what Xiang and his friends had been doing to Bao and me. Whitey grabbed him by the shoulders, and he kept slamming his head to the floor. Calling him a monster. Over and over. Like he was pounding a hammer."

Bile crept up into Rachael's throat and she swallowed hard, sending it back down.

"And then Xiang started shaking all over and then he stopped, and there was blood from his head on the mat," Choua continued. "And Xiang, his eyes were all rolled back in his head. Vong yelled, 'You kill! You kill!' And Whitey, he just…he just shook his head like he couldn't believe it. That's when he told me to go call 911."

Rachael couldn't keep her tears back. She let them trickle down one by one. Choua went on.

"But I didn't call 911. I saw that little box, and I thought of what Whitey had done to Xiang. And I thought Xiang wasn't the only one who deserved to die. So I took the gun, and I came downstairs with it. Vong was kneeling by Xiang and Whitey was too. Bao was in the corner with her arms over her head. I raised the gun and I pointed it at Vong's head. Whitey looked up and saw me and he yelled, "No, Choua!" But I did it anyway. I pulled the trigger."

Oh, God, oh God! Rachael breathed as the tears kept sliding down her cheeks.

Choua was silent for just a moment, and then she continued. "Whitey came over to me and took the gun out of my hands," Choua said. "I didn't even know I was shaking until he took it and held me in his arms. Then I could tell. He asked me why I did it. And I said I did it for Bao. Vong had told me he would leave Bao alone if I did what he said. But he lied to me. He hurt her anyway. Not himself. But he was the one who held her down. He held her down. So I shot him."

"And Xiang? Who is he?" Rachael whispered.

Choua turned to Rachael and her gaze was steel. "Xiang brought the guys to the basement. He was the one Vong owed money to. He was the one who demanded Vong get girls for him and his friends. I'm glad he's dead. And you know what? No one misses him. No one is wondering where Xiang is, are they? There aren't police walking up and down the streets asking about Xiang, are there? 'Cause no one misses him except the ones that are just like him. And they won't call the police."

"What did my brother do with…Xiang?" Rachael said. The words were like shards of glass in her mouth.

"He told me not to worry about it. I don't know what he did with him. And I don't care. He told me Bao and I didn't have to worry about a thing. That he'd take care of everything."

Rachael nodded. "So he took you home that night?"

"Yes."

"And came back later to tell you and Bao what to say if the police were to question you."

"Yes."

"He told you that if he had to, he would tell the cops he shot Vong Thao."

Choua nodded. "Whitey said he was the guilty man, he was the one who would pay the price for having killed someone. He said I shouldn't have to. That I had already paid too high a price. Bao too."

"And you and Bao agreed."

"Whitey told us it was why he had been born. To help us."

Emotion roiled up within her, and it took a concerted effort to keep her head.

"Is that true?" Choua said. "Is that why he was born?"

Rachael wiped at her cheeks with her hands. "Yes, Choua. I think it's true."

Choua looked up at Rachael's face, at the stains the tears had left. "He didn't mean to kill Xiang. That was an accident."

Rachael nodded.

Choua turned her head to look out the passenger window. A few more kids had arrived to play since she had sat down in Fig's car.

"It was too much for Bao," Choua murmured. "She knew I was the one who shot Vong Thao. She knew Whitey had killed Xiang. She was having nightmares. It was too much for her."

Instinctively Rachael reached over and touched Choua on the shoulder. "I meant what I said the other day. Bao is lucky to have you for a sister, Choua. She really is."

Choua didn't move away, didn't try to dislodge Rachael's hand. "She misses our parents. She doesn't even remember our dad, but she misses him anyway."

"Of course," Rachael said.

Choua was silent for a moment. "What will happen to me?" she asked. "Will I go to prison?"

Rachael stroked her shoulder. "I don't think so, Choua."

"Will I get taken away?"

"Not forever, Choua. You're still a child. What you've been through would be a nightmare for even an adult. No judge is going to treat you like an adult just because you've had to bear an adult-sized burden."

Choua sighed. "I guess I have to go to the cops."

"Yes."

"Should I go there now?"

Rachael thought for a moment. "Is your aunt at home?"

"For a little while longer. Then she has to go to work."

"How about if I take you home. You can call Sgt. Pendleton and ask him to come over while your aunt is still there. Then you can tell him."

Choua nodded. "Can you call him for me?"

"Sure." Rachael reached inside her purse for her cell phone and pressed the numbers for Sgt. Pendleton.

The phone clicked into Pendleton's voice mail. At first Rachael was miffed that Pendleton wasn't answering, but then it occurred to her that delaying his visit with Choua would give her time to talk to Josh before the police descended upon him and new charges were filed.

"Sgt. Pendleton, this is Rachael Flynn," she said after the beep. "It's a few minutes before three on Tuesday. I am in my car right now taking Choua Lee home. She called me and asked to see me today. She has something she needs to tell you."

TWENTY-EIGHT

Rachael felt strangely calm as she waited for Josh to arrive from his jail cell. Her heart was heavy, but it didn't feel broken. It felt weighed down with an enormous burden that she knew, in time, would not seem as heavy.

When she had first arrived at the jail, the jailer returned from the cellblocks and told her that her brother had declined her visit. She had sent the jailer back with a message: *I have spoken with Choua.*

She hoped he wouldn't decline a second time.

A moment later the knob turned and Josh walked into the room. He looked a bit agitated. He slid into the chair opposite her.

"Hello, Josh," Rachael said.

"Why are you here, Rachael?" he said almost rudely.

"I told the jailer to tell you why I was here. Didn't he tell you?" Rachael shot back.

Josh stared at her. Rachael recognized the look. Josh was trying to determine how much she knew.

"You spoke to Choua," Josh said dryly.

Rachael nodded. "She called me, Josh."

He shook his head. "No way."

"Yes, she did. I ran into her when I went to visit John Tsue at the teen center. I gave her my card."

"What were you doing over there?" Josh yelled. "I never asked you to go over there!"

"What difference should it have made, Josh? If you had really killed Thao, it shouldn't have made a difference that I went to see John Tsue. And you should know I didn't approach Choua, she approached *me*. She recognized me, Josh. You showed her my picture."

Josh looked away.

"She called me and asked for my help, Josh. She wanted *help*."

Her brother raised his eyes. This was something he understood. "What did she want?"

"Josh, Bao isn't doing well. She was taken to some sort of psychiatric facility yesterday. Choua doesn't even know which one. She said living with the story the three of you concocted was proving too much for Bao. She was having nightmares. She slit her wrists."

Josh closed his eyes but said nothing.

"Josh, Choua appreciates everything you tried to do for her and for Bao. But it's been too much for her too. You get to live a secluded life here in the jail with your secret, but they had to live out there in the real world. It was too hard."

"What did she tell you?" Josh whispered, opening his eyes. They were shiny with emotion.

Rachael leaned forward and immediately her own eyes filled with tears. She reached for Josh's hand. "Everything, Josh. She told me everything."

Josh looked away from Rachael and her outstretched arm. "I really thought I had found a way to redeem myself for what I had done. I should've known it wouldn't work. There will never be a way. Never."

"Josh, it was an accident! You didn't mean to kill that man. You didn't know that what you were doing was killing him. That's very different than aiming a gun at the back of a man's head and firing."

"It isn't different."

"Yes, it is!"

"She's told the police then? It's over?" Josh asked. His voice was heavy.

"Sgt. Pendleton could be at her house right now. I don't know. But, yes, it's over."

Joshua brought a shaking hand to his brow and rubbed it. "I wanted to do this for them. I was ready to do it."

"Josh, no one doubts your compassion for these girls—least of all me."

Joshua looked at her as he brought his hand away. "You don't... really know me, Rachael. Not really."

"Tell me what happened, Josh. Tell me and I will tell *you* what I know about you."

He gazed at her with eyes bereft of hope.

"Tell me, Josh."

Her brother seemed to ponder for a few minutes the loss of his plan of deliverance for the two girls. Then he cleared his throat.

"Bao," and at the mention of her name, Josh's voice broke away. He closed his eyes and then opened them. He began again. "Bao was coming to the teen center more and more and hanging around me like a scared dog shadows its owner. It was weird, not normal. It was like she was both afraid of me and afraid to be apart from me. I kept talking to her and encouraging her to come. Then one afternoon she started asking about heaven and how to get there. So of course I got all excited and told her how Jesus made a way for her to be in heaven one day. And right then and there she prayed to receive Christ, Rachael. It was so awesome!

"But then...then she asked *when* she would get to go to heaven. I told her at the end of her life, she would go there. And she asked... she asked..."

Joshua's voice broke away again and his eyes filled with moisture. He screwed his eyelids shut. Several seconds later he opened them, resolve etched in his face.

"She asked me how to end her life so that she could go, Rachael. She was asking me how she could commit suicide so she could go to heaven! I asked her as gently as I could why such a lovely girl with her whole life ahead of her wanted to die, but she wouldn't tell me. By this time everyone else was gone, and it was time to lock up. But she was terrified to leave. That's when she told me she was supposed to go to her cousin's store that night, but she didn't want to go. I told her I was sure she didn't have to and she just said yes, she did. So I took her home to talk to her aunt, but she was at work. Choua was there.

"So I asked Choua why Bao might be afraid to go their cousin's store, and Choua went berserk. She started yelling at Bao and asking her questions. Bao began to cry. I didn't know what to think.

"I finally got out of Choua that their cousin is a not a nice guy and that him asking Bao to come to his store wasn't good. Bao said she was supposed to be there at nine o'clock that night. I told them I would go talk to him for her. But both Bao and Choua got very agitated about my going. So I said maybe we should call the police and let them handle it, but they reacted even worse to that.

"I had some suspicions at that point that these girls were being pressured to do things they didn't want to do. But I had no proof. I had never even met their cousin. Somehow I convinced them to let me take them to the store and we'd settle it."

"So you came back for them at nine," Rachael said.

"Yes," Josh said. "We went to the back entrance, to the basement. That's where Vong Thao was waiting. He was so ticked that I was there. He started yelling at me. Most of it I couldn't understand. I did hear him tell me to get out, that I was trespassing. Choua started yelling at him then. I had no idea what they were saying to each other. I looked back at Bao, and she was off in a corner with her hands over her ears.

"While Choua and Thao were arguing, four or five other men—I'm not sure how many—came down the same stairs into the basement. One was clearly the leader. Thao called him Xiang. He was angry that Choua and I were there too, and he joined in the argument. The other men left when he turned to them and shouted something at them.

Then Xiang made what appeared to be a threatening remark to Thao. Thao looked very afraid."

Josh stopped for a second, and Rachael waited.

"What happened next?" she finally said.

"I asked if either of the men spoke English. Xiang turned to me and, in broken English, told me I didn't belong there and that I'd better get back to my own neighborhood before something bad happened to me.

"Well, I was ready to leave, that's for sure. So I told the girls to come with me...but they didn't move. Xiang told *me* to just go. And I said, 'Not without the girls.' Xiang said the girls were Thao's family, and I had no business being there...that I was trespassing on private property.

"Choua turned to Xiang and yelled something, and Xiang backhanded her across the face. She fell to the floor. I rushed to help her up, and I knew I had to get those girls out of there. I told Choua, 'Come on, we're leaving.'

"But Choua said to me, 'He lied to me. He said nothing would happen to Bao if I did what they said. But they did it anyway!'

"'Did what? What did they do?' I asked. But I knew. I knew, Rachael! These girls had been sexually assaulted. I wanted to throw up right there. But Xiang came up to me and said, 'This does not concern you. Get out.'"

As Josh talked, Rachael could picture it all. Sketches by Trace, Fig, Brick, and Sidney filled her mind. Her brother continued.

"I was still kneeling down by Choua, but I stood then and looked at Xiang and I said, 'How could you do such a thing? They're just children!' And he said, 'This is none of your business! And you better not try to make it your business. You're getting in way over your head. And if you so much as breathe a word to the cops about what you *think* you know, I will hunt down everyone that matters to you. You get me?'

"Then I said, 'You won't get away with this!' and Choua, at my feet yelled, 'He already does! He already gets away with it. He and all his friends. All the time.'

"That's when I knew there had been others. Not just Choua. Not just Bao. I yelled, 'How many others?' and I was so mad I was shaking. I kept yelling 'How many others?'"

Rachael felt her own anger rising within her as Joshua continued.

"That's when I snapped, Rachael. I just couldn't keep it inside, all the anger and rage. I lunged at him, and he wasn't expecting it.

"We fell to the ground and I...I don't know Rachael, something within me just exploded. I grabbed Xiang by the shoulders and banged his head against the floor over and over. I was screaming the whole time, 'How could you do such a thing? How could you do such a thing? You're a monster! A monster!'

"I kept at it even when Thao yelled at me to stop and tried to pull me off. When Xiang's eyes rolled back in his head and I saw that the floor mat was stained with blood, I stopped. Adrenaline was still coursing through me. Xiang started convulsing on the floor, and Thao was yelling at me. Bao was still in the corner cowering. Choua had risen. She was standing there, watching me.

"The convulsions stopped, and Xiang just lay there with his eyes open. The puddle of blood on the mat wasn't getting any bigger. I knew he was dead. He was dead, and I had killed him. I couldn't believe it, Rachael. It happened so fast. Then I told Choua to go upstairs and call 911.

"But when Choua came back down, she had a strange look on her face. Thao was kneeling at the body, saying Xiang's name, and I was kneeling on the other side, in shock at what I had done. Out of the corner of my eye I saw Choua raise her arm. I saw the gun too late. I yelled but she was already squeezing the trigger. Thao fell over dead, just like that."

Joshua, overcome with emotion, stopped.

"And then you rushed over to Choua," Rachael continued. "You took the gun and embraced her. You asked her why, and she said she did it for Bao because Thao held her down."

Josh nodded.

"You decided then and there you would take the blame for what had happened that night," Rachael added. "You decided if the police began to suspect the girls, you would step in and confess."

Josh nodded.

"So you took the girls home? And then you went back?"

Josh nodded again. "I put Xiang in my car, along with the gun and the floor mat. I drove to Legion Pond out by Lake Elmo. I figured no one would see me there. I buried Xiang and the floor mat on the east side. I threw the gun into the water. Then I came back and drove Xiang's car to a different neighborhood in Frogtown. I left the keys on the dashboard. It was a nice car. I figured someone with a fondness for stealing cars would take it. I'm sure that's what happened. It was gone the next morning."

"And you went back to see the girls after you had done those things?"

"Yes. Choua seemed dazed but okay, but Bao…Bao looked like it was already starting to eat away at her. She turned to me and asked me if Vong Thao and Xiang were in heaven now with Jesus, now that they were dead. And I just grabbed her in my arms and said heaven is not a place for men like that. Not a place for men like that."

Josh put his hands over his face and his body shook. Rachael whispered his name and again reached across the table with her arm. A second later Josh let one hand fall away from his face. He grabbed her hand resting on the table. His grip was fierce with regret and fear.

"It *is* still a place for a man like you, Josh," Rachael whispered. "You didn't mean to kill that man. I know you didn't. God still has his hand on you. *He still does.*"

Joshua said nothing at first, but his grip on her hand lessened. "How did you know there was someone else in the basement, Rachael?"

"What?" She had heard him, but hers was the automatic response of someone who is thrown by a question that has no ready answer.

"How did you know there was someone else in the basement?"

In her mind Rachael went back to the drawings. First she saw the one Fig did of the embodiment of evil floating down the wooden stairs. The recollection of that insight alone—that there were dark forces at work in that basement—caused her to shiver. Joshua surely felt it. His hand on hers tightened.

"Rachael?"

Then she remembered standing at Fig's dining room table, staring at the drawings and imagining—no, deducing—that there had been a fifth person in the room by no other means than gut instinct. Where had that intuition come from? She recalled how on Sunday she'd implored Trace to call Fig and get Brick and Sidney to come back over to the loft and sketch a scenario of a fifth person being in the basement. Sidney had scoffed because she had no proof.

But the idea wouldn't leave her alone.

"Rachael?" Josh said again.

"I don't know how I knew," she finally said.

Josh stroked her hand gently. "I think I do," he said and his voice sounded sad and proud at the same time. "I think it's you God has his hand on. You, Rachael."

TWENTY-NINE

Rachael stood against Fig's car in the Ramsey County Jail parking lot watching the waning sun glisten off the dome of the cathedral of St. Paul a few miles away. Gazing at its serene stateliness kept her mind from traveling in a million directions at once. If she were to take her eyes off it, she knew she would be assailed by too many thoughts, too many aches.

The mind can only handle so many surprises at once.

Joshua's declaration was the most insistent of thoughts that barraged her as she waited to see if Sgt. Pendleton would return to the police station before she left. The notion that God had his hand on her in some kind of special way seemed absurd. She knew God was present, even present in her life, but to imagine that she had something to offer the world as unique as Josh did was as foreign a thought to her as daffodils in a Minnesota winter. Josh was the one with the passion for the mistreated, albeit a passion that sometimes ran to the extreme.

And yet she had felt stirrings lately. She had perceived things that didn't have a textbook explanation.

They weren't tangible objects you could stick a thumbtack in.

They were more like musings of her mind that seemed to originate somewhere other than the physical world.

For someone who dealt with facts and evidence, the idea that she was a receptor for divine insights was debilitating. If it were true, she wouldn't be able to put it in plain words. Trace would probably try to understand, and Josh obviously did already. But she knew there was no rational explanation for what had happened to her the past few days. As she leaned against the car, she couldn't help but wonder if God had granted her one-time insights just to help Joshua. Or had she always been intuitive when it came to matters of truth and deception? Is that why she became a lawyer in the first place? Because she couldn't remember ever wanting to be anything else. Ever.

"God, what have you been up to?" she whispered. She cast a glance back at the jail. She wasn't truly sure what to make of what had happened in the past few hours. She was even less sure of what lay ahead. In the moments before he was led back to his cell, Josh had again gently refused to let Rachael represent him. New charges were sure to be filed within the next twenty-four hours. He would still need a good lawyer, but he wasn't going to let her fill that need.

"I can't have you making excuses for me, Rachael," he said.

She begged him then to continue to let Maggie Fielding represent him. "You made some terrible mistakes, Josh. But you're not a terrible man. I've seen what terrible people can do. You're not like that."

He smiled weakly. She could tell he found that comment sadly comical.

"If you really think I have insights into the truth, Joshua, then who are you to doubt my word?" she said with a slight smile.

His grin had lengthened.

"I'll be seeing you," she promised.

Their visit ended then, and she had come out to the parking lot to contemplate the revelations of the day and wait for Pendleton's car to appear.

She wouldn't be able to wait much longer. McKenna had surely awakened by now. Rachael reached into her purse and pulled out her phone. Fig hadn't called. She pressed the speed dial for his number. In two rings, he picked up.

"*Buon Journo, Raquel,*" he quipped.

"Hey, Fig. You doing okay?" Rachael heard no screaming in the background. A good sign.

"Yes. We're fine. The heiress woke up about an hour ago, but this time I didn't spill the bottle you left for us. She sucked it right down. Jillian's here now, and we're taking turns telling McKenna sixteenth-century riddles. Jillian and I are winning."

"That's great, Fig. Is Trace there too?"

"He came back awhile ago from meeting with the real estate agent. I sent him downstairs to work."

Rachael smiled. "You're the best, Fig. Really."

"Yes, it's true. But please tell no one."

"Sure. I'll be leaving here in just a few minutes, okay?"

"Certainly, kumquat."

"Thanks, Fig."

"You sound sad, Rachael. Did you get more bad news today?"

Rachael sighed. Fig was weird, but he was perceptive. And kind. "Sort of," she responded.

"Oh, dear. Would it help if we had sushi for dinner tonight?"

"Fig, I think Trace and I are going to have to grab something on the road. We're going to have to go to St. Cloud tonight. I have to talk to my parents."

"Rachael, is everything all right?"

She was silent for a moment.

"No. But it will be. In time I think it will be."

At that moment, she saw Sgt. Pendleton pull into the parking lot.

"I've got to go, Fig. I'll be home soon. Bye." She clicked off the phone and slipped it back in her purse. She watched as Pendleton got out of his car. He immediately turned to her.

He had seen Rachael when he drove in.

The policeman walked toward her.

"So you've been to Choua's?" Rachael asked when he had closed the distance between them.

He nodded.

"Is she going to be okay?" Rachael asked spontaneously.

"I'm optimistic," Pendleton said, cocking his head. "Thanks, for your help with this. I feel like I owe you an apology. You were sure from the beginning that your brother was covering for the girl."

"You don't owe me an apology," Rachael said quickly.

Pendleton hesitated and then nodded toward the jail. "I suppose you've visited with your brother?"

"Yes. I wanted to hear the truth from him myself."

"And did you?"

"Yes. He told me where the body is. He buried it at Legion Pond out by Lake Elmo. Eastern shore. The floor mat is there too. And the gun."

"I figured."

There was a momentary pause.

"That guy Xiang threatened Joshua, you know," Rachael said. "He told Josh that if he went to the police, he'd hunt down the people Josh cared about."

Pendleton shook his head. "Your brother would have been a lot better off if he had just called us."

"But it never occurred to Josh to do what would be better for *him*, Sergeant. That's not how my brother thinks. He's different. Special. He wanted to do what was best for the girls."

"Well, he didn't do that either. This farce wasn't the best thing for those girls."

"An intellectual might have figured that out. Josh doesn't think with his brain; he thinks with his heart."

"Yeah, well, that's the kind of stuff that makes my job so interesting."

Rachael smiled. "That's the kind of stuff that makes this broken world a lovelier place."

Pendleton opened his mouth to say something and then decided against it. He extended his hand. "It's been a pleasure to know you, Ms.

Flynn. I'm sorry it was under such horrific circumstances. I hope New York is good to you. I think you're probably a very good lawyer."

"Thank you, Sergeant," Rachael replied, shaking his hand. "And New York has been good to me. But I'm coming home."

Telling her parents about the events of the day was not as difficult as Rachael had feared it would be. Her mother cried, of course, and Cliff put his hands over his own eyes more than once. But in the end Rachael believed her parents came to the same weighty conclusion she had: Josh had accidentally killed a corrupt man in the heat of an emotionally charged moment. He had just learned the young girls he was trying so hard to protect had been victimized in the worst possible way.

It had not been the act of a man bent on murder.

"So what happens now?" Eva asked when Rachael finished.

"Well, the police will go search for the body of that other man. Then they will file a new police report with the new confessions: Choua's and Joshua's. The county prosecutor will file new charges against Josh. I'm hoping they will go with a voluntary manslaughter charge, but that's out of my hands. Murder two with intent was worse, Mom. Manslaughter is a little different. Josh won't get near the prison time as he would've with murder two."

"But that can't be all," Cliff said quietly. "He lied to the police. He destroyed evidence. He disposed of a body."

Rachael nodded. "Yes. There will be other charges, I'm afraid."

"So," Eva said, pausing. "So he will be in prison for a long time?"

Rachael shrugged. "I don't know, Mom. I don't know which charges the county will go with. And the court has to abide by mandatory sentencing laws. It could be five years or ten or fifteen. It all depends on what the prosecutor's office charges him with and what the judge will say. Josh doesn't want a trial, so there won't be a jury."

No one said anything else for several moments.

"In all my dreams and desires for Joshua, I never thought in a million years he would end up in prison for killing someone. I just never saw it that way," Eva murmured.

Cliff closed his eyes and turned his head away from the group.

"He was such a good boy, wasn't he, Cliff?" Eva continued. Her voice sounded detached and speculative. "You know, I don't think we ever once had to spank him or discipline him or even send him to his room for hurting anyone. He got into trouble, but it was never for hurting anyone. It was for coming home late or reading under the covers past bedtime or leaving his clothes on the bathroom floor. But never for hurting anyone."

"I need to walk the dog," Cliff said abruptly. He rose from his chair.

"Want some company?" Trace asked tentatively.

Cliff paused for a moment. "Sure. That'd be nice."

Rachael watched as her father and husband walked out of the room. In her lap, McKenna fiddled with Rachael's wedding ring.

"He'll be all right," her mother said quietly when the sounds of Kipper's toenails on the kitchen floor had disappeared and the back door had opened and shut. "He just has to process things in his own way."

Rachael nodded. "We're all like that, I think."

Eva wordlessly reached for McKenna, and Rachael handed her over.

"It's so amazing to me that she has her whole life ahead of her. She's like one of Trace's blank canvases, isn't she?" Eva said, kissing McKenna on the forehead.

"Yes," Rachael whispered. "Yes, she is."

"Rachael, I promised myself I would never give you parenting advice unless you asked for it, but if I may be so bold, don't stand in the way of who McKenna must become," Eva said gently, looking only at her granddaughter. "Don't stand in her way and don't *make* her way. Just walk with her on her way. And love her for who she is, not for who you'd like her to be."

"That's good advice, Mom. Thanks," Rachael replied softly.

The two women sat in silence. Rachael watched as her mother cuddled McKenna, whispering things like "Grandma loves you, precious." She found herself imagining that Nana probably had held her that way when she was a baby. Nana surely had embraced her, kissed her, and prayed over her that God would keep her forever in the palm of his hand.

THIRTY

Late-morning sunlight bathed the new hardwood floor of the nearly finished loft. Rachael held McKenna in her arms as she and Trace walked through the airy openness of the empty rooms. All around them was the aroma of fresh paint, sawdust, and polish.

It was the fragrance of new things.

McKenna made a gurgling sound and it echoed. She made another one and the sounds blended.

"If we want, we can move in before the end of the month," Trace said as they returned to the main room. His voice ricocheted off the barren, twenty-foot walls.

"I suppose it would make sense to get settled before the first snow-fall," Rachael said.

"Yikes! Did you have to mention the word *snow?*"

"Let's not forget now what it was like to live here, Trace. You know we're going to have more snow in Minneapolis than in Manhattan."

Trace wrapped his arms around her from behind. "I know it. I just don't want to think about it right now. Although falling snow is going to look quite lovely from these enormous windows." He tipped his head toward the tall panes of glass that spanned the wall ahead of them.

"Sort of like our window-wall back in Manhattan," she said.

"Yep. Sort of."

Her cell phone rang at that moment, and she handed McKenna over to Trace. McKenna began to coo loudly, and Trace took her upstairs.

"Hello?" Rachael said.

"Rachael, this is Will Pendleton."

She hadn't talked to the sergeant since their conversation in the parking lot two days earlier.

"Hi," she said.

"Say, I just thought I'd tell you we've located the body," he said.

Rachael hesitated a second before answering. "I guess that's good news."

"Divers found the gun too. Early this morning."

"I see."

"Rachael, the press is going to enjoy this story, I'm afraid. It's not often that a man pleads guilty to a murder he didn't commit and then hides the evidence of the one he did."

She sighed briefly. Yes, it was not the average story. "I understand."

"And your name has come up. We haven't been able to hide nor would we choose to hide the fact that you had a part in cracking this, so consider yourself warned. You might be getting some phone calls from the media this afternoon."

Rachael couldn't help but grimace. It wasn't that she minded talking to the press. She had done so several times back in New York when a high-profile case came the firm's way. But this wasn't like those situations. This was about her brother. And yet she wanted people to know the truth about him. He wasn't some renegade vigilante with a bent toward violence. Josh was the most compassionate man she had ever known. Nothing had changed about her estimation of him.

"Thanks for the heads-up," she said.

"You're welcome."

"So is he…is the dead guy who Josh said he was?"

"Ronnie Xiang was bad news," Pendleton said. "And it's true what Choua said about him. No one reported him missing because the only people who missed him were slimeballs like him. He had never been convicted of anything, but he had been arrested more than once on drug charges. This is the first we'd heard of him being involved in a child prostitution ring. To tell you the truth, I would have liked to have seen him in court for this rather than on a slab in the morgue."

Rachael ignored the comment. "What about those other men who were in the basement before Xiang yelled at them to leave?" she asked.

"Well, unless Choua and Bao agree to help us identify them, I don't know that we'll be able to chase them down. Choua hasn't been as cooperative in describing the men who've abused her as I would like. And Bao isn't in a position to participate in this investigation at all at the moment."

Rachael thought of the young girl whom she felt she knew intimately, but had never really met.

"Will Bao be okay?"

"She's young. She's getting good care. It's really up to her, I guess. Her aunt told me she thinks in time Bao will be able to rise above it because of what her name means in Hmong."

"What does it mean?" Rachael asked.

"Butterfly."

Rachael let the image of a delicate swallowtail float across her mind before speaking again. "Will, have you heard from Emily Lonetree yet? Do you know what Josh will be charged with?"

"I've been too preoccupied with the body search and the new case with Choua. I haven't talked to her," Pendleton said. "But I really don't think any of the charges will surprise you, Rachael. Between your statement and Joshua's and Choua's, there's enough evidence to show that Joshua acted impulsively and under duress with regard to the homicide. The county will probably come down harder on him for obstruction of legal process and making a false statement, since he did those with more of a clear head. She won't bring any charges against him that you wouldn't bring if you were her, I'm sure of that."

"All right," Rachael sighed. "When's his next court appearance, do you know that?"

"Probably tomorrow."

"Okay."

"Say, Rachael," the sergeant said. "Were you being serious when you said you were moving back to the Twin Cities?"

"Yes. I was."

"Will you be looking for a job here then?"

"Possibly."

"Just thought I'd tell you there are openings in the county attorney's office. I'll put in a good word for you. I know you're a defense lawyer back in New York, but you might want to think about what you could bring to the prosecutor's office here in St. Paul. You've got—I don't know—a nose for the truth."

She smiled. "Thanks for the compliment. I'll keep it in mind."

"So long, Rachael."

"Goodbye, Will."

She clicked the phone off and went to find Trace and McKenna. She wanted to make a quick trip to see her brother before heading back to Fig's.

Rachael sat across from her brother and noticed that the yellowish bruise under his eye was nearly gone. Only if one looked close could he see traces of a night gone terribly wrong.

"They found the gun too," she was saying.

Josh just nodded. His demeanor was solemn, but he didn't seem lifeless like he had in days past. He appeared to be in deep thought as Rachael relayed the news that the body of Ronnie Xiang had been found as well as the gun and floor mat.

"And the girls? Are they okay?" he whispered.

"Yes, Josh."

"How do you know?"

"Well, Bao is in a really good treatment center. One of the best, Josh. And Choua's at a therapeutic group home for the moment. She's getting counseling, and Sgt. Pendleton is working with the county prosecutor on the charges that will be filed. She won't spend the rest of her childhood in juvenile detention, Josh. I'm sure of it."

Josh nodded. "And what about me?"

"I don't know yet, Josh," Rachael said. "You won't spend the rest of your life in prison, I'm sure of that too."

Josh smiled ruefully. "There isn't any reason why I shouldn't."

Rachael leaned forward. "Oh yes there is. There are a lot of reasons."

"Name one."

"You didn't intend to kill that man. It was an accident, Josh. He threatened you. He indirectly threatened me and Trace and McKenna. Mom and Dad too. He abused young girls in the worst possible way. And you tried everything in your power to get those girls out of that basement!"

"I crushed his skull, Rachael."

"You didn't mean to."

Josh shook his head and grinned savagely. "But that's just it. I did want to. I did, Rachael."

"You wanted justice, Josh. You didn't set out to murder Xiang."

"Ah yes. Justice. And what kind of justice will there be for me then? I killed a man."

"And you will go to prison for it, Joshua," Rachael answered. *But not for the rest of your life.*"

Josh was silent for a moment. "Isn't that what I deserve, Rachael?" he finally said. "An eye for an eye? A life for a life?"

Rachael sat back in her chair. "What you deserve, Josh, is mercy. If you deserve anything, it's mercy."

"Why? Why do I deserve mercy?"

A thousand images of Joshua reaching out to those cared for by no one else quickly filled her brain. Too many to name. How many lives had her brother touched? How many hours had he labored for those who had lost everything? How many children had he lured away from the horror of substance abuse by simply befriending them? How many widows' houses had he painted or fixed or cleaned? How many hearts had he kept from giving up on life? On God?

"Because you love God. And you love people like he does," she said softly.

Joshua looked at her. A splinter of hope shimmered in his eyes.

"And does he still love me?" he whispered.

"You know he does."

"How can he forgive me for what I've done?" Joshua looked down at his hands, the hands that had crushed a man's skull.

"Because that's his very nature, Josh."

Josh didn't look at her, but he reached across the table between them. She took his hand in hers. "It's his very nature," she whispered, wanting the echo of those four words to stay with him long after she left.

They sat that way for several quiet moments before the jailer opened the door to take Joshua back to his cell. Her brother stood and squeezed Rachael's hand. "Thank you," he murmured. It was so softly spoken, Rachael wondered for just a moment as he turned and walked out of the room if he had said anything at all.

Rachael and Trace stood outside Fig's front door, listening. They had just returned from the Ramsey County Jail. On the other side of the door they heard laughter, music, and loud noises.

Trace put his hand on the knob, turned it, and poked his head in. Behind him Rachael looked over his shoulder.

Fig was standing in the center of the room wearing his signature fedora, leather pants, and a Hawaiian shirt. He was holding a large piece of paper in his hands. Next to him was an easel. Across from him were Brick and Sidney, sitting on bar stools at the island countertop, laughing. They all had art pencils in their hands.

Fig turned at the sound of the door opening. "Don't come in!" he yelled. "Close the door! It's a surprise!"

Trace threw him a curious glance, but Fig shooed him with his hands. "Close the door, Trace! We've got a surprise for the kumquat!"

Trace closed the door and looked at Rachael.

"I hate it when he calls me that," Rachael muttered.

Trace grinned.

"What are they doing?" she said.

"I think they want to surprise you with something."

A look of impatience wrinkled Rachael's face. "I've had more than my share of surprises lately, don't you think?"

"I doubt this one will involve the police," Trace offered.

"Just one more second!" they heard Fig yell through the closed door.

McKenna gushed a one-syllable reply.

"Okay! You can open the door!" said Fig from the other side.

Trace turned the knob, and Rachael stepped in ahead of him. Brick and Sidney were still on the bar stools but the pencils were gone. Fig had turned the music down on the stereo and was standing by the easel, which was now facing the front door and was covered by a bath towel.

Trace closed the front door. "Aren't you guys supposed to be at work?" he said to Brick and Sidney.

"I don't have afternoon classes on Thursdays," Brick said.

"My reason for being here is a little more purposeful," Sidney said. "We can get to that later."

"I asked them here to celebrate your moving back to Minneapolis," Fig said.

"A celebration in the middle of the afternoon, Fig?" Trace sounded dubious.

"Well, Sidney picked the time. I didn't really care when. But then Brick came over, and you guys hadn't come back yet, and so we decided to sketch one last drawing for our Rachael."

Rachael wasn't sure she wanted to see one last drawing. Fig led her to the easel anyway.

"Ready?" But before she could answer, Fig whisked the towel away.

There, clamped to the easel, was a cartoon sketch of all of them sitting in the new loft with cartoon furniture inside it. Seated around the standing caricature of herself were Fig and Jillian, Brick, Sidney and his wife and son, Trace, her parents, and Joshua—smiling and calmly sitting there with a crowned McKenna in his lap waving a scepter. On the walls were prints of Madison Square Garden and the Manhattan skyline. On the cartoon coffee table were cups of espresso and triangles of baklava.

The images made her smile. All of them.

She touched the penciled lines of Josh's tranquil face.

"It's a wonderful drawing. Thanks, guys."

Fig smiled. "Do you know what you're doing?" he said, pointing to the cartoon drawing of herself.

Rachael looked at her likeness. She was standing in the center of the people she loved, as if addressing them, holding a magnifying glass and a notebook.

"It looks like I'm giving you all a lecture," she said.

"You're telling us who really killed JFK, smarty-pants!" Fig crowed.

She elbowed Fig. "Very funny."

"She *is* a smarty-pants," Fig said, turning to Sidney and Brick and speaking in a serious tone. "She figured out the whole thing with her brother. Just like one of those TV psychic cops that sees ghosts."

"Fig!" Rachael exclaimed.

"Say, about that whole thing with your brother," Sidney said, getting off his stool and coming toward her. "I've got friends in the news department at the paper who really want to talk to you about what you did and how you did it. They know I know you, Rachael. They really want to talk to you. That's the real reason I came over. I told them I'd convince you somehow to tell them what happened."

Rachael breathed in deep. She cast a look at the smiling caricature of Josh sitting with McKenna in his lap.

"I wouldn't be able to tell them anything above what the police tell them. I can't say anything that would jeopardize Josh's case. And I can't talk about the girls by name. They're juveniles."

"I'm sure they'd be okay with that."

"If I talk to them, it will be to tell them the kind of man Josh is, not the kind of crime he committed."

"Whatever you say, Rachael."

She hesitated a moment. "When do they want to speak to me?"

Sidney cleared his throat. "There's actually a reporter and a photographer sitting in a van across the street waiting for me to call them."

Rachael's eyes grew wide. "They've been waiting all this time?"

"Well, about an hour I guess. We didn't know when you and Trace would be getting back. They wanted to wait. They really want the story."

Rachael looked back at the drawing.

"Are you sure you want do to this, Rachael?" Trace's face was lined with concern.

She nodded. "I'm sure."

"Great. I'm going to call them up." Sidney withdrew his cell phone from his pocket.

"I'm going to see if I can get McKenna to lie down," Rachael took her daughter from Trace and walked back to the guest room.

Her true desire, though, was to be alone just for a moment before the reporter came up to the loft. She carefully placed McKenna in her portable crib and began to gently pat her back. A few moments later she heard the intercom by the front door squeak a greeting and Sidney say, "Come on up."

Rachael stood. McKenna wasn't asleep. She might even begin to cry and complain during the interview. Life was like that. Full of surprises that foil even the simplest of plans.

She heard the men talking in the other room. And she heard Trace say, "She'll be right out."

Rachael closed her eyes and sent a prayer heavenward for a clear mind. She opened them and, for a moment, she stood at the window looking at the spot where the moon had been the night before. It was nowhere in sight now, not even the near-transparent suggestion of it. But she knew it was there. When darkness fell, she would see it again.

She walked out of the room and closed the door softly behind her. In Fig's living room two strangers stood and looked her way. They looked hopeful.

Sidney came forward. "Rachael, this is Cory Stellman. He's a staff writer at the *Star Tribune*. And this is Hector Margolis, a photographer with the *Strib*."

"How do you do?" she asked, shaking their hands.

"Thanks for speaking to us, Ms. Flynn. We really appreciate it," Stellman said. His tone was grateful; his smile, genuine.

"Please call me Rachael. Shall we sit down?"

Sidney, Brick, and Fig moved away from the living room and took the bar stools, which kept them apart from the intimacy of the interview but would allow them to hear every word.

Rachael sat down on the couch, and Trace sat next to her. Stellman and Margolis took the chairs opposite them. The reporter pulled out a minicassette recorder.

"Do you mind?"

Rachael shook her head and Stellman pressed the "record" button.

"Where would you like to start, Rachael?" Stellman asked.

Out of the corner of her eye, Rachael saw the drawing Fig, Brick, and Sidney had hastily drawn that afternoon. She could see Joshua's face. His gentle eyes. His hands around McKenna's fragile body. In her mind, she saw his sleeping eight-year-old body stretched across her bedroom floor, ready to rescue her from demons. She recalled the way his eyes shone when he came home from the revival meeting convinced he had been touched by the very finger of God. She heard the echo of his voice saying, *This is the reason I was born,* as he whispered it to a scared, abused orphan in a dirty place of dashed hopes.

Rachael leaned forward. "Let me tell you about my brother..."

A NOTE FROM SUSAN

Writing about difficult issues isn't easy. The subject matter in *Widows and Orphans* is troubling to say the least. Most of us know the streets of poor, urban areas are often unsafe. And where there is poverty, there is often crime. But this tale is not a commentary on Hmong culture. Or any culture. Depravity occurs in every culture and on every kind of street. As does compassion, courage, and sacrifice.

It is worth mentioning that the Hmong people living in northern Laos secretly assisted the CIA and the American military during the Vietnam War at great personal risk, saving thousands of American lives and losing many of their own. When Saigon fell and American troops pulled out, the Hmong people, who had fought against communist forces, were targeted for genocide. Thousands escaped by crossing the Mekong River into Thailand, but many—including children and infants—died in the attempt. Hmong refugees began arriving in the United States in 1975. There are now more than 40,000 Hmong living in Minnesota alone, with the greatest concentration living in St. Paul. You can learn more about Hmong culture by visiting www.hmongcenter.org.

Discussion questions for this book as well as my other titles with Harvest House are available on my website at

WWW.SUSANMEISSNER.COM

You can also email me by visiting my website. I love hearing from readers! You are the reason I write.

Yours in Christ,

Susan Meissner

Coming in January 2007! The second book in
the Rachael Flynn Mysteries series...

STICKS AND STONES

The sequel to *Widows and Orphans*

Lawyer Rachael Flynn has only been at her new job in the Ramsey
County District Attorney's office for four months when she receives
an unsigned letter: "A body is going to be found at the River Terrace
construction site. He deserved what he got, but it was still an accident. You understand about accidents; I've read the papers. You need
to know it wasn't supposed to happen."

Her colleague Sergeant Will Pendleton, rushes to the building site of
a multimillion-dollar condominium complex in suburban St. Paul.
Two days later the predicted body is found, but to everyone's astonishment, the young man's remains have been buried for at least twenty-
five years.

While DNA experts work to identify the body, Rachael continues to
receive notes. The anonymous writer is clearly looking for absolution
and admits to confiding in Rachael because of how she handled the
recent and very publicized homicide involving her brother, Joshua.

The remains are finally identified as those of Randall "Bucky" Buckett,
a bully who terrorized neighborhood children until he ran away at
the age of fifteen.

Rachael and Will turn their attention to finding the people who
suffered the most at Bucky's hands—those he tormented, who might've
felt at one time that Bucky "deserved what he got."

As Rachael becomes immersed in the victim's tortured past, she is
drawn to the neighborhood where the long-ago bullying took place—
and to an abandoned house that no longer exists, but seems to call
out to her nonetheless...

ABOUT SUSAN MEISSNER

Susan Meissner is an award-winning newspaper columnist, pastor's wife, high school journalism instructor, and novelist. She lives in rural Minnesota with her husband, Bob, and their four children. If you enjoyed *Widows and Orphans,* you'll want to read Susan's other novels....

WHY THE SKY IS BLUE

What options does a Christian woman have after she's been brutally assaulted by a stranger...and becomes pregnant? Happily married and the mother of two, Claire Holland must learn to trust God in all things.

A WINDOW TO THE WORLD

Two girls are inseparable until one is abducted as the other watches helplessly. Years later the mystery is solved—and the truth confirmed that God works all things together for good. Named by *Booklist Magazine* as one of the top ten Christian novels of 2005.

THE REMEDY FOR REGRET

Tess Longren finally has a job she enjoys as well as a proposal of marriage from the man she loves, but she can't seem to grasp a future filled with promise and hope. She can't seem to move past her mother's death. A masterful novel about courage, stamina, understanding the limitations of an imperfect world, and realizing the vast resources of a loving God.

IN ALL DEEP PLACES

Acclaimed mystery writer Luke Foxbourne lives a happy life in a century–old manor house in Connecticut. But when his father, Jack, has a stroke, Luke returns to his hometown of Halcyon, Iowa, where he reluctantly takes the reins of his father's newspaper. Memories of Norah—the neighbor girl who was his first kiss—haunt Luke as he spends night after night alone in his childhood home. Soon he feels an

uncontrollable urge to start writing a different story…Norah's story…
and his own.

A SEAHORSE IN THE THAMES

Alexa Poole intended to spend her week off from work quietly recu-
perating from minor surgery. But when carpenter Stephen Moran
falls into her life—or rather off her roof—the unexpected happens.
His sweet, gentle disposition proves more than she can resist and now
she's falling for him.

Her older sister, Rebecca, has lived at the Falkman Residential Center
since a car accident left her mentally vulnerable and innocent. Now,
17 years later, she has vanished. Alexa fears the worst. As she begins
the search for Rebecca, disturbing questions surface. Why did the car
Rebecca was riding in swerve off the road killing her college friend,
Leanne McNeil? And what about the mysterious check for $50,000
found in Rebecca's room signed by her friend's father, Gavin McNeil?

Fans of Susan Meissner also enjoy the fiction of

ROXANNE HENKE
Coming Home to Brewster series...

AFTER ANNE

"A dear dear friend gave me *After Anne* several weeks ago.... Your book was awesome and should be sold with a box of Kleenex!" —*From California*

"I felt as though the characters were my best friends. The last time I cried this much was when I read James Patteron's *Suzanne's Diary for Nicholas.*" —*From North Carolina*

"I could hardly put the book down. Oprah should know about this!" —*From Oregon*

"*After Anne* is probably my favorite [book of the year]. This moving story of an unlikely friendship between two women will have you laughing and crying and longing for a relationship like theirs." —*From Christianbooks.com*

"We read *After Anne* for our book club in our MOPS (Mothers of Preschoolers) group in Fargo and all fell in love with it. We all kept saying even if you cannot make it to book club, this is a book you have to read." —*From North Dakota*

And book number two,
FINDING RUTH

"I read *Finding Ruth* after I finished *After Anne* and I thought this book couldn't be as good...but sure enough you did it again! You are my favorite author." —*From Virginia*

"I just finished reading the last page of *Finding Ruth*...the tears went down my cheeks as I read it...But what kept me so on the edge...was your showing me Brewster town. I could see everyone, even their laugh lines." —*From California*

"Your book couldn't have come to me at a better time. I struggle with contentment or lack of. Thank you for a touching story that fit quite nicely into my life. I was moved by it. If I had my way, your book would be topping all the best-seller lists." —*From Kentucky*

"I chose your book from the new fiction section at our public library without realizing it was a Christian book...I could hardly bear to put it down."—*From Indiana*

And book number three,
BECOMING OLIVIA

"I've been burning up the e-mail lines telling anyone who will listen that your books are required reading. Please hurry with number 4!!!!"—*From Indiana*

"Just finished *Becoming Olivia*. Loved it!...Your Christian insight and faith shine through as realistic and practical without coming off 'preachy.'"—*From North Carolina*

"I could not put it down! I could relate to so many of the things Olivia went through, especially the struggle with depression and anxiety...*Becoming Olivia* was the first of your books that I have read, and I look forward to reading the others. Thank you!"—*From South Dakota*

"I've just read *Becoming Olivia* and am so moved. There are many words to describe the book, but none seem adequate enough."—*From Ohio*

"I just finished *Becoming Olivia* and had to write and tell you how much I loved it. I have read all 3 of your books...but *Becoming Olivia* especially spoke to me...I know that this had to have been a difficult book for you to write, but you did a superb job, as always."—*via e-mail*

"I cried and laughed through the whole book, finishing it in under two days! This was the very first Christian fiction book I have read and I want more! I cannot wait to find your other two books so I can read them."—*via e-mail*

And about book four,
ALWAYS JAN

"I just finished reading *Always Jan,* and, like your other books, I loved it...God has truly given you a beautiful talent...one which I pray you will continue to use so that we can share in His goodness and mercy through your stories."—*From Dorothy*

"I just finished your book, and man! This is your best work yet!"—*From Nancy*

"I just finished reading the fourth book in the Brewster series. Wow! What a read…Life can sure be difficult at times and a good uplifting honest book is a treasure."—*From a housewife and mother in Indiana*

And the final volume in the Coming Home to Brewster series,
WITH LOVE, LIBBY.

"I just finished the book last night and I was sad when I was finished as it was so good that I wanted more. Whenever I purchase your new book, I think that it can't be as good as your last one but you prove me wrong. You do have a special gift!!"—*From Brenda*

"I just finished reading *With Love, Libby.* It was my favorite book of the series!!!"—*From Jeanette*

"I finished your last book last night. I have to tell you that I loved it."—*From Trish*

"It was a fabulous, tear-jerking, wonderful, "stellar" read. I really enjoy the way you write and how you weave the story."—*From Judy*

"It was with sadness that I finished *With Love, Libby.* I enjoyed it immensely, and felt like I could walk into the little town and know people. I will miss them."—*From Kathy*

The Million Dollar Mysteries
Mindy Starns Clark

Attorney Callie Webber investigates nonprofit organizations for the J.O.S.H.U.A. Foundation, giving the best of them grants ranging up to a million dollars. In each book, Callie comes across a mystery she must solve using her skills as a former private investigator.

A PENNY FOR YOUR THOUGHTS

Callie finds herself looking into the sudden death of an old family friend of her employer. But it seems the family has some secrets they would rather not have uncovered. Almost immediately Callie realizes she has put herself in serious danger. Her only hope is that God will use her investigative skills to discover the identity of the killer before she becomes the next victim.

DON'T TAKE ANY WOODEN NICKELS

Callie finds herself helping a young woman coming out of drug rehab and into the workforce...who's suddenly charged with murder. What appears to be routine, though, explodes into international intrigue and deadly deception.

A DIME A DOZEN

Callie finds herself involved in the life of a young wife and mother whose husband has disappeared. But in the search for him, a body is discovered, which puts Callie's job on hold and her new romance with her mysterious boss in peril.

A QUARTER FOR A KISS

Callie finds herself on her way to the beautiful Virgin Islands. Her friend and mentor, Eli Gold, has been shot. This unusual—and very dangerous—assignment sends Callie and her boss, Tom, on an adventure together to solve the mystery surrounding the shooting.

THE BUCK STOPS HERE

Callie finds herself in the middle of an intense investigation of a millionaire philanthropist and NSA agent—Tom Bennett, her boss and the man she hopes to marry. When Callie overhears a conversation in which her boss implicates himself in her late husband's fatal accident, Tom's association with the NSA prevents him from answering her questions. But she must have answers.

HARVEST HOUSE
PUBLISHERS